Creatures Unbound

There were four of the things now, shuffling on in single file, awful in their unhurried but relentless pursuit. Four monsters from the same ghastly mold. And now as their hissing swelled to a snakepit chorus he noticed the mouths from which the sound spewed forth. Each was an obscene slit equipped with two long, needle-pointed fangs . . .

FESTIVAL OF FEAR

Stuart David Schiff, editor of the World Fantasy Award–winning *Whispers* magazine, presents a chilling collection of today's top horror talents. *Whispers III* includes nightmarish visions by the masters of the macabre: Ramsey Campbell, Dennis Etchison, Frank Belknap Long, Karl Edward Wagner, Fritz Leiber, and many more. So prepare yourself for the scariest time of your life—and enter the world of . . .

WHISPERS III

Books edited by Stuart David Schiff
from Jove

WHISPERS

WHISPERS II

WHISPERS III

WHISPERS III

EDITED BY STUART DAVID SCHIFF

JOVE BOOKS, NEW YORK

All of the characters in this book
are fictitious, and any resemblance
to actual persons, living or dead,
is purely coincidental.

This Jove book has been completely reset
in a typeface designed for easy reading and
was printed from new film.

WHISPERS III

A Jove Book / published by arrangement with
Doubleday & Company, Inc.

PRINTING HISTORY
Doubleday edition published 1981
Jove edition / January 1988

ISBN: 0-515-09363-7

Jove Books are published by The Berkley Publishing Group,
200 Madison Avenue, New York, NY 10016.
The name ''JOVE'' and the ''J'' logo
are trademarks belonging to Jove Publications, Inc.

PRINTED IN THE UNITED STATES OF AMERICA

10 9 8 7 6 5 4 3 2 1

For the Chapel Hill Gang,
the Drakes,
the Wagners,
and the Wellmans

ACKNOWLEDGMENTS

"The Dead Line," copyright © 1979 by Stuart David Schiff for *Whispers* #13–14, reprinted by permission of the author.

"Heading Home," copyright © 1978 by Stuart David Schiff for *Whispers* #11–12, reprinted by permission of the author's agent, Kirby McCauley.

"Who Nose What Evil," copyright © 1979 by Stuart David Schiff for *Whispers* #13–14, reprinted by permission of the author.

"A Fly One," copyright © 1979 by Stuart David Schiff for *Whispers* #13–14, reprinted by permission of the author.

"The Button Molder," copyright © 1979 by Stuart David Schiff for *Whispers* #13–14, reprinted by permission of the author.

CONTENTS

PREFACE

It is with great pleasure that I present *Whispers III*. Like its predecessors, it is an anthology of fantasy and horror and is *both* a Best of *Whispers* magazine *and* an original collection. It is my full-time goal to generate new fiction in the fantasy-horror field. This book does just that.

In the following pages you will see the length and breadth of today's horror and fantasy genre. The stories run the gamut from contemporary horror ("The Dead Line") to heroic fantasy ("King Crocodile") to traditional horror ("Heading Home"). Still, many of the stories herein defy easy classification. "A Fly One" may best be described as strange. "Who Nose What Evil" might be called weird and unusual. And Karl Edward Wagner's "The River of Night's Dreaming" is really difficult to categorize as it slices and slithers its way through contemporary horror to psychological terror to traditional horror. Yes, the vast scope of the fantasy-horror field is well covered. I am firmly convinced that the genre's addicts will feed their habits well with *Whispers III*.

Stuart David Schiff
Whispers Press
70 Highland Avenue
Binghamton, N.Y. 13905

My "discovery" of Dennis Etchison has been one of my greatest pleasures from doing Whispers *magazine. I have used more of his stories in my books and magazines than those of any other author. I am very pleased to note his entry into the "Big Time" with his novelization of* The Fog *having already sold more than 300,000 copies. Dennis's last two* Whispers *stories have led off the last two* Year's Best Horror *stories. "The Dead Line" is one of those masterworks. It pushed two already-typeset stories out of an issue of* Whispers, *something I had never done previously. I think you will agree, though, that this tale cried out for print.*

THE DEAD LINE
by Dennis Etchison

1

This morning I put ground glass in my wife's eyes. She didn't mind. She didn't make a sound. She never does.

I took an empty bottle from the table. I wrapped it in a towel and swung it, smashing it gently against the side of her bed. When the glass shattered it made a faint, very faint sound like wind chimes in a thick fog. No one noticed, of course, least of all Karen. Then I placed it under my shoe and stepped down hard, rocking my weight back and forth until I felt fine sand underfoot. I knelt and picked up a few sharp grains on the end of my finger, rose and dropped them onto her corneas. First one, then the other. She doesn't blink, you know. It was easy.

Then I had to leave. I saw the technicians coming. But

already it was too late; the damage had been done. I don't know if they found the mess under the bed. I suppose someone will. The janitors or the orderlies, perhaps. But it won't matter to them, I'm sure.

I slipped outside the glass observation wall as the technicians descended the lines, adjusting respirators, reading printouts and making notations on their pocket recorders. I remember that I thought then of clean, college-trained farmers combing rows of crops, checking the condition of the coming harvest, turning down a cover here, patting a loose mound there, touching the beds with a horticulturist's fussiness, ready to prune wherever necessary for the demands of the marketplace. They may not have seen me at all. And what if they had? What was I but a concerned husband come to pay his respects to a loved one? I might have been lectured about the risk of bringing unwanted germs into the area, though they must know how unlikely that is with the high-intensity UV lights and sonic purifiers and other sanitary precautions. I did make a point of passing near the Children's Communicable Diseases Ward on my way here, however; one always hopes.

Then, standing alone behind the windows, isolated and empty as an expectant father waiting for his flesh and blood to be delivered at last into his own hands, I had the sudden, unshakable feeling that I was being watched.

By whom?

The technicians were still intent on their readouts.

Another visitor? It was unlikely; hardly anyone else bothers to observe. A guilty few still do stop by during the lonely hours, seeking silent expiation from a friend, relative, or lover, or merely to satisfy some morbid curiosity; the most recently acquired neomorts usually receive dutiful visitations at the beginning, but invariably the newly grieved are so overwhelmed by the impersonalness of the procedure that they soon learn to stay away to preserve their own sanity.

I kept careful track of the progress of the white coats on

the other side of the windows, ready to move on at the first sign of undue concern over my wife's bed.

And it was then that I saw her face shining behind my own in the pane. She was alert and standing for the first time since the stroke, nearly eighteen months ago. I gripped the handrail until my nails were white, staring in disbelief at Karen's transparent reflection.

I turned. And shrank back against the wall. The cold sweat must have been on my face, because she reached out shakily and pressed my hand.

"Can I get you anything?"

Her hair was beautiful again, not the stringy, matted mass I had come to know. Her makeup was freshly applied, her lips dark at the edges and parted just so, opening on a warm, pink interior, her teeth no longer discolored but once more a luminous bone-white. And her eyes. They were perfect.

I lunged for her.

She sidestepped gracefully and supported my arm. I looked closely at her face as I allowed her to hold me a moment longer. There was nothing wrong with that, was there?

"Are you all right?" she said.

She was so much like Karen I had to stop the backs of my fingers from stroking the soft, wispy down at her temple, as they had done so many, many times. She had always liked that. And so, I remembered, had I; it was so long ago I had almost forgotten.

"Sorry," I managed. I adjusted my clothing, smoothing my hair down from the laminar airflow around the beds. "I'm not feeling well."

"I understand."

Did she?

"My name is Emily Richterhausen," she said.

I straightened and introduced myself. If she had seen me inside the restricted area she said nothing. But she couldn't have been here that long. I would have noticed her.

"A relative?" she asked.

"My wife."

"Has . . . has she been here long?"

"Yes. I'm sorry. If you'll excuse me—"

"Are you sure you're all right?" She moved in front of me. "I could get you a cup of coffee, you know, from the machines. We could both have one. Or some water."

It was obvious that she wanted to talk. She needed it. Perhaps I did too. I realized that I needed to explain myself, to pass off my presence before she could guess my plan.

"Do you come here often, Emily?" It was a foolish question. I knew I hadn't seen her before.

"It's my husband," she said.

"I see."

"Oh, he's not one of . . . them. Not yet. He's in Intensive Care." The lovely face began to change. "A coma. It's been weeks. They say he may regain consciousness. One of the doctors said that. How long can it go on, do you know?"

I walked with her to a bench in the waiting area.

"An accident?" I said.

"A heart attack. He was driving to work. The car crossed the divider. It was awful." She fumbled for a handkerchief. I gave her mine. "They say it was a miracle he survived at all. You should have seen the car. No, you shouldn't have. No one should have. A miracle."

"Well," I told her, trying to sound comforting, "as I understand it, there is no 'usual' in comatose cases. It can go on indefinitely, as long as brain death hasn't occurred. Until then there's always hope. I saw a news item the other day about a young man who woke up after four years. He asked if he had missed his homework assignment. You've probably heard—"

"Brain death," she repeated, mouthing the words uneasily. I saw her shudder.

"That's the latest Supreme Court ruling. Even then," I

went on quickly, "there's still hope. You remember that girl in New Jersey? She's still alive. She may pull out of it at any time," I lied. "And there are others like her. A great many, in fact. Why—"

"There *is* hope, isn't there?"

"I'm sure of it," I said, as kindly as possible.

"But then," she said, "supposing . . . What is it that actually happens, afterwards? How does it work? Oh, I know about the Maintenance and Cultivation Act. The doctor explained everything at the beginning, just in case." She glanced back toward the Neomort Ward and took a deep, uncertain breath. She didn't really want to know, not now. "It looks so nice and clean, doesn't it? They can still be of great service to society. The kidneys, the eyes, even the heart. It's a wonderful thing. Isn't it?"

"It's remarkable," I agreed. "Your husband, had he signed the papers?"

"No. He kept putting it off. William never liked to dwell on such matters. He didn't believe in courting disaster. Now I only wish I had forced him to talk about it, while there was still time."

"I'm sure it won't come to that," I said immediately. I couldn't bear the sight of her crying. "You'll see. The odds are very much on your side."

We sat side by side in silence as an orderly wheeled a stainless steel cleaning cart off the elevator and headed past us to the observation area. I could not help but notice the special scent of her skin. Spring flowers. It was so unlike the hospital, the antisepticized cloud that hangs over everything until it has settled into the very pores of the skin. I studied her discreetly: the tiny, exquisite whorls of her ear, the blood pulsing rapidly and naturally beneath her healthy skin. Somewhere an electronic air ionizer was whirring, and a muffled bell began to chime in a distant hallway.

"Forgive me," she said. "I shouldn't have gone on like that. But tell me about your wife." She faced me. "Isn't it

strange?'' We were inches apart. ''It's so reassuring to talk
to someone else who understands. I don't think the doctors
really know how it is for us, for those who wait.''

''They can't,'' I said.

''I'm a good listener, really I am. William always said
that.''

''My—my wife signed the Universal Donor Release two
years ago,'' I began reluctantly, ''the last time she renewed her driver's license.'' Good until her next birthday,
I thought. As simple as that. Too simple. Karen, how
could you have known? How could I? I should have. I
should have found out. I should have stopped your hand.
''She's here now. She's been here since last year. Her
electroencephalogram was certified almost immediately.''

''It must be a comfort to you,'' she said, ''to know that
she didn't suffer.''

''Yes.''

''You know, this is the first time I've been on this
particular floor. What is it they call it?'' She was rattling
on, perhaps to distract herself.

''The Bioemporium.''

''Yes, that's it. I guess I wanted to see what it would be
like, just in case. For my William.'' She tried bravely to
smile. ''Do you visit her often?''

''As often as possible.''

''I'm sure that must mean a great deal.''

To whom? I thought, but let it pass.

''Don't worry,'' I said. ''Your husband will recover.
He'll be fine. You'll see.''

Our legs were touching. It had been so long since I had
felt contact with sentient flesh. I thought of asking her for
that cup of coffee now, or something more, in the cafete-
ria. Or a drink.

''I try to believe that,'' she said. ''It's the only thing
that keeps me going. None of this seems real, does it?''

She forced the delicate corners of her mouth up into a
full smile.

"I really should be going now. I could get something for him, couldn't I? You know, in the gift shop downstairs? I'm told they have a very lovely store right here in the building. And then I'll be able to give it to him during visiting hours. When he wakes up."

"That's a good idea," I said.

She said decisively, "I don't think I'll be coming to this floor again."

"Good luck," I told her. "But first, if you'd like, Emily, I thought—"

"What was . . . what is your wife's name? If you don't mind my asking?"

"Karen," I said. Karen. What was I thinking? Can you forgive me? You can do that, can't you, sweetheart?

"That's such a pretty name," she said.

"Thank you."

She stood. I did not try to delay her. There are some things that must be set to rest first, before one can go on. You helped remind me of that, didn't you, Karen? I nearly forgot. But you wouldn't let me.

"I suppose we won't be running into each other again," she said. Her eyes were almost cheerful.

"No."

"Would you . . . could you do me one small favor?"

I looked at her.

"What do you think I should get him? He has so many nice things. But you're a man. What would you like to have, if you were in the hospital? God forbid," she added, smiling warmly.

I sat there. I couldn't speak. I should have told her the truth then. But I couldn't. It would have seemed cruel, and that is not part of my nature.

What do you get, I wondered, for a man who has nothing?

2

I awaken.

The phone is silent.

I go to the medicine cabinet, swallow another fistful of L-tryptophane tablets and settle back down restlessly, hoping for a long and mercifully dreamless nap.

Soon, all too soon and not soon enough, I fall into a deep and troubled sleep.

I awaken to find myself trapped in an airtight box.

I pound on the lid, kicking until my toes are broken and my elbows are torn and bleeding. I reach into my pocket for my lighter, an antique Zippo, thumb the flint. In the sudden flare I am able to read an engraved plate set into the satin. Twenty-five Year Guarantee, it says in fancy script. I scream. My throat tears. The lighter catches the white folds and tongues of flame lick my face, spreading rapidly down my squirming body. I inhale fire.

The lid swings open.

Two attendants in white are bending over me, squirting out the flames with a water hose. One of them chuckles.

Wonder how that happened? he says.

Spontaneous combustion? says his partner.

That would make our job a hell of a lot easier, says the other. He coils the hose and I see through burned-away eyelids that it is attached to a sink at the head of a stainless steel table. The table has grooves running along the sides and a drainage hole at one end.

I scream again, but no sound comes out.

They turn away.

I struggle up out of the coffin. There is no pain. How can that be? I claw at my clothing, baring my seared flesh.

See? I cry. I'm alive!

They do not hear.

I rip at my chest with smoldering hands, the peeled skin

rolling up under my fingernails. See the blood in my veins? I shout. I'm not one of them!

Do we have to do this one over? asks the attendant. It's only a cremation. Who'll know?

I see the eviscerated remains of others glistening in the sink, in the jars and plastic bags. I grab a scalpel. I slash at my arm. I cut through the smoking cloth of my shirt, laying open fresh incisions like white lips, slicing deeper into muscle and bone.

See? Do I not bleed?

They won't listen.

I stagger from the embalming chamber, gouging my sides as I bump other caskets which topple, spilling their pale contents onto the mortuary floor.

My body is steaming as I stumble out into the cold, gray dawn.

Where can I go? What is left for me? There must be a place. There must be—

A bell chimes, and I awaken.

Frantically I locate the telephone.

A woman. Her voice is relieved but shaking as she calls my name.

"Thank God you're home," she says. "I know it's late. But I didn't know who else to call. I'm terribly sorry to bother you. Do you remember me?"

No luck this time. When? I wonder. How much longer?

"You can hear me," I say to her.

"What?" She makes an effort to mask her hysteria, but I hear her cover the mouthpiece and sob. "We must have a bad connection. I'll hang up."

"No. Please." I sit forward, rubbing invisible cobwebs from my face. "Of course I remember you. Hello, Mrs. Richterhausen." What time is it? I wonder. "I'm glad you called. How did you know the number?"

"I asked Directory Information. I couldn't forget your name. You were so kind. I have to talk to someone first, before I go back to the hospital."

It's time for her, then. She must face it now; it cannot be put off, not anymore.

"How is your husband?"

"It's my husband," she says, not listening. Her voice breaks up momentarily under electrical interference. The signal re-forms, but we are still separated by a grid, as if in an electronic confessional. "At twelve-thirty tonight his, what is it, now?" She bites her lips but cannot control her voice. "His EEG. It . . . stopped. That's what they say. A straight line. There's nothing there. They say it's non-reversible. How can that be?" she asks desperately.

I wait.

"They want you to sign, don't they, Emily?"

"Yes." Her voice is tortured as she says, "It's a good thing, isn't it? You said so yourself, this afternoon. You know about these things. Your wife . . ."

"We're not talking about my wife now, are we?"

"But they say it's right. The doctor said that."

"What is, Emily?"

"The life-support," she said pathetically. "The Maintenance." She still does not know what she is saying. "My husband can be of great value to medical science. Not all the usable organs can be taken at once. They may not be matched up with recipients for some time. That's why the Maintenance is so important. It's safer, more efficient than storage. Isn't that so?"

"Don't think of it as 'life-support,' Emily. Don't fool yourself. There is no longer any life to be supported."

"But he's not dead!"

"No."

"Then his body must be kept alive . . ."

"Not alive, either," I say. "Your husband is now—and will continue to be—neither alive nor dead. Do you understand that?"

It is too much. She breaks down. "H-how can I decide? I can't tell them to pull the plug. How could I do that to him?"

"Isn't there a decision involved in *not* pulling the plug?"

"But it's for the good of mankind, that's what they say. For people years from now, even for people not yet born. Isn't that true? Help me," she says imploringly. "You're a good man. I need to be sure that he won't suffer. Do you think he would want it this way? It was what your wife wanted, wasn't it? At least this way you're able to visit, to go on seeing her. That's important to you, isn't it?"

"He won't feel a thing, if that's what you're asking. He doesn't now, and he never will. Not ever again."

"Then it's all right?"

I wait.

"She's at peace, isn't she, despite everything? It all seems so ghastly, somehow. I don't know what to do. Help me, please . . ."

"Emily," I say with great difficulty. But it must be done. "Do you understand what will happen to your husband if you authorize the Maintenance?"

She does not answer.

"Only this. Listen: this is how it begins. First he will be connected to an IBM cell separator, to keep track of leucocytes, platelets, red cells, antigens that can't be stored. He will be used around the clock to manufacture an endless red tide for transfusions—"

"But transfusions save lives!"

"Not just transfusions, Emily. His veins will be a battleground for viruses, for pneumonia, hepatitis, leukemia, live cancers. And then his body will be drained off, like a stuck pig's, and a new supply of experimental toxins pumped in, so that he can go on producing antitoxins for them. Listen to me. He will begin to decay inside, Emily. He will be riddled with disease, tumors, parasites. He will stink with fever. His heart will deform, his brain fester with tubercules, his body cavities run with infection. His hair will fall, his skin yellow, his teeth splinter and rot. In the name of science, Emily, in the name of their beloved research."

I pause.

"That is, if he's one of the lucky ones."

"But the transplants . . ."

"Yes, that's right! You are so right, Emily. If not the blood, then the transplants. They will take him organ by organ, cell by cell. And it will take years. As long as the machines can keep the lungs and heart moving. And finally, after they've taken his eyes, his kidneys, and the rest, it will be time for his nerve tissue, his lymph nodes, his testes. They will drill out his bone marrow, and when there is no more of that left it will be time to remove his stomach and intestines, as soon as they learn how to transplant those parts too. And they will. Believe me, they will."

"No, please . . ."

"And when he's been thoroughly, efficiently gutted—or when his body has eaten itself from the inside out—when there is nothing left but a respirated sac bathed from within by its own excrement, do you know what they will do then? *Do you?* Then they will begin to strip the skin from his limbs, from his skull, a few millimeters at a time, for grafting and re-grafting, until—"

"Stop!"

"Take him, Emily! Take your William out of there now, tonight, before the technicians can get their bloody hands on him! Sign nothing! Take him home. Take him away and bury him forever. Do that much for him. And for yourself. Let him rest. Give him that one last, most precious gift. Grant him his final peace. You can do that much, can't you? *Can't you?*"

From far away, across miles of the city, I hear the phone drop and then clack dully into place. But only after I have heard another sound, one that I pray I will never hear again.

Godspeed, Emily, I think, weeping. *Godspeed.*

I resume my vigil.

I try to awaken, and cannot.

3

There is a machine outside my door. It eats people, chews them up and spits out only what it can't use. It wants to get me, I know it does, but I'm not going to let it.

The call I have been waiting for will never come.

I'm sure of it now. The doctor, or his nurse or secretary or dialing machine, will never announce that they are done at last, that the procedure is no longer cost-effective, that her remains will be released for burial or cremation. Not yesterday, not today, not ever.

I have cut her arteries with stolen scalpels. I have dug with an ice pick deep into her brain, hoping to sever her motor centers. I have probed for her ganglia and nerve cords. I have pierced her eardrums. I have inserted needles, trying to puncture her heart and lungs. I have hidden caustics in the folds of her throat. I have ruined her eyes. But it's no use. It will never be enough.

They will never be done with her.

When I go to the hospital today she will not be there. She will already have been given to the interns for their spinal taps and arteriograms, for surgical practice on a cadaver that is neither alive nor dead. She will belong to the meat cutters, to the first-year med students with their dull knives and stained cross-sections . . .

But I know what I will do.

I will search the floors and labs and secret doors of the wing, and when I find her I will steal her silently away; I will give her safe passage. I can do that much, can't I? I will take her to a place where even they can't reach, beyond the boundaries that separate the living from the dead. I will carry her over the threshold and into that realm, wherever it may be.

And there I will stay with her, to be there with her, to take refuge with her among the dead. I will tear at my body and my corruption until we are one in soft asylum. And there I will remain, living with death for whatever may be left of eternity.

Wish me Godspeed.

Author's Afterword: It is not often that a writer is able to point to a specific source of inspiration for a piece of fiction. However, I believe in giving credit where it is due. Some of the ideas explored in this story were raised by Willard Gaylin, M.D., president of the Institute of Society, Ethics, and the Life Sciences in Hastings-on-Hudson, New York, in his article entitled "Harvesting the Dead." In particular, it is Dr. Gaylin who coined the terms "neomort" and "bioemporium," two words which I find I cannot improve upon. Readers interested in learning more about the legal and medical ethics involved in such matters are therefore directed to the September 1974 issue of *Harper's Magazine,* where Dr. Gaylin's article first appeared.

Ramsey Campbell has won both the British and the World Fantasy Awards. The esteemed Stephen King recently wrote that "Britain has supplied more than its share of good writers of the supernatural, and it may be that Ramsey Campbell is presently the best of them." Ramsey's original tale, "The Chimney," in Whispers I *earned the World Fantasy Award as Best Short Fiction of 1977 and the following macabre gem landed a prominent slot in 1979's* Year's Best Horror *anthology.*

HEADING HOME
by Ramsey Campbell

Somewhere above you can hear your wife and the young man talking. You strain yourself upward, your muscles trembling like water, and manage to shift your unsteady balance onto the next stair.

They must think he finished you. They haven't even bothered to close the cellar door, and it's the trickle of flickering light through the crack that you're striving toward. Anyone else but you would be dead. He must have carried you from the laboratory and thrown·you down the stairs into the cellar, where you regained consciousness on the dusty stone. Your left cheek still feels like a rigid plate slipped into your flesh where it struck the floor. You rest on the stair you've reached and listen.

They're silent now. It must be night, since they've lit the hall lamp whose flame is peeking into the cellar. They can't intend to leave the house until tomorrow, if at all.

You can only guess what they're doing now, thinking themselves alone in the house. Your numb lips crack again as you grin. Let them enjoy themselves while they can.

He didn't leave you many muscles you can use; it was a thorough job. No wonder they feel safe. Now you have to concentrate yourself in those muscles that still function. Swaying, you manage to raise yourself momentarily to a position from which you can grip the next higher stair. You clench on your advantage. Then, pushing with muscles you'd almost forgotten you had, you manage to lever yourself one step higher.

You maneuver yourself until you're sitting upright. There's less risk that way of your losing your balance for a moment and rolling all the way down to the cellar floor where, hours ago, you began climbing. Then you rest. Only six more stairs.

You wonder again how they met. Of course you should have known that it was going on, but your work was your wife and you couldn't spare the time to watch over the woman you'd married. You should have realized that when she went to the village she would meet people and mightn't be as silent as at home. But her room might well have been as far from yours as the village is from the house; you gave little thought to the people in either.

Not that you blame yourself. When you met her—in the town where you attended the University—you'd thought she understood the importance of your work. It wasn't as if you'd intended to trick her. It was only when she tried to seduce you from your work, both for her own gratification and because she was afraid of it, that you barred her from your companionship by silence.

You can hear their voices again. They're on the first floor. You don't know whether they're celebrating or comforting each other as guilt settles on them. It doesn't matter. So long as he didn't close the laboratory door when he returned from the cellar. If it's closed you'll never be able to open it. And if you can't get into the laboratory he has killed you after all. You raise yourself, muscles shuddering with the effort, your cheek chafing against the wood of the stair. You won't relax until you can see the laboratory door.

You're reaching for the top stair when you slip. Your chin comes down on it, and slides back. You grip the wooden stair with your jaws, feeling splinters lodge between your teeth. Your neck scraped the lower stair, but it has lost all feeling save an ache fading slowly into dullness. Only your jaws prevent you from falling back where you started, and they're throbbing as if nails are being driven through their hinges with measured strokes. You close them tighter, pounding with pain, then you overbalance yourself onto the top stair. You teeter for a moment, then you're secure.

But you don't rest yet. You edge yourself forward and sit up so that you can peer out of the cellar. The outline of the laboratory door billows slightly as the lamp flickers. It occurs to you that they've lit the lamp because she's terrified of you, lying dead beyond the main staircase—as she thinks. You laugh silently. You can afford to. When the flame steadies you can see darkness gaping for inches around the laboratory door.

You listen to their voices upstairs and rest. You know he's a butcher, because once he helped one of the servants carry the meat from the village. In any case, you could have told his profession from what he has done to you. You're still astonished that she should have taken up with him. From the little you knew of the village people you were delighted that they always avoided the house.

You remember the day the new priest visited the house. You could tell he'd heard all the wildest village tales about your experiments; you were surprised he didn't try to ward you off with a cross. When he found you could argue his theology into a corner he left, a twitch pulling his smile awry. He'd tried to persuade you both to attend the church, but your wife had sat silent throughout. It had been then that you decided to trust her to go to the village. You'd dismissed the servants, but you told yourself she would be less likely to talk. You grin fiercely. If you'd been as inaccurate in your experiments you would be dead.

Upstairs they're still talking. You rock forward and try to wedge yourself between the cellar door and its frame. With your limited control it's difficult, and you find yourself leaning in the crack with no purchase on the wood. Your weight hasn't moved the door, which is heavier than you have ever before had cause to realize. Eventually you manage to wedge yourself in the crack, gripping the frame with all your strength. The door rests on you, and you nudge your weight clumsily against it.

It creaks away from you a little, then swings back, crushing you. It has always hung unevenly and persisted in standing ajar; it never troubled you before. Now the strength he left you, even focused like light through a burning-glass, seems unequal to shifting the door. Trapped in the crack, you relax for a moment. Then, as if to take it unawares, you close your grip on the frame and shove against the door, pushing yourself forward as it swings away. It returns, answering the force of your shove, and you aren't clear. But you're still falling into the hall, and as the door chops into the frame you fall on your back, beyond the sweep of the door.

You're free of the cellar, but on your back you're helpless. The slowing door is more mobile than you. All the muscles you've been using can only work aimlessly and loll in the air. You're laid out on the hall floor like a laboratory subject, beneath the steadying flame.

Then you hear the butcher call to your wife, "I'll see," and start downstairs.

You begin to twitch all the muscles on your right side frantically. You roll a little toward that side, then your wild twitching rocks you back. About you the light shakes, making your shadow play the cruel trick of achieving the roll you're struggling for. He's at the halfway landing now. You work your right side again and hold your muscles still as you begin to turn that way. Suddenly you've swung over your point of equilibrium and are lying on your right side. You strain your aching muscles to inch you forward, but the laboratory is feet away, and you are by no means moving in a straight line. His footsteps resound. You hear your wife's terrified voice, entreating him to return to her. There's a long pondering silence. Then he hurries back upstairs.

You don't let yourself rest until you're inside the laboratory, although by then your ache feels like a cold stiff surface within your flesh, and your mouth like a dusty hole in stone. Once beyond the door you sit still, gazing about. Moonlight is spread from the window to the door. Your gaze seeks the bench where you were working when he found you. He hasn't cleared up any of the material that was thrown to the floor by your convulsion. Glinting on the floor you see a needle, and nearby the surgical thread which you never had occasion to use. You relax to prepare for the next concerted effort, remembering.

You recall the day you perfected the solution. As soon as you'd quaffed it you felt your brain achieve a piercing alertness, become precisely and continually aware of the messages of each nerve and preside over them, making minute adjustments at the first hint of danger. You knew this was what you'd worked for, but you couldn't prove it to yourself until the day you felt the stirrings of cancer. Then your brain seemed to condense into a keen strand of energy that stretched down and burned out the cancer. That was proof. You were immortal.

Not that some of the research hadn't been unpleasant. It had taken you a great deal of furtive expenditure at the mortuaries to discover that some of the extracts you needed for the solution had to be taken from the living brain. The villagers thought the children had drowned, for their clothes were found on the river bank. Medical progress, you told yourself, had always involved suffering.

Perhaps your wife suspected something of this stage of your work or perhaps they'd simply decided to rid themselves of you. You were working at your bench, trying to synthesize your discovery when you heard him enter. He must have rushed at you, for before you could turn you felt a blazing slash gape at the back of your neck. Then you awoke on the cellar floor.

You edge yourself forward across the laboratory. Your greatest exertion is past, but this is the most exacting part. When you're nearly touching your prone body you have to turn round. You move yourself with your jaws and steer with your tongue. It's difficult, but less so than tonguing yourself upright on your neck to rest on the stairs. Then you fit yourself to your shoulders, groping with your perfected mind until you feel the nerves linking again.

Now you'll have to hold yourself unflinching or you'll roll apart. With your mind you can do it. Gingerly, so as not to part yourself, you stretch out your arm and touch the surgical needle and thread.

David Drake's The Dragon Lord *was recently published to wide acclaim. It is an intricately constructed heroic fantasy novel that weaves around and through the Arthurian legend as only a cynic like Drake could do. Lawyer Drake's writings run the gamut from hard science fiction to traditional horror. This heroic fantasy done especially for* Whispers III *is a successful blend of accurate research and talented writing.*

KING CROCODILE

by David Drake

The freshest of the twelve crocodile heads had been staked up only a few hours before. All twelve grinned back at Khati and the brown majesty of the Nile beyond him. In his pleasure the scarred, blocky man flexed the great shoulder muscles which had stood him in good stead when he was only a member of Nar-mer's bodyguard. For his proven loyalty to the Great House, Khati had been picked as one of the hundreds of new stewards chosen from the army. Nar-mer had ground pretty kingdoms like millet in a grain mill in his drive to the reed-choked mouth of the Nile. Now he needed trustworthy managers for the estates he had confiscated from princes and a few priesthoods—and the villages in which the new estates were located could use a loyal presence.

Many men had refused the honor and advancement, however. It meant permanent exile from the villages in the

South that had been all their world before Nar-mer had made them soldiers. Khati had his own reasons to accept and become Steward of the lands Nar-mer took from the Temple of Sebek in Usuit. The Great House hated the crocodile god and his scaly avatars, but it did not hate them as fiercely as Khati did.

"Psemthek caught this one?" Khati asked, pointing to the freshest crocodile head, and that of a nine-footer. Its eyes were glazed, but they had not yet sunken into the skull.

"Psemthek and Ro," Hetep agreed. Khati's slim secretary was, like every freeman in the village but the Steward himself, a native of Usuit. His willingness to discuss his neighbors would have made the young servant invaluable to Khati even without his ability to read and write. "They were born together, they farm together—they stood their turn catching crocs together, of course. Ro's married and Psemthek isn't, but there's some stories about that, too."

"I heard them shouting when they carried the carcass into town," Khati said. "Heard their neighbors cheering them, too. There'll be a feast, of course, since the meat won't keep . . . but it's more than that. People are really glad there's one less crocodile. It means that in my three months in Usuit, I've done what the Great House wanted done here . . . and what I wanted. People don't bow to Sebek's children, they don't pray to them, *sacrifice*—"

Khati caught himself before the words began to tumble out. The sweat was bright on his forehead. After a moment's silence the thickset Southerner forced out a little chuckle, as if fury had not been about to don his flesh like a garment. The laugh rattled. It was as unnatural as a skeleton dancing. "Now they can set out hooks for crocodiles," Khati continued in a normal voice. "It's just another duty to the Great House. It's a little easier than chopping reeds in the irrigation canals; and besides, there's a lot of meat for you and your friends if you're lucky enough to bring one in. Bring in one of the filthy, man-slaying vermin . . .''

Hetep cleared his throat experimentally. ''Psemthek'll probably be inviting you to their feast. Do you want to go, or . . . ?''

''Umm, right,'' Khati said. ''I used to eat crocodile, back—home. Occasionally. Didn't particularly like it, too much sulphur aftertaste even when it's fresh. But I couldn't eat it now. There's the Council meeting tonight anyway. Go on back, make amends for me, and fix me the usual supper at the house. I'll be along in good time.'' Khati's eye fell on the bundle of mats and jars at the edge of the bank. He added, ''Oh—you might remind the fellows that they left their gear here when they carried the meat back.''

Hetep nodded and began trotting along the path, bare feet flashing in the sun. A good man, Khati thought, though he'd been associated with the Temple of Sebek until Narmer had confiscated the lands. Perhaps Khati ought to learn more about his secretary . . . ?

When Khati looked back, he blinked to see the priest Nef-neter standing beside the staked heads. The priest's gray beard was neatly trimmed and tufted beneath the wrappings of gold wire. That gold and the priest's scarab ring were the only remaining signs of the affluence he had known when the Temple of Sebek was the largest land-holder in Usuit. Now the Temple had no property but that on which it stood, a room of mud bricks on a hummock in the marsh.

''You won't stop this sacrilege of your own accord, will you?'' Nef-neter said. His voice was so calm as to be arrogant.

''Twelve in three months,'' Khati replied, letting his growing anger move words instead of the muscles bulging over his torso. ''Hooked deep in the guts, then pounded on till their brains squirted out their ears.'' That was exaggerated, but Khati was using his tongue as a weapon—as both men understood perfectly.

"I wonder," the priest mused aloud, "just what it would take to get you to end this—foulness." He was twisting the scarab ring on his thumb, heavy silver set with a gray-green stone so lustrous that it mimicked translucence.

Khati touched his own thonged amulet, a lapis lazuli carving of Hequit, the frog goddess of his home village. "You could have a god come down and order me to stop, Nef-neter," he said. "Then I'd think about it. For now, what I've thought about is your labor duty for the Great House. From here on out, you'll man a hook and line every day—until you've killed a crocodile yourself."

Still Nef-neter refused to burst out in anger. "The others have had the choice of"—the priest's lips moved silently, then continued—"*that* sacrilege, or the usual work. Cutting reeds, repairing the dikes."

"And you don't," Khati agreed, replying to the unspoken question. "Besides that, nobody's going to bring you food any more. I know they've been doing that and I haven't stopped it, but I'll stop it now. You don't eat anything but what you scavenge from the marsh until you've brought in a crocodile— *priest*."

Nef-neter had already begun walking back to his hut. "I'll take you at your word, Councilor," he replied quietly over his shoulder.

The ex-guardsman scowled as he stalked away. He didn't have the authority to give those orders alone, only the Village Council as a whole did; but Khati had the right to name or replace the other Councilors. Right of conquest, in Nar-mer's name. The right that made Khati, a Southerner with no property of his own, the superior of every other man in Usuit. Khati was sparing of his power—he knew that if he pushed too hard, well . . . any man could die on his sleeping bench with a wadded cloak pressed over his airways. But in this one thing he would not be balked.

Ahead of Khati lay Anpu's shipyard, built on fertile land near the water. The yard justified its location with its profits. Its existence slightly diminished the food supply that was the life of the whole region, but Anpu and his three sons lived very well indeed.

The yard was alive with the sound of chattering tools. On the ground sat a circle of a dozen slaves, each holding a bundle of split reeds with his feet. By stuffing additional splits into the unwrapped ends of the bundles, the workmen formed solid cones of papyrus. When the individual bundles were complete, they would be joined into fishermen's skiffs or even larger vessels to carry trade and rich men up and down the Nile.

But Anpu's endeavors were not limited to the reed boats of past ages. Using wood imported from regions where it was less scarce, he and his most skilled craftsmen were building one of a series of large, hollow-bellied vessels. Such wooden ships were able to venture safely even into the salt sea north of the Delta and come back laden with cedar and unguents and ores. They were responsible for most of Anpu's wealth and the fact that his name was well known beyond the boundaries of the district.

The main path from the river to the village proper ran beside the boatyard. As Khati turned onto it, the pattern of stone tools thudding and clicking changed. The Steward looked up. Anpu stood at his bench, his flint adze resting on the rib he had been shaping. He was a stout, dark man with muscles formed and hardened by decades of labor no less heavy than it was skilled. His flat, beard-fringed features could never have been handsome, but they were further disfigured by a fresh scar on his nose. It had been left by the hook which had held him in Nar-mer's slave gang. Anpu's wealth had not kept him from being conscripted by Mekhit, his king, for the army which first faced the Southerners' slashing advance. In the aftermath of that campaign, Anpu's sons had ransomed their father, preserving him from ritual execution or a short, brutal life in a distant holding of the Great House. Nothing, however, could take back the humiliation of the hook.

From other parts of the yard, the faces of Anpu's sons

now mirrored their father's scowl. The slaves kept to their tasks, afraid to call a greeting but unwilling to glower at the enemy of their owner. Khati felt the touch of the god tense his grip on the mace he now carried only as a symbol of authority. He had met Anpu's sort, perhaps the shipwright himself, in the blood-blinding haze of that afternoon. Mekhit's line had been bright with standards and metal-edged weapons. For all that, it had shattered like chaff from the millet when Khati's mace flailed into it.

He was no longer guardsman of the Great House, but rather the Steward in Usuit; and Anpu was Second Councilor and richest man in the village entrusted to Khati's care. There was no point in wishing for the return of the old, simple days of force and slaughter, for they would not return here if Khati did his duty as he was expected to.

Besides, it could be that Anpu had better and more personal reasons to hate Khati than anything that had happened in the past.

The fields spread to either side of the narrow path. They were dusted green with the first shoots of millet and studded with the stooped bodies of the men and women cultivating the grain. The raised walls of irrigation ditches laid the cropland out into narrow strips and allowed the owners to survey the fields during the floods without wading. The folk called cheerful greetings which Khati returned as he walked toward the village itself. The houses were built on the higher ground to the west, beyond the floods' reaches and thus infertile. The Steward realized how fortunate he was that Usuit's first season under his leadership promised to be a good one for crops.

Most of the villagers were still in the fields, so the single row of houses beyond seemed quiet. Psemthek and Ro, however, had gathered a coterie of idlers and servants around them in the low-walled forecourt of Councilor Besh's house. The Councilor's wife ran a tavern there as a sideline to her husband's landholdings. Khati waved as he passed the group. Ro, taller and a few minutes older than his brother, broke off in the middle of a song and tried to stand. When he slumped back on the adobe bench, his cup sloshed a swallow or two of the fresh, potent barley beer. Psemthek cursed his brother blearily. Ro called in good humor, "Come on over tonight, Khati. Have a drink and help us eat Sebek."

Khati only waved again, smiled, and walked on.

"If you won't drink beer with Ro, perhaps you'll have a cup of water here?" called a musical voice from Anpu's house.

Khati looked up, a smile forming of its own accord. The courtyard walls were six feet high, but the gate only came up to Anit's shoulders and framed her head in the opening. Anpu's second wife was younger than his sons by the first. Her father had been an official in the court of Mekhit. Nar-mer's conquest had beggared the family, so the ship-wright had picked up Anit as a bargain. And then again . . .

"My husband just sent up a jar drawn from the center of the channel," Anit added, nodding her head to emphasize its coiffure of ringlets and pins. "Cold and clear."

"Umm," Khati mumbled, glancing westward as if to judge the sun's height.

Anit swung the gate toward her to open it. She was wearing a richly embroidered kilt instead of the plain linen Khati would have expected. Also, she had rouged her bare nipples. She smiled. "You're sure you wouldn't prefer beer anyway?" she asked.

"Ah, no . . ." Khati was frozen, one foot raised to step through the gateway.

"What's the matter?" Anit asked. Then, no longer coy, she added, "Are you afraid?"

"Of failing?" Khati said. He was suddenly calmer. The question had clarified what was going on in his mind. "The Great House thought I could run a village for it. I've got to work with a lot of other people if I'm going to succeed. Your husband doesn't like me, but we can work together. Now." He reached out gently and pulled the door shut. "I'll come drink with you some evening when the rest of the family's home," he said.

It was hard to tell what thoughts were going on behind Anit's calm face. Her right index finger was drawing a small X in rouge on her cheek.

As he walked off, Khati said, "I'll see you tonight at the Council meeting."

It was already getting late. Women were scurrying down the street with last-minute purchases for the meals they would shortly cook. Occasionally a laborer with shouldered hoe trudged toward house or tavern. Those who passed Khati exchanged friendly waves with him. The Steward's house was on the far south end of the village. Two stone pillars framed the gate. They had been systematically defaced, but Khati spat at the nearer one anyway. When Khati replaced Nef-neter as the dwelling's resident, the gateposts had been carven crocodiles.

"Good, good, I was beginning to think I should have told the cook to wait," called Hetep from within the house. "Will you eat inside or out?"

"Oh, bring me a plate out here, I suppose," Khati replied. "But bring me a washbowl first. My skin always crawls after I talk to Nef-neter."

Hetep chuckled as he brought out a flat bowl of water and, across his forearm, a linen towel. "I don't know that you're fair to him," the younger man said. "Want wine with the meal?"

"Yeah—no, wait, not with the Council meeting tonight. Just water, I suppose." Khati was dipping his mug full from the wide-mouthed jar in the shade when his servant returned with fresh bread and a savory dish of pork and leeks. "You were a servant in this house before I came, weren't you?" the Steward asked abruptly.

Hetep set his platter carefully on the table. "That's right. Though originally the house was mine. Well, my mother's." The younger man looked at his master. "But perhaps you already know that story?"

Khati squatted down at the low table and began eating.
"Not a word of it. Have a seat and tell me. And draw
yourself some beer—you don't have a cursed meeting to
go to."

Hetep dipped a mug of water and squatted across the
table from Khati. "My father died before I was born," he
said. "Mother turned to the Temple for help, for running
the estate, for raising me. She made me a ward of the
Temple if anything should happen to her."

"The Temple. Sebek."

"The god Sebek," Hetep agreed. "And so, since . . . a
crocodile took her in the river when I was five, Nef-neter
raised me. He would have liked me to become his acolyte,
I think, but he never forced me. When he saw that I really
didn't have the vocation, he had me trained as his steward
instead." The young man smiled. "So now I'm the steward of the Steward of the Great House. A rather diluted
majesty, but a pleasant life for all that."

Khati paused and looked at his servant. "You could—
live in the house of the beast that killed your mother?"

"For fifteen years Nef-neter was a friend to me," Hetep
answered quietly. "I don't turn on friends because I—dislike
their gods."

Khati let his anger pass slowly. "That's a good way to
be," he said, and he spooned more of the pork into his
mouth.

Hetep brought out a small harp. He began singing the
melancholy songs of farmers and boatmen and lovers. War
and human conflicts eased from the courtyard. Khati smiled
at the younger man in appreciation, but he said nothing
until Hetep began to croon about a girl whose love crowned
her like the flowers do the reeds.

"Not that," Khati snapped.

Hetep's fingers melded the chords into others as gracefully as if he had planned to do so. "Why not?" he asked.

Khati stared at the calm young face across the table

from him. "Because my wife used to sing that to me," he said at last. "It was her favorite, I guess."

The secretary continued to stroke a soothing background from his harp. His lips were silent, but his eyes probed mildly until Khati said, "She died while I was on campaign. She wasn't too pregnant yet that she couldn't help set the fishing weirs. A crocodile got her." The scarred guardsman took a deep breath. "They caught the beast a few days later and beat it to death. But it's a big river. There's enough of the vermin in it to keep me busy the rest of my life."

"Men aren't supposed to understand the gods," Hetep said, "but it may be that gods do the most good when they least seem to." Then he swung into a Delta lyric about ducks in the reeds and the mist that rises from the river at dawn. Hetep was still singing when Khati reached over and squeezed his shoulder in comradeship. Then the Steward walked out of the courtyard, down the lighted street toward Anpu's house and the Council meeting.

Psemthek and Ro, the latter still trying to sing as the pair of them stumbled toward their gate, met Khati in the street. "Councilor!" Psemthek shouted, "come have a drink now!"

Khati saw the gate quiver ajar, displaying the worried face of Psemthek's wife—or was she Ro's? The panel closed again. A servant, too drunk to carry his lamp lighted, straggled behind the brothers.

"Psemthek!" Ro gasped before Khati could beg off again. "We didn't fetch the gear from the river bank!"

"So?"

"There was beer left!"

Without a further word, the two men turned and began pacing determinedly back toward the track to the river.

"Hey!" Khati called, "you'll fall in a ditch and drown!"

The brothers ignored him. One of them had started to sing again. The Steward shook his head and continued on his way. A moment after he had passed Ro's house, the gate opened. The woman he had seen before slipped out, cloaked and cowled. She did not look at Khati as she followed after her man—or men—at a discreet distance. Khati smiled. It was not only the gods who looked after drunken men.

Because of the numbers sometimes attending, Village Council meetings were held in the courtyards of Councilors' houses. The Councilors Senti and Besh, both of them large landholders, were already talking to Anpu when Khati entered. A scattering of citizens with petitions huddled against the inner walls, waiting to be called on at the Council's pleasure. As Khati swung the gate closed behind him it was caught with a querulous squeal by Sanekht the brickmaker. Sanekht, the fifth member of Council, was an ancient man with a twisted body and a mind far gone in mushy senility as well.

Khati apologized to Sanekht, then nodded to the others present. He took his seat at the center of the low bench across the courtyard from the gate. The other four Councilors sat down without delay. Hor-nef, the scribe, cleaned his pen and poised it over a fresh roll of papyrus.

"The third channel's important to more than just *my* farm," Senti continued to Anpu in a lower voice than before, "and as grown up as it is, only about half the water that should be is getting through it. We need—"

"Call to order," Khati grunted. He raised the millet cake and beer mug set out for the purpose. "First," he prayed, "we thank the gods for the past well-being of our village, and we pray for their continued indulgence."

The gate creaked open. All eyes in the courtyard turned from Khati to the thin figure of Nef-neter, framed by the posts. "Do you thank *all* the gods, Councilor?" the old priest demanded. "Are you willing to end your blasphemy, then?"

The rage poured into Khati and shackled his tongue. The beer began to tremble in the libation mug. From a long distance away he heard Anpu saying, "You're out of

order! Sit down until you're called!'' Two of the shipwright's husky sons were moving toward the intruder.

"One moment further!" Nef-neter said. "You think to
offend Sebek, and of course you do. But remember that
Chaos itself sometimes takes the form of a crocodile. Repent while you still have time and—"

The mug shattered in Khati's hand, beer spurting in a
high arc as the Steward's grip pulverized the earthenware.
Khati stood. "Get him out," he croaked, pointing with
fingers that wanted to twist around a mace hilt, "or—"

Anpu's sons grasped Nef-neter by both arms. They
hustled him back into the street. The priest's scarab ring
winked in the lamplight. The old man looked neither
surprised nor discomposed, merely patient as if he were a
statue in the hands of workmen.

"I've warned you," he said. His body stiffened.

The double scream was loud, even though it came all
the way from the riverbank. No one in the courtyard
moved. A hacking bellow deep as distant thunder swelled
over the screams, drowning them and leaving only silence
when it passed on.

Khati was the first man through the gate, shouldering
the priest aside as he moved. The Steward had carried his
mace to the meeting as a symbol of authority. Now it was
in his hands and a weapon again, polished and quick to
crush the skulls of the enemies of the Great House. Khati's
feet found the path to the river as much by memory as by
the light of the thin moon. Behind him he could hear
others coming, cumbered by fear and whatever arms they
could snatch up in an instant.

Someone was stumbling toward him from the river.
Khati braced himself in the center of the narrow path and
cried, "Hold it right there!"

The figure sank down. "Sebek," a woman's voice
moaned. "The god took them both!" It was Ro's wife,
utterly distraught. She had lost the cape she had worn as
she left her house.

Khati pushed on by her, running the rest of the way to the river. It had happened on the bank very near the shipyard. One of the brothers—the light was too dim for identification, even though the face was undamaged—lay scattered across the path and reeds. Huge clawed footprints—how large they were Khati refused for the moment to recognize—had trampled the ground and crushed in the victim's torso. The head and limbs lay each at a little distance from the body, joined by pseudopods of the great central blood-splash. All the pieces seemed to be present.

There was no sign of the other brother.

Khati knelt, looking at the track scraped through the reeds. Men came running up behind him. Anpu was among the first. He carried the only metal weapon in the village, a copper-bladed spear with sharp edges and a point like an asp's tongue.

"What happened?" the shipwright demanded.

"The god came!" wept the woman in the background. "The god took my men!"

Khati morosely traced a footprint with his index finger. Even the webbing between the digits had been impressed in the blood-softened earth. He said nothing.

From the darkness Ro's wife continued to cry, "The crocodile god took them!"

The murmur of the crowd had begun before dawn as villagers began to gather in front of Khati's house. The sound had grown with the number of those waiting. Now it had the sibilance and power of the air before a windstorm rips out of the western desert. Only once before had Khati seen the whole population of Usuit assembled: on the day he had arrived and announced Nar-mer's initial edicts for the village.

That day Khati had been backed by a company of the Bodyguard of the Great House. Now he was alone except for Hetep, who brought his master a breakfast of milk and figs—and did not mention that the other servants had left the house.

Khati eyed the wall. It would be wide enough to stand on. He thumbed toward it and said, "Give me a lift, Hetep. If I've got to talk to them all, I want them to hear me."

The younger man nodded solemnly and locked his hands into a yoke for his master's foot. Khati stepped onto the hands and lurched upward, drawing himself erect atop the wall in a single motion.

"People of Usuit!" he roared. Gods, there were thousands of eyes on him. But they weren't hostile, not yet. It was just that they'd come to him for an answer to the spiritual catastrophe which had struck the village. And he'd damned well better have an answer . . . "Today, I'm going to lead a party out on the river. We'll hunt the crocodile that attacked Psemthek and Ro last night."

The crowd sucked in its collective breath, an awestruck antistrophe to Khati's words. From his vantage point, the Steward could see Anpu and his family near the front of the plain of faces. Senti, Besh, and even old Sanekht were close by too. Khati's shadow carpeted a long track across his audience in the light of the rising sun.

"That's if it hasn't run away and hid already," Khati continued. "They're slimy cowards, those beasts, and they'll run from a village of brave folk like this one. But if it's still here, we'll smash its skull and drag it ashore to spit on, me and your other Councilors." *That* brought some unexpected interest, Khati thought grimly. "The Council will meet here to make final plans. We'll send for a few volunteers to fill out the crew. I want all the rest of you to go home, now, go back to work. Otherwise you'll be in the way of our taking care of this skulking vermin."

"My people," another voice cried, "repent of this madness!"

There was a sudden space in the dense crowd, setting Nef-neter apart like a negative halo. Fear marked the surrounding faces, but not the hatred Khati knew was warping his own countenance into something hellish as he gazed down at the priest.

"Your sins have brought Chaos down on you," the priest said, his arms high, his scarab blinking, "but there is still hope if you—"

"Vermin!" Khati shouted, feeling the god starting to don his form. He gestured with his clenched fist, roped to his body with sinews that ridged and rippled the dark skin. "A word, a word more and your head will be on a pole while we use your body for bait!"

Nef-neter fell silent. He was a priest, after all. Perhaps he could see that it was no man but a god of fury that stood splay-legged addressing him.

"Now go!" Khati ordered the crowd. "All but the Council."

They were streaming away even as Khati leaped back within his courtyard. His flesh was trembling so that Hetep, who had just opened the gate to a giggling Sanekht, reached out an arm to steady his master.

Anpu was close behind the brickmaker. "What sort of a joke is this?" he demanded. His white nose scar stood out the brighter when his face was flushed. "How is paddling up and down the river going to help rid us of that crocodile?"

"Wait till the others are here," Khati answered, too weak to be other than calm.

The shipwright's family had entered with him, his three lowering sons and his wife who was younger than the youngest of the sons. Anit's hairdo was simpler than before, though pins of horn and ivory still set off the rich black of it. She wore no makeup this morning. Her naked eyes were more intimate, her breasts more tender.

Senti and Besh were together but otherwise unaccompanied. Hetep closed the gate behind them and barred it.

"Anpu, we'll need a boat," Khati said without preliminaries. He was master of his body again and master, he thought, of the problem as well. "A good-sized one, something impressive. We'll take nets, spears; maybe twenty men, that'll be enough for the show.''

''The crocodile isn't going to come and meet us, you fool!'' Anpu burst out. ''We'll only be wasting our time and stirring up a little of the bottom mud.''

''That's right,'' Khati agreed easily, ''but it's not a waste of time.'' Surprise tinged the faces turned toward him.

''The crocodile is real,'' he explained, ''but it wasn't here before. You all saw the size of the prints, that wasn't something we'd have overlooked if it'd been any while in the district.'' He'd phrased that wrong. The expressions of the others proved they had indeed seen the blood-soaked prints and that they would rather not have been reminded of them. ''If it came here, it'll leave again. It's just like a flood, it comes but it doesn't stay. What we're going to do is go out on the water and prove that it's safe to the others who don't understand these things. Otherwise nobody'll go fishing, nobody'll work the fields for months, and we'll lose half the crop for nothing.''

''It'll have dragged old Ro down into its den,'' Sanekht chuckled. He slobbered a little, then wiped the spittle into a smear of mud with his unwashed hands. ''Let him get good and ripe for a while before it eats him. Maybe a week before it needs to go hunting again. 'Course, to fill a belly *that* big it might take—''

''When it comes out again, it'll leave!'' Khati said loudly to silence the old man. ''Now, who else do we take in the boat?''

''It's already too hot,'' Besh grumbled, putting his shoulder against the boat. The vessel slid a foot farther down the bank and hung up again. ''We should've waited till afternoon.''

''A pass up and down the river now'll convince people to get themselves back to the fields,'' Khati grunted behind him. Only half the twenty crewmen were wading through the muddy shallows to launch the craft. Nar-mer's Steward did not care to make an issue of the others' reluctance. The men had agreed to join what they thought was a dangerous enterprise, and that was an offer he would not have been able to compel in peacetime. Anpu and his sons were on the shore too, but that was arrogance and not fear.

And after all, Anpu had provided the boat. Its bow was now bobbing free on the brown water. The hull was papyrus. Sanekht had repeated with senile insistence that, "Crocodiles won't touch a papyrus boat," and no one else had seen a reason to argue with the old man. The frapped ends of the vessel spired up higher than a man could stand, and there was a reed deckhouse just forward of the steering oar. Apart from those embellishments, the vessel was thirty feet of clumsy artifice with thicker bulwarks than its hull cavity justified. Even Anpu seemed to look with scorn at his creation. The shipwright stood like a toad erect, his bright-bladed spear a slim tower beside him.

The stern of the boat floated free. "Start loading," Khati called. "Some of you on shore bring the nets and spears, will you?"

While those who had launched the craft held it steady, the most fearful of the men on shore scampered through the shadowed water and rolled aboard. Anpu and his sons followed more deliberately, the muddy Nile slapping their calves but not the kilts bound high on their loins. As the shipwright braced himself to board, Khati said, "Let me borrow your spear while we're at this. It'll look more impressive than my flint will."

Anpu's scar blazed. "Let your king give you a metal blade—if he thinks that you're worth it. Or buy the copper yourself. You won't touch what's mine. Not a *thing* that's mine!" He climbed the fat gunwale.

"Then you'll plant your ass in the bow and use your damned toy if we *do* find something!" Khati snapped.

Anpu looked down coldly at the Steward. He shuffled forward without a reply.

Leather thongs had been woven into the papyrus bundles to serve as oarlocks. Khati took one of the bow oars. Hetep knelt beside him at the other. The sycamore thwart was not wide enough for the Steward's broad shoulders and those of another man as well, but Khati had been in the Bodyguard too long to take a place farther back where the belly swelled and gave more room. Even though it was no battle they were about to enter . . .

"Pull!" called Huni, a fisherman chosen as steersman in the hope that he would not ground them ignominiously on a mudbank. Khati pulled, fouling his oar with that of the man kneeling before him. He started to curse but realized there was no point in it; they were not a trained crew, only a symbol.

Huni sent them downriver a quarter mile or so, smoothly enough. Then he ordered the boat about. They began to stagger south again against the current. The oars rubbed in places that agricultural implements did not. Men began to mutter as their skin sloughed.

"Bring her up to the end of the fields and then head 'er in," Khati ordered. The morning mist had been burned from the water, leaving the surface that remained a bronze mirror reflecting the sun. Besh had been right: they should have waited for a cooler hour. But from the houses above the cropland, people were watching. Now and again a figure carrying a hoe or bird-switch walked carefully down into the fields.

Khati glanced over his left shoulder, catching in the corner of his eye the determined sternness of Anpu posing in the bow. Jutting from the reeds was the hillock bearing the linen-swathed Altar of Sebek, a triangular block as high as a man's thighs. The rude hut in which Nef-neter lived had been thrown up beside the altar after Nar-mer confiscated the house in the village. Worship had always been at the altar site, however, despite the mud and insects there, despite the wealth that had been available to raise a temple west of the fields—or at least clear of the marsh.

"All right, let's swing her," Khati called.

Anpu shouted, "Wait!"

All the oarsmen paused. Khati muttered under his breath and twisted. His shoulder bumped Hetep's. The younger man leaned aside. Ahead of them the opaque water was shadowed from beneath in a blur as long as the boat, and the shadow was coming nearer. The tendons of Anpu's legs swelled beneath the skin as the shipwright poised his spear to thrust with both hands.

One of Anpu's sons stood up amidships, rocking the craft dangerously. "Sit down, you soul-burned fool!" Khati snarled back at him. The guardsman was groping beside him for the shaft of his spear. He did not take his eyes off the huge blotch in the river. "Hetep," he said, "slide back out of my—"

The water sluiced over the bony scutes of a head more than a yard long. Behind it, the whole length of the crocodile was breaking surface. Its tail was bent in a flat *S* which shot the body forward faster than the boat could have been rowed to escape. Khati saw the flaps which had closed the nostrils flare open as the snout raised. The beast's gums were white except for the dark mottlings where leeches writhed among the great teeth.

Anpu squawked like a hen in a civet's jaw. He drove his spear downward. The burnished copper struck the reptile between its dilated nostrils. The metal bent back like a plantain leaf. The shipwright dropped his weapon and cried out again, this time in certain fear and no defiance. Khati grabbed Anpu's sash in his left hand to keep the squat man from falling backward.

The armored head glided over the bulwark and a black-clawed foreleg slashed at Anpu. The veins were bright in the webbing where the skin stretched wide between the digits. Khati balanced his spear to jab at the eye glowing like mother-of-pearl beneath its membrane. The other fore-

limb reached into the boat and the bow plunged under tons
of the reptile's weight. Something green flashed among the
horny claws and the blood spraying from Anpu's thigh.
The sash tore and the shipwright pitched forward, over the
monster that was tearing at him.

When the crocodile slipped back, the boat broached like
a leaping dolphin. It threw Khati into a tangle of Hetep
and four other oarsmen. An anchor-stone clacked against
the base of his skull, dimming into pale pastels the colors
of everything he saw. The guardsman struggled to his
knees, regardless of the shouting men around him. He still
gripped his spear.

Anpu was floundering naked in the water. The jaws rose
straight up on either side of his waist. They were twin
wedges armed with three-inch teeth. The shipwright
screamed. His scarred nostrils were as white as the gums
closing about him. Soundlessly, the crocodile sank back
into the river. Anpu continued to scream until the brown
water frothed across his face. It bubbled once more, turning red as it quieted.

A harp had been playing, cool and thin in the evening
breeze. Now it seemed to have stopped. Khati raised up
carefully from the reed mattress on which he had flung
himself as soon as he reached his house. His head still
buzzed with gall and the blow it had taken from the
anchor.

"Hetep!" the Steward called. His voice cracked. The
house was dark and close and still. "Gods grind his bones,"
Khati murmured as he stood and walked out into the
lamplit courtyard.

Hetep was there on a bench by the gate. His harp was in
his hands, but he fingered it so gently that the strings were
silent. When he felt Khati's eyes, he jumped up. "Master?" he said.

The night beyond the walls breathed.

"Where are they?" Khati demanded.

Hetep dipped up a gourd full of water and waited for Khati to drink. Then he said, "They're out at the altar, I suppose."

Khati flung the gourd. It clacked on the hard soil, leaving a dark zigzag in the dust. "Suppose! Suppose! You know they're out there, praying to that foulness!"

The guardsman stalked to the gate and into the street beyond. He did not bother to close the panel behind him. The back of his head prickled as hairs twitched in the dried blood which Hetep had been unable to sponge wholly away while Khati slept.

"Khati," the younger man said urgently, "let them be. They won't bother you, they don't dare to. If you . . . disappeared, the Great House would just send another Steward who would crush a dozen skulls while he was at it."

The narrow track that wound from the house that had been Nef-neter's to the altar in the reeds was steeply slanted. Behind Khati, his servant's voice continued, "They need you for appearances. And it doesn't matter what people want to pray to, not if the taxes come in and the King gets his labor quotas—"

"Shut up!"

"Master, they won't kill you, you're killing your—"

"Shut up!" Khati snarled, turning toward Hetep for the first time since he left the house. *"You* can watch babies wrapped in flowers and laid out in the reeds for Sebek—if you want. *You* can watch parents kiss the snouts of the creatures fat and stinking with the flesh of their children, watch them pray, 'Greatest god, spare me again this coming year; but if you chose me from your water, what ecstasy!' I'm going to die someday no matter what, and I'll die before I watch that happen!"

"Master," Hetep said to the guardsman's back, "I didn't go with the rest of them."

Khati paused in mid-stride. He turned again. "Maybe you should have," he said, "my friend."

The only illumination was the moon and a pair of rushlights on the covered altar. The flickering tallow was more to mark Nef-neter than to brighten the scene. The priest was speaking in thin-lipped triumph from the mound. The silent mob that had greeted Khati at his house in the morning now faced the slim priest of Sebek in a great half-circle. Those at the back could not hear the words, but they moaned responsively with the ones nearer the front. Many were in mud to their knees, holding their smallest children and oblivious to the bites of insects still unsated with their blood.

There were a few scowls, a few curses as Khati began to shoulder his way through the crowd. Then the people looked at his face and swept back, still-voiced, from the Steward's advance. In his wake the villagers eddied, unwilling to close too swiftly the gap Khati had plowed among them. It was as if a pasture had been sundered by the advance of a young challenger, striding straight and fiery-eyed toward the eminence on which the herd bull awaited him.

Nef-neter pointed at his rival. "God's will *shall* be done, whatever the wishes of men!" the priest roared to the crowd. They moaned worshipfully.

Khati pushed up to the firmer ground of the hillock. He stepped through the last row of villagers, two paces from the altar. One of the inner circuit of listeners was Anit, her coiffure ragged from inattention. Anpu's sons flanked her.

Nef-neter glared from behind the altar as if it were a breastwork against Khati's charge. The flames were mushy daggers to either side of the old man's face. "Why do you defy a god?" he demanded loudly.

The Steward turned his back on the priest and his covered altar. It was no physical attack he feared. The villagers were spread in a broad fan, a moraine of humanity spilling down the mound. None of them was any closer to the river than the altar stone itself was. "My people!"

Khati shouted, "what madness drives you to worship this belly-crawling filth?"

There was no sound from the crowd. Then, from behind Khati, came a bellow that was not of man or of men.

Khati turned without speaking, already aware that he had lost. A dull, boat-huge torso rose from the surface of the river fifty yards away. Reeds and their fellows kept most of the villagers from seeing the crocodile, but no one could be in any doubt as to what had appeared. It was the dark epiphany of a god.

Nef-neter was silent and so motionless that only the reflected flames moved on his eyeballs. The crocodile made another sound, more of a grunt this time than a roar because its jaws were gripping something. Water sprayed high as the beast thrashed.

"Oh, aye, they don't have teeth that can cut like a dog's," mumbled somebody nearby in the crowd—was it old Sanekht? "That's why they like meat to get ripe, so when they twist it—"

The crocodile's wedge-shaped skull slashed sideways and up like a slinger's arm. The river exploded in white foam. Something sailed up and away from the burden still gripped in the terrible jaws. The missile plunged past the frozen priest. It slammed one of the rushlights from the altar before spinning into the crowd.

In the river, the crocodile had sunk again. Anit was struggling to her knees, her left hand gripping by the hair the object that had knocked her to the ground. Only the scarred nostrils served to identify Anpu's head. The neck, savaged by great conical teeth, had parted under the whip-lash shock of the crocodile's jaws. As if he were dreaming, Khati saw the young woman reach back into her hairdo and come out of it with an ivory pin in her hand, six inches long and pointed. It had been carved in the shape of a crocodile. Anit's dainty hand covered the grinning jaws, but the jutting tail glinted as she drove it toward the Steward's throat with a scream.

Hetep stepped in front of her, his body blocking hers as his right hand drew her arm back and loosened its grip on the weapon. Untouched, Khati fell full-length on the ground. Beyond him, he heard Nef-neter cry, "Lord Sebek!" and the crowd gave back the cry a thousandfold, "Lord Sebek! Lord Sebek!"

Then there was nothing but the dark.

Sunlight and Hetep's worried face greeted Khati when he opened his eyes. The servant's air of concern amused Khati, because he himself was calm. He had thought he could rule this village for the Great House; events had proved him wrong. But Khati was still of the Royal Body-guard. He could find a way to die with honor.

"Any breakfast handy?" Khati asked with a smile.

Hetep blinked in amazement. "Something, sure. Shall I bring it now?"

"Right. And then set out my best clothes. I want to make a good impression."

After his bowl of barley-and-cheese porridge, Khati went back into his bedroom. There, in a narrow alcove covered by a hanging of embroidered linen, Khati kept his weapons. Although the smooth-headed mace had always been the tool he best wielded when the god wore his flesh, there were also six javelins in the alcove. Khati chose a pair of them, short-shafted throwing weapons with three-inch flint points. He carried the weapons into the courtyard with him. Using his strength and a saw whose stone blade was set in a wooden back, Khati cut each shaft six inches behind the head. When Hetep, still frowning, had brought a bobbin of stout flaxen cord, Khati bound the shafts side by side with a wicked flint point jutting out to each end.

"You're going to bait that and hope the crocodile catches it in its throat?" Hetep ventured.

"Something like that."

"I don't see how it can work," the younger man added after a pause.

"Well, it may not," the guardsman agreed. He had buffed his limbs with a mixture of oil and sand. A slight sheen from the oil danced over his skin even after he scraped himself off with an ebony strigil.

"Well, what're you going to bait it with?" Hetep asked.

"Me." Khati began dressing. His best kilt that he would not leave for another man. The fillet with three red-dyed kite feathers marking him a champion of champions, death in human guise.

"Khati, you can't do this to yourself! Just by being here you've made people aware that—" Hetep looked at his master's eyes, his friend's, and the words stopped.

Khati left his papyrus sandals—they would be in the way of his paddling—and his mace. He thrust his knife through the sash of his kilt, however. Like the strigil, it was of ebony. Even so dense a wood would not take a useful edge, but neither would the blade shatter as flint might against a skull or a chief's bangles of shell and turquoise. In his time, Khati had slammed the point through ribs, withdrawn it, and thrust it in again. The memory turned his thoughts red, and he began to tremble slightly.

Hetep followed him out of the house. "At least tell me what I can do to help," he begged.

Khati smiled wryly. "You can tell the next man the Great House sends here what happened to me." The servant opened his mouth to protest, but Khati cut him off. "Believe me, if there were another way I could see for you to help, I'd ask you. I'm not a saint, and I want that—creature—dead more than anything else in this life or the next." He looked at Hetep. "More even than I want to die now myself. But this is going to work alone if it works at all. You'll be a lot more useful in the future."

"If they let me," Hetep said.

"Then run, get out now!" snapped Khati. "I'm sorry, but if I knew a way to change things I'd already have done it!"

Hetep sighed. "I'll be back at the house," he said quietly. "I'll have dinner ready when you get home."

The shipyard was closed, but Anpu's three sons were there in heated conclave under a split-reed canopy. Khati stepped through the gate. One of the big men growled and stood, his hand snaking for a nearby maul. His two brothers pulled him back.

"What do *you* want?" one of them demanded.

"That," Khati replied. He pointed at one of a half dozen net-stringer's floats leaning against the back fence. They were the simplest of craft, single bundles of reeds bent and flattened a little so as not to roll in the water. The user rode the bundle, either kicking with his feet or stroking to alternate sides with a short paddle. Khati's hands would be full, so he must kick . . . "I want to go out in the water alone."

The one who had reached for the maul flushed and shouted, "You'll have nothing from here, you goat-licker, except—"

"Hapi!" snapped his eldest brother. Hapi fell blankly silent. The brother who had stood in the boat when the crocodile first surfaced said, "Take it and get out. The House of Anpu is shut of you and your king."

Khati nodded. He shouldered the float and strode away. It was an awkward burden but light enough to be handled alone by a strong man.

As the guardsman stepped out through the gate again, one of the brothers called, "Do you think the crocodile will send you back with your nose pierced, Councilor?"

Khati did not answer.

The track torn through the reeds when the crocodile attacked Ro and Psemthek made a smooth, brown entrance to the stream. Khati stepped into it, feeling the crushed stems twist under his weight. Mud spurted between his toes like a thing alive. When the ripples began to slap his kilt, he set the float in the water and climbed gingerly aboard. Holding his double-pointed weapon flat against the bundle in front of him, he kicked out beyond the reeds. The hammering sun dried the linen of his kilt stiffly against his hips.

Khati's feet no longer touched the bottom, but the water was still fairly shallow and its current mild. He thrust steadily upstream, aided by the breeze that blew against his back. Eyes followed Khati's slow progress. The whole village was at work today. Usuit had made its peace with the new king, as it had with Nar-mer before. It is not for men to concern themselves with the struggles of the gods.

And if now and then a child would wail on Sebek's altar as the new king waddled up from the Nile—it is not for men to quarrel with the ways of gods.

Nef-neter stood now at that altar, still and erect as he stared eastward. Khati glared up at the priest who had defeated him, but the sun was bright and the distance too great for eye contact. Nef-neter could have been carved from sandstone for all he seemed to move.

Ahead of Khati the surface fluxed, but the tops of the nearest reeds bent also. A stray gust had troubled the water, not something below it.

Water riffled again. This time there could be no doubt of the eyes that rose from beneath. Bulbous and high-set, they could have been a frog's but for their size. With his left hand Khati fingered the charm of frog-faced Hequit that hung against his own breast. The cord parted. Before Khati could grab it, the amulet had splashed into the water.

The body shadowing the tawny surface could have been no thing on earth but one, and it was approaching very swiftly. The crocodile had slid from its den somewhere under the bank and was moving to take the bait.

Khati began whispering a prayer, not for victory but of thanks. Nothing mattered but that he had another chance to kill. The float bobbled sideways skittishly as Khati shifted. He kept his weapon hidden as far as possible against the papyrus.

The crocodile twisted its length into an *S* through which all the monstrous bulk was driven forward. The blunt snout cut the surface in a *V* of spray. The jaws opened and the forelegs flattened back against the pale belly plates.

Khati shouted and thrust his weapon out vertically to the rush, but the jaws closed short of his hand and the double points. The bundled reeds of the float shredded as the teeth crushed through them. The float had been driven backward by the beast's charge, but the reptile was sinking now with the tiny vessel in its jaws. The papyrus did not have enough buoyancy to keep the great creature on the surface.

Khati tried to jump free. His kilt was tangled in the separating float. As his torso slid under water, the guardsman drove one end of his weapon at the crocodile's jaws as if he held an ordinary knife. The blade slashed deeply across the white gums. The float wobbled. A membrane drew across and back over the eye focused on Khati. He struck again but the jaws shifted, opening slightly, and then closed even tighter in a double palisade of teeth. Half of the weapon was within the crocodile's mouth, but it lay horizontal and harmless like a bit to which no reins were attached.

Khati's right wrist was held by the interlocking rows of teeth. They were cones, pointed to grip but without shearing edges to meet and dismember prey. Because wadded papyrus still jammed the creature's gape, the tooth in the upper jaw that pinned Khati's wrist to the gum below did not even break his skin; but the Steward could not escape without cutting off his right hand. That he had neither the time nor the tools to accomplish.

The crocodile was still sinking. The float had broken apart. Shreds and sticks of papyrus mottled the golden surface as Khati went under. He reached out with his left hand, skidding a thumb across bone and scales as hard as bone as he struggled to find the creature's eye.

It was getting darker, getting cold. Khati should have filled his lungs before the crocodile pulled him under the

Nile, but there had not been time to think. There was never enough time. Perhaps the knife would reach what his bare hand could not.

But suddenly it was too cold for even that. There was time now, however, all the time in the world—until the last spot of light went out.

Khati awoke, but for a moment or more he did not realize it. Then, though his eyes and ears told him nothing, the fetor and sharp objects in the muck brought him to an awareness that he lived. He thrust out his hands, touching earthen walls on either side. When he tried to stand, the roof caught him at once and threw him prostrate. Khati's eyes were dancing with lights now, visual echoes of the pulse behind his retinas. He vomited, only a little water with the taste of mud and bile. While unconscious he must have lost his breakfast and most of the water he had swallowed on the way to drowning.

When Khati reached forward, he touched scales and the great teeth which had dragged him beneath the surface. He knew where he was and why. Sometime this night or the next, the crocodile would awaken and tug its prey back from its den into the Nile for dismemberment.

The beast did not appear to be breathing; its nostril flaps were closed. Khati's own breath was quick and ragged until he slowed it deliberately. He knew that the pain which sledged his temples might as easily be from the foul air as from the battering his head had taken during the past day.

Whatever was breathable in the den had to have come from the outside. Turning very slowly in the tight place, Khati retreated from the crocodile. The tunnel shrank almost immediately and ended.

Nef-neter had threatened the village with Chaos if it defied him, but the crocodile had not shown itself to be an enemy of order. Only of order which Nef-neter himself had not imposed. And the sun of the crocodile's foreclaws had picked out a green scarab ring like the one the priest wore . . .

Khati squirmed onto his back in the slime of the den. It was a mixture of finely divided silt and scraps of the crocodile's previous victims. The wooden knife was still in Khati's sash. He slipped it out and jabbed at the low ceiling above him. Dirt fell on his face.

The den was a tight workplace which grew tighter each time the ebony chopped up into the clay. Crocodiles dig by thrusting their clawed forefeet deep into the mud and squirming backward. The double armloads of muck are dumped in the river. Since the monster's bulk filled the den as fully as a sword does its sheath, there was nowhere for Khati to pile dirt save around his body.

Each upward stroke of the knife rammed a wedge of pain up Khati's sinuses as well. He did not really feel the dirt cascade over his face and chest. After half a dozen blows, he paused and brushed the accumulation back toward his feet. When he kicked it farther, his toes brushed the scaly horror below him in the den. Khati froze as terror overmastered pain, but the crocodile was as motionless as a corpse. Edging forward, giving his body a little twist to clear more of the dirt from his clammy skin, Khati resumed his attack on the ceiling.

To a man in total darkness, the world is everything beyond the hairs fringing his flesh. In the den, that world was clay and the heat which crushed and corroded away all the strength that once had been Khati's. He found that he had driven a shaft as long as his arm and no wider than that. He could reach no farther. His legs to the waist were mounded over by earth, his face and chest were caked with it; and all he had done was prove that the open air was still farther above him. Mumbling a curse, Khati began to widen the narrow upward track.

If it really pointed up. Khati had no direction in the blackness, no trustworthy instinct when each blood-pulse tried to split his skull with its hammering. But the dirt pattered onto his closed eyelids—that was proof enough. Besides, there was no choice. Only by cutting like a machine into the earth could Khati control the agony that wracked him.

Because of that machine-like pace, the guardsman bloodied his knuckles with a second blow bare-handed at the rock that had torn the knife from his hand. He paused, letting the new red pain wash over him. Then he reached out with both hands, touching the exposed surface. Raising the knife again—the point had splintered raggedly—Khati probed gently at the stone. It was rounded and at least as large as his head. When he had scraped the edges clear, he found they were locked by other stones, all held together by a matrix of alluvial silt. Khati was beneath a pavement—or a cairn.

The air was getting very dense.

Carefully, Khati worked the stone free. When he slid it past his body and against the pillow of dirt between him and the crocodile, an unnoticed edge flayed a patch of skin from his chest. The stone rested under the soles of his feet, giving him a better purchase as he worried out the block beside it and then a third. Khati's knees were high up against his chest, but he was through the rock stratum. He thrust his battered knife up with all his strength.

The blade wedged in a second layer of rocks. Despite the ebony's toughness, the wood snapped apart between the stress of Khati's thrust and the inflexible stone.

Khati was breathing very deeply, but there was no oxygen. His lungs filled with white fire at every breath, twisting and unraveling like burning wool. Only his chest moved, but he was not resting, not gathering strength. His strength had been dissipated. Nef-neter had defeated him, the scaly vermin behind had defeated him; and Death would soon come by to take the wager. And yet—

Fury, the god that had been with Khati all through his life, strode closer now. Fury had carried him a dozen times into blocks of opposing spearmen and brought him through, reeking of brains and blood, with no conscious memory of the blows he had struck. The red haze soaked into his tattered flesh, quenching the fire in his lungs. Fury set Khati's shoulders against the stones above him. It straightened his legs against the stones beneath. What is flesh to stone?

But stone is nothing to a god!

Slowly, but with the certainty of an air bubble rising through a marsh, Khati's shoulders lifted. Stones and earth burst upward above him. The sun-blasted air sluiced over his torso like an ice bath. Khati saw nothing, heard none of the screams from the crowd that watched him lever himself upright from the ground.

When the rage lifted its blinders from his eyes, Khati saw that he stood behind the Altar of Sebek. It was uncovered now for the first time in his memory. Nef-neter beside it had again been haranguing the villagers. The priest turned and his eyes grew as blank as the glaring sun. The crowd gaped at Khati as if he were a god in truth and not merely the flesh a god had worn.

The altar was the fossilized skull of a crocodile larger than the one denned beneath it; and tied to that altar, dressed in a set of Khati's own clothes, was Hetep.

Nef-neter raised his hand. On it shone his gray-green scarab, twin to the one on the foreclaw of the great crocodile. His lips began moving soundlessly. Then his eyes glazed again and the priest's body stiffened into an immobility equal to that of the monster when Khati had shared its den.

Khati strode to the altar. His body was without feeling, save for the blissful anodyne of oxygen rushing into his lungs to burn away the pain. Two of Anpu's sons stood beside Hetep. They fell back at Khati's advance, wild terror flickering across their faces.

The fossil altar was grimly complete down to hooked teeth longer than a man's thumb. If stone had once filled the cavities of the skull, it had since been leached out by acidic waters or painstakingly drilled away by generations of priests. A papyrus cord through the fossil's eye sockets bound Hetep's wrists. Khati gripped it with both hands. His eyes looked into those of his servant.

Hetep tried to smile. Blood and bruises marred his handsome face. "I don't have a meal ready after all," he whispered. "You should dismiss me."

Khati twisted his hands and the cord between them tore as if rotten. Hetep stood. His sash sagged with the weight of Khati's mace. For his sorcery, Nef-neter had made the servant as close an analogue to the master as was possible.

Reeds shuddered in the Nile as the crocodile rose.

The crowd sighed; a dry, mindless sound like wind through the papyrus.

Hetep flexed his hands. He looked down at the river, the waves washing to either side as the creature clambered ashore. "Master," he began, "we'd better . . ." He stopped when he realized that no one was listening to him.

The crocodile grunted as it came. There was no screaming panic, even among the villagers standing on the side slopes of the hillock with a perfect view of the creature. A god was coming. Mud-brick houses had not even the pretense of security.

Khati's form was no longer his own. His last conscious thought was not of the crocodile beginning to mount the hill on high, splayed legs. Instead Khati was remembering his first battle, an array of black-glittering spearpoints bearing down on Nar-mer's standard. His hand had sweated on his mace haft then as he watched them. After that afternoon, even his comrades of the Guard had looked at him in awe, but Khati himself could not recall an instant of his slashing attack. His mind had been smothered in a haze of blood.

As it was now.

The villagers were keening, but the advancing crocodile gave a triple grunt louder than the thousands of human throats.

"Khati!" Hetep was shouting. "We've got to run!"

Khati shrugged off his friend's hand without really noticing it. He knelt, touching the fossil skull at the back and side of its jaw.

"Master, you can't move that, it weighs—"

Khati stood, his skin flushing black with the sudden exertion. The blood in his ears roared louder than the crocodile a dozen feet away. The beast's right foreleg extended, mirroring Nef-neter's frozen gesture. The scarab rings of priest and monster blazed at one another. The jaws were open, the ragged teeth cruel and wide enough to gulp the sun. Khati's own mouth was a rictus of flesh as tense as bone. He wheezed with mindless strain as he hurled the four-hundred-pound altar down at the oncoming crocodile.

Khati fell forward as he released the missile. His mind and body were no longer the pawns of fury, but the heaping abuse of past hours had spent him totally. Through the tumult of shouting and the crocodile's explosive bellows, Khati heard the familiar *thock!* of his own mace on a skull. His eyes flashed him a tumbling kaleidoscope of impressions. One flicker was Hetep, standing over Nef-neter's body with the bloody mace in his hands. The priest's soul would never again reenter the flesh in which it had been born; the back of the old man's skull bore a dent the size of the macehead.

And the crowd of villagers was crying, "Khati! Khati!"

The sunlight was a bath soaking poisons from the scars and bruises which still colored Khati's skin. He turned from the Nile. The two skulls on posts grinned back at him. That of the crocodile had been partly cleaned by birds and insects. The scavengers even picked at the brains where the cranium had been pulverized by the impact of the stone altar. Nef-neter, however, had been spared by everything but the sun itself. That had drawn the skin away from the priest's teeth in black ridges.

Khati stood, hands on hips, and began to laugh. In the

fields, men and women heard their leader. They nodded toward the sound and trembled; and the prayers they muttered were for mercy from a god still more terrible than Sebek.

Hugh B. Cave's Murgunstruum *(Carcosa, 1977) collected
the very best of his horror fiction from the 1930s. The
writing level of them was so high that the volume won
1978's World Fantasy Award for Best Collection over such
contemporary writings as found in Fritz Leiber's* Swords
and Ice Magic *and our own* Whispers I. *I am proud to
boast that* Whispers *magazine, David Drake, Karl Edward
Wagner, and myself were all partly responsible for Hugh's
reentry into the fantasy-horror field, and that "The Door
Below" is only one of several new Cave stories I have
ready for publication.*

THE DOOR BELOW

by Hugh B. Cave

Lifting his gaze from the island lighthouse ahead to the
gathering gray clouds above, the man stopped rowing and
said, "It looks like rain, Wendy. Can't we do this some
other time?"

The girl who shared the skiff with him said gaily, "Alan
Coppard, I do believe you're scared! Why, we're nearly
there!"

"You know I don't scare. But—"

"Oh, come on, Al. What if we do get a little wet?
When we get back, I'll dry you and you dry me. Okay?"

In spite of his dark mood, Alan smiled. You had to
smile at this girl. She not only said things he had never
heard a girl say before; she did things he hadn't known
were done. Things that made him feel ten years younger
than he was. Her age, instead of thirty-four.

He was a lucky man, he realized. Two weeks ago he

had been mired in a miserable marriage with no hope of escape, never dreaming he would be here with the liveliest, best-looking girl on the *Star-News* payroll.

Of course, he had known he would be at the beach. He had rented the cottage a month ago, convinced that millionaire Roy Bolke's disappearance was a fake—and if he could prove it was, his future as a journalist would be assured. But he had never anticipated that by the time his vacation actually rolled around, dear Elaine would have walked out on him—calling him "crass" and "soulless," no less—to start proceedings for a divorce.

"Okay?" the barefoot girl in jeans and halter said again.

"Well, if you think—"

"You know what I really think, Al Coppard? You're not altogether convinced Danny Marshall was lying."

"The hell I'm not. Why else would I be giving up my vacation? I just don't think I'm going to get at the truth by snooping around an abandoned lighthouse."

"Well," she said, "you ought to see where it's supposed to have happened, even if it didn't."

Alan turned again to look at the island as he rowed toward it. It was visible from the cottage but didn't look the same close up. The distant view was like a hackneyed painting, he thought, having no impact, being in fact rather homey and comfortable. Close up, there was something threatening in the way those huge rocks rose out of the sea. "Tread here at your risk," they seemed to challenge.

The lighthouse too was different at close range. It was not white, as he had supposed, but gray as a weathered granite graveyard marker, and now that it had been shut down, the glass at its top was, of course, dark. The shaft looked like a fairy-tale giant blinded in combat but still erect and grimly defiant, sullenly awaiting the return of its foe. Hey, he thought, that's pretty good. I must remember that and use it.

"Al," Wendy Corwin said.

"Yes?"

"I'm sorry. It *is* a creepy place. What did you say it's called?"

"Dolphinback. But when I get through tearing that kid's story apart, they'll be calling it Liars Light."

There were few places on the island where it was possible to tie up a boat and step ashore, he discovered. The best appeared to be a sheltered fissure, resembling a miniature ferry slip, that must have been used by the lighthouse keepers before the "incident." Some iron mooring rings had been set in the rock there.

"This must be where Joe Marshall and the boy tied up the *Ariel* when they brought her in," he said while looping the skiff's painter through a ring.

Nine-year-old Danny Marshall—if you accepted his story—had been fishing off the rocks when his grandfather came out of the lighthouse and told him there was a boat in trouble. Joe Marshall had been talking on the radio with the boat's owner, Roy Bolke, when suddenly the man broke off the conversation. Wondering what could have happened, Joe went to the tower to see if he could pick up the boat with binoculars. He could, but saw only one person on board—a woman who was running back and forth as though demented while the boat drifted.

So, according to Danny, the two had rowed out to see what was wrong. Not only because it was their duty to do so, but because Joe knew Roy Bolke well. Joe had been the millionaire's chauffeur for years, and had become keeper here only after smashing himself up in one of Bolke's fancy sports cars.

The rope fast, Alan helped his companion ashore, admiring the competent way she used her pretty feet. "Watch your step now," he cautioned. "We don't want any accidents in this godforsaken place."

With the agility of a ballerina she danced up the natural stone staircase and turned with hand outthrust to wait for him. When he had toiled up to her, she said, "There's a thing I'm not clear about, Al. Danny and his grandfather rowed out to the yacht from here, and when they got there, the woman Joe had been watching through the glasses had vanished?''

''That's what the kid said. There were just the two bodies—Bolke at the wheel and his wife in the cabin. Their clothes were in shreds, and both bodies had small deep marks all over them—punctures of some sort, Danny insisted—but there was no blood anywhere. The missing woman's clothes were on the deck and not torn, he said. We're supposed to believe she stripped them off and tried to swim ashore or to the island here.''

''So Danny and Joe brought the yacht here?''

''If you believe the boy. But night had fallen by then so they decided to wait till morning before doing anything more. Then when Danny awoke in the morning he found Joe dead in bed. Right in the same room with him—if you're a believer in fairy tales—Joe had been killed by the same thing or things that killed the two on the boat. Pajamas shredded, same puncture marks on the body, same unexplained absence of blood. Anyway, the kid says he jumped into their dinghy and rowed ashore to tell the police.''

Solemnly nodding—which meant she didn't believe a word of it either—Wendy took him by the hand and tugged him toward the lighthouse. But Alan resisted.

''Hold on a minute. Now we're here, let's have a look at the island first.''

''You said it was going to rain.''

''*You* said if we got wet, we'd dry each other. So let it rain.''

The place hardly deserved to be called an island, Alan noted. It was a mass of stone half an acre in extent, its top a field of smooth planes tipped at assorted angles and its edges nearly everywhere plunging precipitously into the sea. It must have been a depressing place for a partially crippled man like Joe Marshall. If Bolke had indeed offered him a profitable escape from here in return for a tale that would cover up a murder—as he, Alan Coppard, firmly believed—Danny's grandfather could almost be excused for snatching at it.

The background for what he believed was simple. Roy Bolke, millionaire founder of a cosmetic empire, was sixty-seven. His wife Amanda had been sixty-five. A few weeks before the happenings at the light here, Bolke had brought back with him, from a visit to Madrid, a stunning, twenty-four-year-old Spanish model named Maria Oviedo. When her English improved he would make her a sex symbol for his cosmetics, he said.

But, of course, the role of public sex symbol was not what Bolke had in mind. Sex, certainly—and no mere symbol. Public, no way.

What Alan Coppard believed, and intended to prove, was that Bolke and his Spanish kitten had conspired to do away with Amanda. Why the elaborate hoax with the help of former chauffeur Joe Marshall? Two reasons. First, Amanda Bolke for years had been deeply involved in spirit-world doings, claiming to have talked time and again with the dead. Second, Dolphinback had a sinister story, dating back forty-odd years, of mysterious drownings and disappearances. Amanda herself had written a book about it.

As they made their way over the canted planes of stone, Wendy was a child at play and Alan a reluctant explorer held back by his feeling that the trip was a waste of time. But as they neared the lighthouse the girl said with a sudden frown, "When the police came out here to investigate Danny's story, what did they find, exactly?"

"The yacht."

"You mean *only* the yacht?"

"That's right. No bodies on board. No trace of Joe Marshall's body which the boy said was in the lighthouse."

"What about the Spanish girl's clothes?"

"Well, they did find those where Danny said they would, on the *Ariel*. But I figure Bolke and Maria were smart enough to leave them there to back up the tale the boy had been coached to tell."

"So with the help of Joe Marshall, Bolke and Maria are far away by now, and Amanda is dead at the bottom of the sea, huh? That's what you think?"

"That's it. And when I prove it—"

"Where's Danny now?"

"Living with his mother, Joe's daughter, in the village. And he's one tough kid, I can tell you. But he'll crack." Alan suddenly realized he had allowed himself to be led to the lighthouse doorway and was about to be walked inside. Annoyed, he took a step backward.

"Come on now," Wendy said with a pretty pout. "You promised."

There was no way he could back down without risking an unwanted change in their relationship, he realized. There was not even a door to deter them. Someone, probably curious visitors, had forced it open despite a No Trespassing notice that must have been nailed up by the police.

Unwillingly he surrendered. It was stupid, though, he felt. He would get his story from the boy, not from prowling around a stupid lighthouse.

Curiosity seekers *had* been here, he saw as he and Wendy entered a living room of sorts. The stone floor, only partly covered with a worn carpet, was littered with cigarette stubs. There appeared to be little damage, however. Perhaps the callers had not stayed long.

For one thing, the room was dark. Though the afternoon still had an hour to run, the windows were small and the panes so coated with salt they let in little light. And heavy, dark ceiling beams added to the uncomfortable feeling one got that the place was a dungeon.

Wondering if the power had been shut off when the lighthouse was closed down—Dolphinback was fed by an undersea cable—Alan hopefully tried a light switch. Nothing happened.

He turned to study the room. It contained a worn sofa and two shabby overstuffed chairs, a smattering of small tables. On the wall were instruments of some sort, perhaps designed to warn the keeper of any malfunction in the light chamber above. An old bookcase, built to fit the curved wall, contained volumes whose titles intrigued him. *Lorna Doone?* Sophocles? *Tarzan and the Jewels of Opar?* Amanda Bolke's *The Mysteries of Dolphinback?* Strange assortment. But then, the local people must have donated their surplus books from time to time.

"What's upstairs, Al?" Wendy asked, startling him a little as she broke the long silence.

"Other rooms, I've been told. Kitchen, bedroom, storeroom—right on up to the light itself."

"Come on, then." She grabbed his hand and pulled him toward a narrow wooden staircase.

"Wendy, don't you think—"

"Oh, don't be *old*, Al Coppard!"

That did it. He followed her up the stairs into a kitchen and stood patiently, hands in pockets, while she satisfied her curiosity. It took her some time to complete her snooping—there were more cupboards and drawers than one would have thought to find in such cramped quarters—and all the while she kept up a running conversation with herself which he found amusing. Then like an eager child on a treasure hunt she climbed the next flight of stairs and, following, he found himself in a bedroom.

It was here Joe and Danny Marshall had slept, and here the boy had awakened to find his grandfather dead that morning—if you accepted his pack of lies. The small, circular room contained two cots, two straight-backed chairs, a table, and a closet. The closet door was locked, Wendy discovered when like a moth to a flame she went straight to it and tried to open it.

"Sorry," Alan said dryly. "Joe Marshall's daughter has the key."

"Huh?"

"Investigators came out here, did what they were supposed to do, then told her she could remove Joe's belongings. Her answer was that as long as she lived she would never set foot on this island again. So they locked Joe's personal things in the bedroom closet here and gave her the key, telling her to come when she felt like it."

Obviously disappointed, Wendy turned toward the next flight of stairs. But Alan, with a frown, held up a hand and said, "Hold on. Isn't that rain I'm hearing?"

It certainly was something. Muffled by the thick walls of the lighthouse, it was still loud enough to be disconcerting.

Wendy's enthusiasm for adventure at last seemed to wane. "Gee, Al, it *is* rain!"

"Let's get out of here."

The rain had brought premature darkness and they had to be careful descending the steep flights of stairs to the base of the tower. It took a surprisingly long time, with both of them stumbling as the darkness thickened. With the increase of gloom came an amplification of the noise, so that when Alan at last groped through the lower room to the door by which they had entered, he was all but deafened by the roar.

There in the doorway he halted, stared out at a wall of falling water, and shook his head in disbelief. "We're not going anywhere," he announced. "Not in this."

Wendy clung to his hand. "Oh, Al, it's my fault."

"Forget it. Come sit down till it eases off a bit."

They returned to the living room and sat, but the room was even more oppressive now than it had been. As the darkness deepened, Alan found he could no longer read the titles in the bookcase, or even see very clearly the face of his companion, though he could see enough to know she was now both contrite and frightened.

Rising from the overstuffed chair he had plopped himself down in, he searched the room for something to relieve the gloom. "There *must* be some lamps around here, in case the power went off," he said. "At least a flashlight." But he could find nothing.

Now for a long time both he and Wendy just sat in silence.

When the roar of the downpour seemed to diminish somewhat, Alan looked at his watch. "Oh Lord, it's after six-thirty. Be dark soon even without this blasted rain. Look, I'm going to bail out the skiff. It'll be half full by now. Give me five or ten minutes, then you come too."

"I'm not staying here," she said quickly. "I'm going with you!"

He glanced around the room and realized he wouldn't enjoy being left alone in it either. Not in darkness. "Okay, come on."

Through the still-pounding rain they groped across the treacherous no-man's-land of stone to where the skiff was tied. There in a state of shock they stood hand in hand, silently gazing down into an empty cleft. The tide had risen. With each incoming wave a rush of snarling gray foam covered the iron ring with its frayed foot of yellow rope attached. The skiff was nowhere to be seen.

Lifting his head, Alan surveyed the stretch of angry, rain-whipped sea between island and shore. Wendy was a first-class swimmer and might make it, but hardly in the dark under conditions such as this. He was no swimmer at all. "Seems we're stuck for the night," he said, wanting to add a few choice expletives but aware he probably shouldn't, because the girl whose hand he held was frightened.

"Oh, Al," she sobbed.

"Take it easy now. It's not the end of the world. We have shelter, and we'll find a light if we look hard enough, I'm sure. Come on, girl. You wanted adventure. Now you've got it."

* * *

He spent only a few minutes more searching the living room for a light, then turned to the stairs. It was ironical, he thought. A hell of a note, really. Here they were in a lighthouse, of all places, and with a wet black night coming down on them they couldn't find even a candle. Ha!

He did have a book of paper matches. With those he searched the kitchen, finding nothing, and then with Wendy at his heels climbed the stairs to the bedroom.

"Our last hope," he muttered as he produced a pocket knife and tried to jimmy the locked door of the closet.

It would not open. Stepping back, he gave it an angry kick that persuaded it. "Ah," he breathed, reaching for a lantern on one of the crowded shelves.

When he shook the lantern, it gurgled. He applied a match and the room filled with yellow light and a smell of kerosene. He let his breath out in a sigh of relief. "Not much, but better than nothing," he said as he sank wearily onto one of the cots. "Whew! For a while there I wasn't too sure."

Wendy sat too. But after a moment of silence she went to the closet and began to investigate its contents. "Here's a radio of some kind, Al. Look." She stepped aside so he could see it on the shelf.

Alan got up. "One of those citizens-band things, I guess."

"The kind people talk to each other with? Can we use it to call for help?"

"If I knew anything about them. Afraid I don't. Anyway, the power's off—remember?"

"Oh."

It probably worked on DC too, Alan thought. But even if old Marshall had some source of DC power around for emergencies—they had it on boats, didn't they?—and even if he recognized it when he saw it, he wouldn't know how to hook it up.

There was another gadget on the shelf, however. "Now

this," he said, reaching for it, "I know about. It's a tape recorder. Uses cassettes. Got batteries in it, too," he added after flipping the back open. "Maybe we can have some music while we wait. You see any cassettes in the closet here?"

She found some and he carried them, with the recorder, back to the cot from which he had risen. In a moment the little bedroom with its flickering yellow light and smell of kerosene was filled with music.

"Beds and Beethoven," Alan said. "Even light of a sort. Not bad for a start. Marshall had good taste in music, anyway."

Wendy was actually smiling again. "And I saw some cans of food in the kitchen, if we get hungry. The stove's electric, though. We'll have to eat the stuff cold."

Alan rose again. "I'll bring some on my way back. Want to get that Amanda Bolke book and see what she said about this place." He reached for the lantern and realized he had a problem. If he took their only light, Wendy would be left in darkness. "Guess you'd better come with me," he said.

They descended to the living room, Alan holding the light high as he led the way. The book in hand, he said, "Hold on a minute," and stepped to the door to size up the weather. The rain was still unrelenting, the night black as pitch now. He could hear the sea assaulting the island: a circle of sound like a ring of wild animals with Wendy and himself helpless in the center.

He was glad to go back upstairs. Somehow the bedroom, high up in the tower, seemed a better refuge.

With the lantern on the table between them, they lay on the cots, Alan with his book, Wendy with her hands clasped behind her head and her gaze fixed on the ceiling as she listened to the music. But presently Wendy got up again, saying, "I just thought of something, Al."

"What?"

"This rowing out to the *Ariel*, finding bodies on board,

and bringing the yacht back here. Wouldn't a lighthouse keeper write up a report of a thing like that if he actually did it?''

"Don't be a dope. Joe Marshall didn't write any report."

"Read your book. I'm going to have a *good* look in this closet."

She really hoped to find something, Alan realized with amusement as he watched her assault the closet's contents. She actually believed at least part of the boy's story. Losing interest, he returned to Amanda Bolke's *Mysteries of Dolphinback*.

A strange woman, Amanda Bolke. Like other very wealthy women he could think of, she seemed to have ridden her hobby with fantastic determination. "Wendy, listen to this," he said, and began reading from the book aloud. " 'It should be obvious to anyone who has delved deeply enough into the history of Dolphinback Island— even before the construction of the lighthouse—that here is one of several very special places where the known and unknown worlds are in juxtaposition. There have been too many unexplained happenings here for us to believe otherwise. If one acknowledges the existence of demons, as one must, of course, if not cursed with a rigidly shut mind, then here is one of the gateways by which such creatures are able to penetrate our world.' ''

"Who published that nonsense?" Wendy demanded, pausing in her exploration of the closet.

Alan looked. "She did, herself."

"Ha!"

"Wait. 'One day when the time is propitious,' she goes on, 'a believer in these matters, with a proper background of study and self-training, will make an effort to deliberately summon these spirit-world creatures from their habitat in this area. It is my own firm belief that their dwelling place, or at least the gateway to it, lies under the sea in the vicinity of the island.' ''

"She's nuts," Wendy said, "but she gives me the creeps."

Alan grinned. "Sure she's nuts. But all this will make my story bigger and better when I break it. And I'll break it, don't worry. This time next month you'll be seeing Al Coppard's name all over the place."

"The new journalism you were talking about, huh?"

"That's it, woman. All you need to do today is get the goods on some well-known character and drag him down. When he's down, you're up."

"Well, all right," Wendy said. "But if you want to read that book, kindly read it to yourself and let me listen to the music."

When the Beethoven ended, Alan tried another tape from the closet. This was a live Boston Pops concert, apparently recorded by Marshall himself from a radio program. It lasted long enough for Wendy to finish taking the closet apart—without finding a single item of interest, she was forced to admit—and when the Pops tape gave way to a professional recording of Mahler, Wendy returned to her cot.

Only for a moment, though. Rising again, she frowned down at the cot and said, "You know, I'll bet *I've* got the bed Danny found his grandfather dead in that morning."

"Danny didn't find anyone dead."

"Well, we don't *know*. Anyway—" Walking over to his cot, she stood there impishly gazing down at him. "Move over, huh? You can even read to me if you like."

Alan didn't read to her. When she was nicely snuggled up to him with her head on his shoulder, he dropped the book and put his arm around her. They lay that way in silence for a time, then undressed and made love.

It was when they were quietly side by side again that Wendy suddenly said, "Al, listen!"

He did so but was aware of nothing unusual—only a diminution of earlier sounds to which he had become accustomed with the passing of time. "Rain seems to have stopped," he said. "Sea's subsiding. That what you mean?"

"No. Listen."

It was hardly a time to confess that his hearing was less than acute. He really tried to absorb what she apparently was hearing but received nothing.

"You don't hear a scratchy noise like—like footsteps?" She was frightened now, he realized. Her warm, moist body—they were both still undressed—had begun to tremble in his embrace.

"Probably water dripping somewhere. From the rain."

"Uh-uh. It isn't water." She slipped from his arms and hurriedly put her blue jeans and white halter back on. As she did so, he saw what looked like a bit of silver chain dangling from a pocket of the jeans and reached out for it.

To his surprise he found himself holding a small cross, apparently of sterling, with a crucified Christ on it. To the brief length of chain was attached a small safety pin of the same metal. Apparently the cross was meant to be pinned to the wearer's clothing.

"Where did this come from?" he demanded, certain it was not hers.

She seemed annoyed. "I found it in the closet."

"Oh-oh. You *are* shy of scruples, aren't you?" He turned the cross over and saw something stamped in the metal, and, his sight being sharper than his hearing, was just able to read it. " 'Cedillo, Guadalajara.' Must be the maker."

"Guadalajara's in Mexico," Wendy said, pouting. "I've been there." She took the cross out of his hand and with a look of defiance thrust it back into her pocket. Then suddenly she said, "Al, listen!"

Obediently he did so but heard nothing.

"Downstairs!" she insisted. "What's wrong with you, Al? Can't you hear *anything*?"

Rising, Alan went naked to the door and opened it.

Annoyed by her censure of him, he stood there fully a minute, straining to hear what she said she had heard.

Nothing.

He realized suddenly that she was at his side, peering into the darkness down there at the foot of the steep stairs. "Well?" he demanded.

"It—it's gone, whatever it was. But I *heard* it. Something was moving around down there, Al. Making the same scratchy footsteps I heard before. Only—only I'm sure there was more than one this time."

Alan was tempted to take the lantern and go down the stairs with it to show her there was nothing down there in the kitchen. His nakedness dissuaded him, and so did his awareness that her hearing *was* better than his. He shut the door and said, "What we need is some lively music, don't you think?" Music she was familiar with, he thought. Something to take her mind off what was supposed to have happened here. Otherwise she might crack up.

She had discovered a dozen or more tapes in the closet and he had played parts of some already. He looked at the others now. Most were prerecorded symphonies, opera excerpts, chamber music. Even the ones bought blank were filled with the same kind of music, according to the scribbled notes on the boxes. One box, however, had no index. Hopefully he inserted that tape into the player.

A man's voice came scratchily from the speaker. ". . . so what we did, Joe, we decided to take the *Ariel* and get away from those pests for a while. You know what bastards they can be with their questions; you used to keep them at bay for me. Since Watergate, every two-bit newsman in the country thinks he's the Spanish Inquisition. So I said to Maria, 'Come on, let's take off and let them find someone else to harass.' And here we are. You know we're close enough I could almost talk to you without this radio, Joe . . .

"You're what? Taping my part of this? Well, I'll have to say something for posterity then, won't I? Maybe I should ask Amanda for some deathless words. You'd get a laugh if you were aboard this boat right now, Joe. You know what she always said about Dolphinback? That crazy book she published? Well, for the past hour she's been in the cabin going through some kind of crazy routine that's supposed to prove everything. Right this minute she's bellowing out some lunatic chant. Can you hear it? Listen while I keep quiet a minute.''

There was a faint background sound of chanting on the tape. Then the voice of Roy Bolke intruded again. ''You hear it, Joe? Yeah? Well, it's been going on like that for an hour. Can you imagine? Maria is scared half to death. These Spanish gals are high-strung, you know. For half an hour she's been begging Amanda to stop it, telling her something awful will happen if she keeps it up. A while ago she came and begged *me* to stop it, and I noticed blood on her blouse where she'd pinned a cross on herself. It was for protection, she said, in case Amanda succeeded in opening that gateway she's been going on about. What I mean, the poor gal is so scared and nervous, she stuck the brooch right into herself, Joe. Right into her breast. But hold on a minute, will you? What is it, Maria?''

Here another voice, a woman's, was audible for a few seconds but was too far from the microphone to be intelligible. Too shrill, too. ''What?'' Bolke said in reply. ''Hell, I can't come now. Somebody has to run this scow. Go tell her I—''

The next sound on the tape was not his, nor could it have come from the girl to whom he was talking. It was a prolonged scream that obviously came from a distance. Then Bolke's voice, returning, was a hoarse yell. ''Oh, Christ! Oh, my God . . .''

And silence.

When the silence had endured long enough to indicate the taping was at an end, Alan stopped staring at the recorder and muttered what he knew was a stupid remark. It was the only one he could think of that would not make matters worse.

"The cross didn't come from Mexico," he said. "There's a Guadalajara in Spain."

Wendy, too, seemed to realize they must control their emotions. "How do you suppose it got here, Al? To the lighthouse, I mean."

"That's more than I can figure out."

It wasn't more than Wendy could figure out, though. After a few moments of silence she said, "Al, I think I know what happened. I mean I really do."

"What?"

"Well, in the first place Amanda Bolke, with her crazy chanting and whatever else she was doing on board the yacht, opened that door or gateway she believed in and conjured something up out of the depths. She and her husband were killed by it, but the Spanish girl was protected by the crucifix she wore. Demons and vampires and such are supposed to fear a crucifix, aren't they?"

"You're nuts," Alan said.

She ignored the comment. "But Maria made a mistake. When she found herself alone with two dead bodies, she stripped off her clothes—with the crucifix pinned to her dress—and tried to swim ashore. Not to make it, because she was unprotected then. You see?"

"You're wasting your time working for the *Star-News*, pal. You ought to be writing shudder movies."

"So we come to Joe Marshall and his grandson," Wendy stubbornly continued. "They rowed out to the yacht and found the two bodies and Maria's clothes. They took the yacht to the island here. Then while examining the Spanish girl's garments Danny saw the cross and fancied it, just as I did when I discovered it in the closet. He took it. And that night, when whatever boarded the *Ariel* came here to the lighthouse, Danny survived because he had the cross in his possession. When he rowed ashore in the morning he must have left it behind for fear he'd be questioned about it."

"You're a genius," Alan said. "So what about the tape? How did it get into the closet here?"

"Well . . . when Joe and Danny went out to the yacht to see what was wrong, Joe must have left the radio and recorder running in case Bolke came back on the air. That makes sense. Then when they got back here Joe was pretty shook up, and my hunch is he just didn't bother listening to the tape until later, when Danny was in bed. Realizing the police would want to hear it, he rewound it intending to take it ashore in the morning. But in the morning he was dead, and *Danny* didn't take the tape because he had no idea it was important."

"Ha."

"Well, can you think of a better explanation? When the police came out here after hearing Danny's story, they wouldn't have thought anything of finding the tape. More than likely there were others around, all of music, so why should that one be special? When the time came to gather up Joe's things and lock them in the closet, the tape went in with everything else and that was the end of it."

"You know," Alan said, shaking his head in not-so-mock amazement, "I never dreamed you had a mind like that. I almost hate to shut you up. The fact is, however, the tape is a fake, a hoax, part of the whole elaborate plot to enable Roy Bolke to escape from a dull marriage and run off with his Spanish doll. Newsmen think they're the Spanish Inquisition, do they? Ha. He'll find out. Now if you'll just stop your fantasizing for a moment and—"

A new sound had filled the room. The recorder, left running, had come alive again after a long silence. A girl's voice was screaming hysterically in Spanish.

Screaming for *help,* Alan realized with an ego-shattering shock as his knowledge of the tongue came back to him. His Spanish was the South American version, acquired during a year in Venezuela, but it was adequate.

"They're coming back!" she was screaming. "Oh Jesus, Mary and Joseph, they're coming back for me! Oh, they're horrible, horrible—I can see four of them coming up over the side. Oh God, I can't stay here! I have to go!''

The rest was a scream that diminished in volume as the girl ran from the yacht's radio. Ran out on deck to strip off her clothes and leap into the sea. *If* this wasn't just a continuation of the fairy tale . . .

Again the recorder was silent. While Alan struggled with his convictions and Wendy sat like a figure carved from wood, it ran on for another minute or two, gently humming, then clicked as the tape came to an end. Total silence filled the room.

I better put my clothes on, Alan thought. This whole thing is phony, but I can't be like this if anything happens. He had always enjoyed the sensation of being naked, but now it filled him with dread. He felt defenseless.

But Wendy's hand was on his thigh, her sharp nails tearing at him as she whispered frantically, ''Al! There's something downstairs again! Oh, my God!''

As before, he strained to hear—and this time *did* hear a rhythmic, rasping sound as though someone were shuffling toward them over a stone floor strewn with sand. But it was not in the kitchen below. It was on the stairs just outside the door.

Wendy screamed. Snatching the Spanish girl's cross from her pocket and thrusting it blindly out in front of her, she leaped to her feet and raced to the door. She jerked it open. Something massive and dark out there—something man-shaped but taller than any man—recoiled from her with a hissing sound as she jabbed the cross at it. Alan had only a glimpse of huge webbed feet and a scaly torso, of upflung arms terminating in long, curled fingers that resembled the talons of a bird of prey.

''Wait!'' he wailed. ''For God's sake, Wendy, wait for me!''

But she was past the thing and gone. He could hear her shrieking at others, on the stairs, to get out of her way. Could hear the slap of her bare feet as she fled through the dark kitchen below. Had she forgotten there was no skiff? Probably she had, but it made no difference. She had the cross, and she could swim . . .

He stopped thinking about Wendy then. Poised for flight, he stared at the doorway and felt his naked body shrivel. The thing at the top of the stairs filled the doorway now, and the lantern's light revealed even more of it. The scales and talons were not its most frightful features. He found himself staring at a huge, scaly head with great bulbous fish-eyes and cavernous nostrils. And he had not believed!

With a hoarse cry Alan snatched the lantern and raced for the stairs at the rear of the bedroom—stairs leading up to chambers he and Wendy had not explored. As he clawed his way to the next room above, he looked back and saw one of the cots go crashing into the wall as the plodding creature kicked it aside instead of walking around it. It was the cot on which he and Wendy had made love.

Behind that horror came a second, and a third.

The stairs ended and Alan found himself in a storeroom, stumbling past a standby generator and drums of fuel . . . past a workbench and mounds of boxes. No refuge here. He groped across it to the next flight of stairs and again looked back as he climbed.

There were four of the things now, shuffling on in single file, awful in their unhurried but relentless pursuit. Four monsters from the same ghastly mold. And now as their hissing swelled to a snakepit chorus he noticed the mouths from which the sound spewed forth. Each was an obscene slit equipped with two long, needle-pointed fangs.

Staggering into the room at the top of the tower, he saw he could go no farther. It was the smallest chamber of all. Its walls were of glass. The space left for running was only a circular catwalk around the lamp.

He, Alan Coppard, new-style mediaman, was trapped in the blind eye of the fairy-tale giant that was, after all, only a prison.

As the first of the creatures plodded inexorably forward, he turned wildly to face it and screamed. But the scream came out a whimper as he sank naked to his knees and covered his eyes with his hands.

Phyllis Eisenstein is making her first appearance in Whispers *with the following poignant yet chilling work. Her stories have appeared in* The Magazine of Fantasy and Science Fiction, Analog, Galaxy, *and* New Dimensions. *Her novel,* Born to Exile, *has appeared in both hard and soft covers.*

POINT OF DEPARTURE

by Phyllis Eisenstein

On Tuesday morning I lost my mind. Tuesday was my day off work, and I was spending it in bed with a good book. When the phone rang, I assumed it would be Mark, calling in a slack minute at the office. I lifted the receiver.

"What can I do for you?" I said.

"You could call me once in a while," replied a female voice.

I didn't recognize the voice, but for a moment I was too embarrassed to admit that, so I played along, hoping that a few additional words would reveal the speaker's identity. "I will in the future, if you want."

"You never call me. You treat me like a stranger."

"Well, I've been pretty busy lately, you know."

With great sadness, the voice said, "Did I raise you to be too busy for your own mother?"

"I'm sorry," I replied as gently as possible, "but you must have the wrong number. You'd better dial again."

"I don't need to dial again, Leah Stern. I know who I'm calling."

I sat up slowly. "This isn't funny."

"I thought I'd invite you to dinner tonight, about seven o'clock. Can you make it?"

"Who is this?"

"I have a nice pot roast. Mark eats pot roast, doesn't he?"

"Who are you?"

"I'll see you at seven, then."

The connection broke, and I was left with a dead receiver in my hand. Dead as my mother, in her grave for thirteen years. The memory of her last days flooded over me: the disinfectant smell of her bedroom, the sunken look in her eyes that pleaded for ever more morphine, the sound of her death rattle rising from her throat, the funeral, black, black, everyone in black. And yet the voice . . . the voice . . . it was hers.

I cradled the receiver. My body felt hot, beads of sweat bursting from my skin at forehead and armpits. My stomach churned. I ran to the bathroom and heaved up breakfast, and then I lay on the floor, gasping against the cool tiles, and I wondered who would be cruel enough to play that kind of grisly joke.

Back at the phone, my first impulse was to call Mark and spill the tale to him. If I sounded distraught enough, he would come home and comfort me in his arms. I paused halfway through dialing and hung up. That was weakness, I told myself; I, who had gone calmly through the last weeks of my mother's life, could not succumb to the cruelty of a phone call. Instead, I called my brother Paul, because I thought he would want to know that someone had been jesting with his mother's corpse.

"Well, well," he said. "A call from my sister. What's the occasion?"

"How are you doing, Paul?" I asked.

"Good enough. Since I last talked to you, Fran and I have been to Munich. Lovely city, Munich. How have you been?"

"I just had a phone call that I thought you would be interested in."

"Yes?"

"From . . . from Mom."

"Oh? What did the old girl want?"

"She invited us to dinner tonight."

"Did she?" There was the sound of rustling papers. "Us too; I have it here on my calendar. You're going, aren't you?"

"Going?"

"She'd be pretty disappointed if you didn't make it. She's really hot for a little togetherness."

My hand began to shake, and I clenched my fingers tighter about the receiver. "Paul, how can we go to Mom's for dinner?"

"Oh, it won't be *that* bad. You can stand her for a couple of hours, can't you?"

"Paul . . ." I said weakly.

"Look, I've got to go. See you tonight at seven." He hung up.

I called Mark.

"Are you all right, honey?" he asked. "Your voice sounds a little odd."

"Darling, Paul is playing a terrible, terrible joke on me, and I don't know what I've done to deserve it."

"What kind of joke?"

"About half an hour ago, someone called claiming to be my mother and inviting us to dinner at her home tonight."

"And . . . ?"

"And when I called Paul to tell him about it, he pretended that it really was my mother."

"Well, was it or wasn't it?"

"Mark, what kind of *question* is that?"

"Wait a minute, don't get hysterical. I only meant, did it sound like your mother?"

"Yes, it did."

"Well, then, it must have been your mother."

"Mark, how could it *possibly* have been my mother?"

"I know she hasn't invited us to dinner in a long time—"

"Dinner? Where would she invite us to dinner? At the cemetery?"

"What?"

"I can just see it: a tablecloth over the grave, chopped liver on the tombstone."

"Leah, what are you talking about?"

"I'll spell it out for you, Mark—how can she invite us to dinner if she's dead?"

"Dead? My God, when did it happen? How—?"

"What do you mean, when did it happen? It happened thirteen years ago!"

There was a silence at his end of the phone.

"Mark? Are you there?"

"Let me get this straight." His voice sounded strained. "You're saying that your mother has been dead for thirteen years?"

"Well, of course she has!"

"Leah, you must have been asleep and had a nightmare. Your mother isn't dead. She's very much alive."

"Mark, she died before I met you."

"Call her if you don't believe me."

"I can't call her; they don't have phones at Rosehill!"

"Listen, Leah, I want you to lie down. Relax. I'll be home in less than an hour. Just relax."

"She's dead, Mark. I was there when it happened."

"Just relax. I love you." He hung up.

Tears of rage choked me. My brother and my husband of ten years—I could scarcely believe it. I threw the phone at the wall.

While I waited for him, I made myself a cup of tea, and

I was sitting at the kitchen table sipping the brew and nibbling cookies when I heard his key in the lock. He hurried toward me and pulled me into his arms, a look of deep concern on his face. I couldn't help admiring his performance.

"You feel warm," he said. "Are you running a fever?"

"I'm not the one who's sick," I said, pushing away.

"Look, I talked to your mother before I left the office. She's fine, and she did invite us all to dinner tonight."

I leaned back against the refrigerator, my arms crossed over my chest. "And where did you call my mother?"

"She's at home. You can call her now if you want."

"At home where?"

"At the house. At *her* house, the house you grew up in."

"Somebody else owns that house now. It was sold after she died."

He tried to touch me, but I fended him off. "Leah, it's your father who's dead, not your mother."

"He's dead too. He died when I was a child. She died when I was an adult."

He grabbed the kitchen phone receiver from its cradle and thrust it at me. "Call her right this minute!"

"That number belongs to someone else now. It has for thirteen years."

He pulled the phone directory from its niche, thumbed through it till he found a page in the middle, and held it out for me to see, his finger stabbing a place in the center column. "Here it is, right here!"

Her name, the address of the house I had grown up in, the old phone number.

I took the directory from him, looked at the cover. It was this year's. The page was bound securely to its neighbors, numbered properly, in correct alphabetical order. "You got a fake listing put in the phone book."

"It's not fake, Leah."

"You want me to think I'm losing my mind."

"No!"

"I just don't understand *why*. Is it money? Some other woman? Mark, you don't have to go through all this!" I felt my mouth shaping the ultimate cliché: "Why are you doing this to me?"

"Oh, my darling, I'm not doing anything, believe me. You're tired. You've been overworked. We'll take a vacation—anywhere you like, I promise!"

I slumped into a chair and put my head down on the table. "This isn't happening," I murmured.

He hovered over me, and at last he put his hand on my neck and stroked gently. "Why don't you lie down on the bed and I'll give you a back rub. You'll feel better."

"My body will," I muttered, "but not my mind." I scraped the chair back, away from him. "I have some phone calls to make."

"You might call your mother."

"Oh, no, not that. You can't get me like that again. Paul hired her, I presume—a nice match on the voice. Very nice."

"Leah, no."

"Go away. I don't want to hear any more lies."

He made himself a cup of instant coffee while I dialed.

I called my oldest friend, the only one left from high school days. She had been in the house those last weeks of my mother's existence. She would remember. Without much preamble, I said, "Gloria, is my mother alive or dead?"

She said, "Is that a rhetorical question?"

"Just answer it."

"Well, she was alive the last time I looked."

"When was that?"

"Oh, a couple of months ago, I guess. During the holidays."

"Did Mark tell you to say that?"

"Mark? No, why should he?"

"Gloria, we've been friends a long time. Like sisters."

"Yes, we have."

"Do you love me as if I were your own blood?"

"You know I do."

"Then why are you lying to me?"

"Lying about what?"

"You know my mother has been dead for years!"

"Leah, are you feeling all right?"

I slammed the phone down, then dialed another number. My Aunt Mildred. She wasn't home. I tried my uncles; one of them answered and confirmed the assertions I had already heard. I began trying long-distance numbers, relatives who hadn't seen me in years, in California, New York, Florida, numbers I didn't know by heart and had to look up in the address book. The same story, over and over again.

And then I ran across my mother's address.

I would never have written it into the book for myself, of course; I had spent too many years in that house to forget its address. But the book had been Mark's originally, from before we were married, and when we began to share our lives, I just added my list to his. Yet, he had no conceivable need for the address; I had long since left my mother's house when he met me.

It wasn't in his handwriting or mine. It was in hers—that spidery, slanted script I had taken to grammar school after each day of absence. I could never forget *it*, either.

Forged, I told myself.

I called Directory Assistance and asked for her number. The operator gave me the one I knew by heart. I didn't dial it.

I picked up my purse. "I'm going out," I said to Mark. "You can go back to work if you want."

"Leah, I think you should lie down—"

"I'm going to my mother's."

He smiled. "I think that's a good idea. Stay the afternoon; I'll meet you there tonight."

"We'll see about that," I said.

Easing my car into the street, I headed south. I hadn't been in that part of the city in years, not since I moved into an apartment of my own after the funeral. No one I knew lived in the neighborhood any more—it was changing, had changed, and the look of it was alien to me. Stores I remembered from childhood had been transformed, some even abandoned; trees had been cut down, houses repainted; the gravel playground of my old grammar school had been covered with blacktop. Yet the block where my mother's house stood looked like an oasis of timelessness, the same lilac bushes everywhere, the same sycamore tree; even the trim on the house was the same pale yellow I remembered. I parked in front of the hedge that I had trimmed so often with hand shears, and I climbed the shallow stairway to the front porch. I rang the bell.

She came to the door.

For a moment I thought I was fainting. The world tilted, and I felt that I was seeing through a long black tunnel. I reached out for the railing, caught it, gripped it like a spar floating in the open sea, my only hope for safety.

She was older than I remembered. Her hair was all gray now, not salt and pepper any more. She would be sixty-four. If she were alive. She said something, but I couldn't hear it clearly, and then she opened the screen door and caught my arm and helped me inside. I staggered to the couch, the old silver couch in the green living room, her arms supporting me, her flesh warm and alive against my own.

She brought me a cup of tea and we talked, though I hardly knew what I was saying. Thirteen years of my life were rolling around in my brain like ball bearings on a plate. How long, I wondered, had it taken me to reconstruct the past, to manufacture her death, the funeral, the years since? A night? An hour? A minute? I had erased her from my memory, and, sitting on the familiar couch, watching her speak half in words and half in gestures that I used myself, that I had learned from her, I could not guess why.

"You were always so close as children," she was saying. "And Mark always seems to enjoy himself when he's around Paul—why doesn't *he* make some effort to get you together more often?"

I clutched at the thread of the conversation, hoping to find some sort of comfort in small talk. "Well, we do live at opposite ends of the city," I said slowly. "He's busy, we're busy, you know how it is . . . Mom." The final word almost choked me, and I covered it with a cough and a gulp of tea. At that moment, I could have used something stronger, but I knew that my mother kept no liquor in the house. Where was my vaunted calm? I realized suddenly that I must have made that up too—a heroic attitude to go with invented adversity.

I leaned back on the couch then, and my hand, which had been shaking just a trifle, steadied. I could be calm. My mother was alive, sitting right in front of me, and I would have to accept that and accept the frailty of my own mind that made me think she was dead. I thought of all the people I had called—I was going to have a fancy time talking my way out of the confusion I had caused them all. But I would be calm now, even if I had never been before, because that was the only way I was going to stay out of a mental hospital.

"Are you interested in helping me make dinner?" said my mother.

"Sure."

In the kitchen, I set my teacup in the spotless sink. My mother opened the refrigerator and began taking out vegetables to go with the roast. I knew where the knives were, the cutting board, the colander. She had kept her kitchen in the same order since I was a small child. While we worked, we talked about my childhood, and Paul's.

Mark called at six o'clock. I answered the phone, told him to come on over. He sounded relieved at the cheer in my voice. I kissed him when he came in the door; I had a lot to make up for.

Paul and Fran arrived exactly at seven. He had gone grayer since I saw him last; *she* was frosting more of her hair these days. Dinner was pleasant. We all had a lot to say, sitting around the table—Mark and I about our business, Paul about his, Fran about the children and the trip to Europe. They had brought a stack of pictures with them, and, more than the castles and the monuments, the photos of their children caught my attention: they had grown so that I hardly knew them any more, and I realized that they had probably forgotten what their aunt looked like.

"You should have brought them along," I said.

"Let them drive the sitter crazy," said my mother. "This is an adult dinner." And yet when she spoke of Paul and me, which she did at length, it was to remember us as children. "The black eye she gave you, Paul—I'll never forget that day. You didn't fight again after that."

"I didn't dare," said Paul. "She had a hell of a punch."

I said, "You asked for it, big brother. You knew I didn't like being teased."

"Of course I knew." He grinned. "That's why I did it. I never expected you to try to kill me."

I sipped delicately at my coffee. "There were times, I recall, when you were very cruel."

Paul shifted in his chair, and his fingers played over the silverware beside his plate. "Well, you know, little sister, you were quite a nuisance. I never could seem to get rid of you—you didn't understand the word 'scram.' "

"I liked to see the two of you together," said my mother. "Then I knew Leah was safe."

"Full-time baby-sitter," muttered Paul.

"I rather enjoyed it myself," I said.

"That was obvious."

"Oh, come on, we had a lot of fun together. Remember when we went to the amusement park?"

He nodded. "I remember that you almost fell off the roller coaster."

"I did not!"

"You stood up, and if I hadn't grabbed your shirt, it would have been goodbye."

"I was holding on to the bar—I wouldn't have fallen out."

"You never told me about that," said my mother.

"There was nothing to tell," I said. "Paul just had an overactive imagination."

He shrugged. "I didn't want to worry you, Mom."

I leaned my elbows on the table and interlaced my fingers. "What I remember best about that day was the episode in the funhouse. When you played that dirty trick on me."

"What do you mean?"

"You convinced me to go in, even though I was afraid of the dark, by saying that I could hold on to your belt. And then, in the darkest corridor, you slipped your belt buckle off and let the strap slide away. And me with it."

"I never did that."

"Didn't you?" I looked down at my fingernails. "I screamed a lot, but then, you probably couldn't hear me above the other screams—the teenage girls whose boyfriends were using the darkness to cop a quick feel."

"I don't remember anything like that."

"I'm sure it wasn't very important to you. Just mildly amusing." I looked up at him and shrugged.

He eased back in his chair, crossing his arms over his chest. "Shall I think of something rotten that you did to me? Are we going to play that kind of game, Leah?"

I smiled. "I did a lot of rotten things to you. That's in the nature of little sisters. They do them because they love their older brothers and want their undivided attention. Don't you see that in your own children?"

"Of course we do," said Fran.

"I loved you so much that I wanted to be with you all

the time," I said, "Sometimes it was hard to do that without being rotten."

"Well, I loved you too," said Paul, "even if you did drive me crazy."

I wondered how many people at the table noticed that both of us used the past tense.

"We did have fun," I said. "All the miles we rode on your bike, the snow forts we built in the backyard, and those terrific museum visits. And every time I asked a question, you knew the answer, or you knew where to find it."

"You certainly asked a lot of questions." He smiled wryly, shaking his head. "But we did have some good times, didn't we? Remember the Bears-Rams exhibition game?"

"What happened?" asked my mother.

"Why . . . nothing, except that it was a great afternoon. The Bears won."

"No, I mean, what happened to the good times? Why don't you do things together any more?"

Paul flapped his hands. "Well, we did both get married, Mom."

"You don't even call each other."

"We're busy, Mom," I said.

"You said that before. But if you really wanted to see each other, you'd find the time. You wouldn't be too busy."

"It's just not practical," said Paul, "with me so far south and Leah so far north."

My mother struck the table with the flat of her hand. "I don't believe that. Not for a moment."

A profound silence followed that statement, and I was about to clear my throat just to break it when Mark said, "We *should* get together more often. I know it's quite a drive from our place to yours, but we could meet downtown for dinner and a movie, only half the distance for each of us."

"I really think that's a great idea," Fran said quickly. "Why don't I take a look at the new movie listings on Friday and give you a call?"

"All right," I said.

And the conversation faltered again, as I wondered if she would call, or if Paul would think of some excuse to cancel. He worked in the evenings sometimes; it wouldn't be hard for him to postpone the projected outing forever. I stared at him, and he looked away.

"Will you call?" asked my mother, aiming the question at Paul, not Fran.

"I can't plan that far ahead," he said.

"You won't call," she said softly. "You never call, either of you. For thirteen years you've avoided each other. Thirteen years—I've counted every one of them. What happened so long ago to make you strangers to each other?" She looked from Paul to me." What happened?"

The number thirteen made a chill run through me. I knew immediately what she was talking about, yet I knew, too, that it happened only in my mind. Looking at Paul, I could almost see the calendars rolling back behind his eyes as he struggled to place the period she spoke of.

"We weren't kids any more by then," he murmured. "We were grown up and going our separate ways. I was married already, and Leah was in college." He frowned. "Thirteen years ago—wasn't that . . . when you were so sick?"

"That was when I had cancer," said my mother. "I'm not afraid to say the word, Paul."

My hands turned clammy and clutched at the tablecloth where it brushed my knees. I felt adrift between fantasy and reality. My mother admitted having had cancer—where, then, did truth leave off and delusion begin? Was it only her death that was false? Was there a reservoir of calm inside me after all, ready to be tapped in crisis? My whole body ached with stiffness as memories flooded over me and I could not tell how many of them were real.

"I remember," said Paul, "Leah nursed you."

"The whole summer," said my mother. "She almost missed the beginning of college because of me."

"But she did a fine job, really fine. The doctor was impressed."

The doctor had looked into my eyes and told me how well I was holding up, alone. I could feel the touch of his fingers on the back of my head, the tongue depressor in my mouth. I could hear his voice: "I don't like those tonsils, young lady. We can't have you getting sick right now." At the funeral he had held my hand.

I felt a headache starting at my temples, and I closed my eyes. To my family gathered around the dinner table, I murmured cautiously, "I remember it being a very grueling time."

"It was hard on you," said my mother, "all alone."

I opened my eyes and looked at Paul. "Was I alone?"

His face turned in my direction, but his gaze didn't meet mine. "Well, I did have to work."

"Yes, I remember that."

"I was pretty tired when I got home at night."

"I know. I was too, only for me it didn't end at five o'clock."

"Leah, I just didn't have time to spend on nursing."

"You didn't have time to waste on your dying mother, you mean!"

There was a sudden, sharp, collective indrawn breath around the dinner table. Everyone was staring at me.

Except my mother. Her eyes were fixed on Paul. "You'll never know, Paul," she said quietly, "how unhappy that made me."

His mouth worked a bit before the next words came. "You know how it was, Mom. That job was important to me, I threw everything I had into it, and when I got home I was exhausted."

"You didn't even call."

"I knew you'd be all right."

"No, you didn't," I said. "You thought she was going to die, just like everybody else did. She looked like a mummy toward the end—with her bones showing through skin like old, yellowed paper. But you wouldn't know about that, would you? You never saw her that way!"

"Leah, please! Not in front of Mom!"

I glanced at my mother, and she shrugged, saying, "I know it wasn't a pretty sight."

To Paul, I said, "Not in front of *you*, you mean. It probably makes you sick just to imagine it."

He looked pale to me, and his fingers were slowly shredding a paper napkin into confetti. "All right," he said at last. "All right. I just couldn't stand watching it, Mom. I just couldn't."

I shouted, "I stood it!"

He started up out of his chair, and his thighs struck the table, making all the glassware ring. He clutched the napkin in one fist. "So I'm not a superman; I'm a coward! Is that what you want me to say? Well, I've said it, damn you! I've said it!"

My mother stretched her arms out over the table, as if to keep Paul and me apart. "Sit down, Paul."

He sat, eyeing me warily.

"So I caused the rift between you," she said. "If I had never had cancer, you'd be friends today."

I leaned an elbow on the table and pressed the palm of that hand to my forehead, to the fierce pain behind the bone. "It was a baptism of fire, and he turned out to be paper while I had to be iron." I peered up at him through narrowed eyelids. "You know, I hated you for years afterward. I hated you for leaving me alone in the house with her, with all the things that had to be done for her. How could you expect me to be even socially cordial toward you after that?"

Coldly he said, "I expected you to be my sister."

"Well, I had expected you to be my brother. Looks like we misjudged each other, in spite of all those years we spent together.'' I turned to my mother. ''Mom, do you have an aspirin? I seem to have a headache.''

She brought the tablet, and as I was washing it down with a glass of water, she laid a hand on my shoulder and said, ''Don't you think that thirteen years is long enough to hold a grudge?''

I lowered the tumbler then, and turned it slowly in my hand, watching the reflections of the dining room lights travel across its smooth surface. ''After thirteen years he's still ashamed of himself. Somehow I find that a pleasant surprise.'' I looked up at my mother. ''Why shouldn't I still hold a grudge?''

Her fingers squeezed my shoulder as she gazed across the table at my brother. ''*I* was hurt, Paul. I know you understand that. I thought I was dying, and of my two children, only one was willing to spend the last weeks of my life with me. I was terribly hurt. But I have forgiven you.'' She looked down at me. ''And I have forgiven you for holding the grudge against him all these years. If I can forgive both of you, each of you can forgive the other.''

Paul and I stared at each other for a long moment, and then he said, ''I really think the whole episode is best forgotten, like a bad dream. Let's talk about something else.''

''But it hasn't been forgotten, Paul,'' said my mother. ''Not in thirteen years.''

''How could it be?'' I asked. ''He never even *tried* to make it up to me.''

''Make it up to you?'' he echoed. ''How could I possibly have made it up to you?''

''You could have started by apologizing.''

His mouth tightened. ''You want me to get down on my hands and knees?''

''That would be all right.''

Paul turned to his wife. ''I think we should go home now, Fran. It's getting late.''

''Both of you, stop it!'' cried my mother. Her fingers on

my shoulder turned to claws, digging deep into my flesh; she shook me hard. "Are you an adult, or are you still the little girl who gave her brother a black eye?"

I gripped her wrist and tried to tear her hand away. "Mom, you're hurting me."

"I'd like to throw you over my knee and spank you, young lady." She let go abruptly. "You're so proud of yourself. You're so smug in the role of martyr." She looked at Mark. "How do you stand her?" Mark had no answer, being busy drinking from an empty water glass, but she didn't wait for one anyway. "Why do you think I invited you all here?"

"I'll bite," said Paul. "Why?"

"To get this out in the open. Because you *don't* forget it, you just let it fester inside you, both of you. After thirteen years, I've had enough!" She put her hands on her hips. "Yes, *I've* had enough. I've watched it for thirteen years and I can't stand any more. If you won't forgive each other for your own sakes, then do it for mine." She glared at me, obviously waiting for me to make the first move, and I shifted uncomfortably beneath that glare.

"It isn't easy, Mom," I muttered.

"Aren't you strong enough to forgive him, Leah? I always thought you were strong enough for anything."

I closed my eyes to escape her, but I could feel her standing beside me. "I might say it, but I don't know if I'd mean it."

"I want more than words, Leah."

"Well, I couldn't give you more than words right now."

"Then say them. It'll be a start."

I opened my eyes, and there was my brother Paul sitting across the table, his gaze riveted on his empty plate. I felt very tired as I said, "All right, Paul. I forgive you. Let bygones be bygones."

He looked up slowly. "I'm willing," he said, "if you're really willing."

I glanced at Mom. "I'll try. I promise to try. For your sake."

She sighed. "Then why don't we do the dishes? The three of us."

Leaving Mark and Fran in the dining room, we went into the kitchen, where we changed off washing and drying the old familiar china. It brought back memories, as Mom had meant it to—so many times we had stood in that very spot, after all the relatives had finished Sunday dinner. We didn't talk much.

Paul and Fran left early; their sitter had school the next day. At the door, Paul turned to me. For a moment I thought he was going to kiss me, one of those perfunctory kisses that we usually gave each other when we parted, but he didn't. Instead, he said, "Come to dinner Friday night. Let the kids start getting used to having their aunt and uncle around."

Mark said, "We're free Friday night."

I said, "Then we'll be there."

Paul looked at me for a long moment. "Are you sure?"

"Yes. I'm sure."

My mother shooed us out shortly afterward, saying she was tired. At the threshold she hugged me hard, very hard, and when she let me go I saw a trace of tears in her eyes.

"Take it easy, Mom," I said. "I'll call you soon."

She smiled. "Tomorrow. Call me first thing in the morning."

"Is there something you want to tell me?"

"Tomorrow." Gently, she pushed me out the door.

Mark eyed me frequently as we drove home, but I was too tired, too emotionally drained to make conversation. We went straight to bed.

The world looked fresher in the morning. I felt like a snake that had just shed its skin, viewing the world through eyes newly unclouded. Mark and I discussed the business day to come as we drove down to the office; I didn't touch on the events of the previous day and neither did he. I cleared a few pressing matters off my desk before I called my mother.

Or tried to call her.

A strange voice answered her number, and the voice and I did a little verbal two-step before I decided I had misdialed. When I tried again, the voice was annoyed. When I had the operator dial for me, the voice was downright abusive.

"Don't you play no more of these games on me," it said finally, breaking the connection with a crash.

I called Directory Assistance, but they had no listing for my mother.

At last I went over to Mark's desk, sat down on a bare corner, and waited till he got off his phone.

He glanced up at me. "Problem?"

"I think so. I can't seem to get hold of my mother."

Both of his eyebrows rose. "Is that surprising?"

"She asked me to call this morning."

He touched my arm. "Leah, are you feeling all right?"

"I'm fine. Why?"

"Because your mother couldn't have asked you to call her. She's dead. She's been dead for years."

Suddenly I wasn't fine at all, and Mark had to help me back to my own chair and bring me a glass of water and a cold washcloth for my face. I babbled then, about the previous day, the dinner, the conversation with Mom, and he made soothing noises, assuring me that it had all been a dream, that I was overworked and that we two would take a vacation as soon as he could arrange it. When I could stand up by myself, he took me home and made me go to bed, but not before I had checked the phone book and the address book and my best friend and found they all agreed that my mother was dead.

"Did I call you yesterday?" I asked Gloria.

"No. Was it something important?"

"No, nothing."

So it was Tuesday that I lost my mind, and Wednesday

that I found it again. A whole day gone from my life, I didn't know where. Mark ordered me to take Thursday off from work, too, so I let him go to the office alone, but instead of sleeping as he had suggested, I drove out to the old house. The neighborhood looked familiar, but not like my thirteen-year-old memories, and I thought I must have actually been there in a mental fog on Tuesday. The house hedge seemed a bit tattered, though, and when I rang the bell, a middle-aged black woman with a baby in her arms answered. Behind her, I could see that the interior decor was no longer green but a dingy beige. I told the woman I had the wrong address.

That night, Paul called. "I just wanted to know if beef stroganoff is okay."

"Okay for what?" I asked.

"For dinner tomorrow night. You haven't changed your mind about coming over, have you?"

I had a little trouble finding my tongue, but at last I said, "When did we make this date for dinner, Paul?"

There was a silence at his end of the line, and then he said, "Well, I don't quite remember. It must have been a while ago, but I'm sure I asked you."

"Oh, you did, Paul. You did. Stroganoff will be fine."

"See you tomorrow, then."

Mark recalled the dinner invitation too, but not when it had been extended. "I should remember, I suppose—it's such an unusual event."

I put my arm around him. "It won't be so unusual in the future. I've been thinking of seeing more of Paul and the family now that the kids are growing up."

"That's okay with me." He kissed me. "Hey, I meant to tell you, your Aunt Mildred called at the office today. She gave me quite a lecture."

"On what?"

"On how you didn't go to the cemetery with her on Tuesday."

"Why should I have done that?"

"Well, you know your Aunt Mildred . . . it seems that Tuesday was the anniversary of your mother's death."

A chill passed through me, and I held him a little tighter. I had put that date out of my mind, had never wanted to keep track of it, had never gone to the cemetery since the funeral, in spite of Aunt Mildred's frequent requests. Now, with her reminder, everything fell into place for me, and I wanted to blurt out my new understanding. I wanted to talk about events that could happen and yet not happen, about ghosts manipulating time and space and people's memories. But I didn't want Mark to get worried again, so all I said was, "I think my mother would want me to care about the living, not the dead."

"That's what I told her. She said you were being disrespectful to your mother's memory."

Against his shoulder, I whispered, "She's wrong about that. She's entirely wrong."

Who could know better than I?

David Campton's fiction never fails to delight and intrigue. It pleases me immensely to have people feel that I discovered him, but David Sutton, among others, used his talents long before I did; however, I may at least lay claim to being his North American connection. In the past half decade I have called upon David's stories eight times in putting together books and magazines. The following is an original done especially for Whispers III.

FIRSTBORN

by David Campton

There were questions to be answered.

As the gale hurled more snow at the window of Harry's cottage I asked myself what I was doing there. The pure malt I sipped was hardly the answer: the local product made a visit to this ice-raked wilderness bearable, but I wasn't here for the whisky. To be honest, I had hoped that, since coming into his late uncle's thousands, Harry might be good for another touch; otherwise, when he suggested the jaunt, I might not have so willingly traded civilisation for cold quarters in a converted barn. But what was a hot-house plant like Harry doing in the highest of the Highlands anyway?

Moreover Harry's elegant Elaine was here too in this croft north of Inverness. Why?—at this time of all times in a woman's life. Surely persons of substance expect their firstborn to be delivered with all the advantages of modern obstetrics. Instead of which Elaine, who at a pinch could always make do with the best, was holding her breath in the whitewashed bedroom next to us, while the local midwife did whatever local midwives do. The atmosphere was charged with unvoiced questions.

At a sharp cry from the next room Harry paused in mid-glass. The Scottish tones of the midwife's response, half-chiding, half-reassuring, were muffled by the closed door. Harry opened his mouth, but only managed a creak from the back of his throat. The expectant father's face shone in the light of the stoked-up fire. His eyes tried to focus on objects beyond the flicker of the leaping flames. He wanted to talk, and only needed enough Scotch in him to flush out the words. At last he plunged.

"Trust you, Gerry," he mumbled.

"Hope so." Detecting a certain lack of conviction in his tone, I hastened to reassure him. "After all, I owe so much to you." The literal truth—all those IOUs.

This comfort induced a wry smile. "That's why it has to be you. Here, I mean. In case . . ." He tossed another log onto the fire. "First you ought to know about . . . Not fair to face you with . . . Of course, it might not after all—in which case there's no harm . . . But if it should be necessary . . ." He kicked the log, sending a burst of sparks up the chimney.

Had I betrayed signs of uneasiness? He patted my shoulder, and paced from wall to wall of the tiny room—four steps each way. "That's why we're out here in the wilds, of course. Nobody else to . . . The midwife's a risk, but money's a great persuader, eh?"

I nodded agreement over the rim of my glass.

"How else did the old boy coax us down to Dorset?" he went on. "Money called. Elaine didn't even query the social life in Dorset, which meant that even she understood the situation. The wolves were gathering—you're familiar with the signs: bills in red with great threatening stamps all over them; 'phone dead; supplies cut off; friends suddenly out of town. At the clink of Uncle's money bags we packed the little we had to pack and accepted what he offered without leaving a forwarding address for our creditors.

"Uncle must have heard a whisper of our little local difficulties, but that didn't explain this uncharacteristic generosity. True, I was his surviving nearest and dearest, but until then he'd hardly acknowledged my existence. I didn't believe his guff about being lonely. He'd lived alone all his life and, being past the seventy mark, must have been used to his own company. For forty or more years he'd devoted himself to making money in the City with a ruthless singlemindedness that ruled out friends. He may have had an acquaintance or two at one time but almost certainly threw them to the sharks whenever profit was involved. Uncle loved Uncle and money, which didn't leave much affection over for anyone else. Not even my beautiful Elaine. He asked specially for Elaine. Obviously in some way or another we were expected to sing for our suppers; but a straw looks like a life-boat to a drowning man. Dorset was the Promised Land.

"Uncle had built the place there just over a year before. Between retirement and moving into this retreat he had lived abroad. He never mentioned those years to us: whatever we learned about them we gleaned from another source. The architect of the new building must have been utterly undistinguished, as not a single aspect of it was designed to catch the eye. The more remarkable features had been added to my uncle's own specifications, and we were only to learn about them in due course. His home was distant enough from civilisation to satisfy a demanding recluse. The taxi fare from the station took away my breath and all but a jingle of small change.

"I suppose it was typical of the very rich that Uncle never considered reimbursing our travelling expenses. So there we were on his doorstep like orphans at Barnardo's, dependent on his charitable whims.

"Oddly we felt neither downcast nor apprehensive. Sunshine helped—remember last May's early heatwave? Although the house was nothing to write home about, the garden was a delight. Bees were busily doing whatever bees are supposed to do, and the flowers were encouraging them. Their scent would have been worth a fortune in a bottle. Elaine seemed to think so too: she paused half-way up the garden path, nose twitching and an expression of silly bliss on her face. That slight indulgence gave Uncle time to establish himself on the front porch with welcoming gestures.

"He was an undersized monkey of a man whose grin stretched from ear to ear exposing an unconvincing set of teeth. His bright eyes twinkled like frost. Obviously we measured up to his expectations. Elaine particularly. He fondled her hand in both his shrivelled paws, and stood on tip-toe to kiss her cheek.

"His enthusing over how much he was going to enjoy having us with him had a ring of the double entendre. As Elaine's eyes met mine over his wrinkled head she raised a questioning brow. I replied with a reassuring smile— whatever lecherous impulses my superannuated relative may have harboured, he was surely past exercising them.

"After which we were introduced to the guest room, then given lunch. The appointments were new and luxurious. I suspected they had been ordered specially for us. The food was as good as deep-freeze and micro-wave could rise to. The wine was excellent. I had a feeling that Elaine was going to be happy for a while. Between meals she was able to stretch out, suitably annointed, on the green velvet lawn exposing herself to the sun; her gleaming skin tanning to the caramel that blended so well with her butterscotch hair. I caught Uncle licking his lips like a small boy at a sweet-shop window. Well, age can have few compensations, and who was I to intrude on his naughty fantasies? I had daydreams of my own.

"I had plenty of time for them, too. The house, equipped

with every modern labour saver, more or less ran itself while Uncle pottered among his plants. In spite of his initial pressing invitations the old boy paid far more attention to his seedlings than to his guests. He presided over meals and presumed that concluded his duties as host. His concentration on the paraphernalia of propagation almost amounted to mania. As an ancient is entitled to his eccentricities, I left him to them. By the third day, though, boredom had led me to the greenhouses.

"We hadn't been warned that they were out of bounds. When I tried one of the doors, and it wouldn't open, I assumed it was merely stuck. I was just heaving on the handle when Uncle bounded up, shrieking.

"I didn't exactly quail, because I'm not the quailing sort; but I must have looked somewhat blasted, because he suddenly cut his wrath short and apologised, giving me the monkey grin with nothing behind it but teeth. On my side I agreed that botanical experiments can be a sensitive area; and on his side he promised a guided tour of the potting sheds.

"While I'm fond enough of fruit and flowers on the table, I've never been one for prying into their private lives. However, I had nothing better to do, and as our comfort depended on keeping Uncle sweet, I trailed behind, playing up an interest I didn't exactly feel.

"The first greenhouse was all orchids. Some were pretty; some were bizarre. Uncle explained he had started with orchids. While still in the full vigour of his late fifties, piling thousands upon thousands, his medico had advised him to take up a hobby—'preparing for retirement,' he called it. Orchids were one of the suggestions. The doctor should have known that my uncle was incapable of doing anything by halves. Orchids became a consuming passion. Retiring years before he was expected to (actually shaking the F. T. Share Index), the relative devoted himself to his new pursuit. He embraced orchidomania as fervently as a religion. New horizons opened up. He had hoped one day to cultivate . . . had I read Wells's 'Flowering of the Strange Orchid'? A pity that one had eluded him, because orchids now commanded less of his time. He reached beyond orchids . . .

"We left the orchid house. The orchid house was not locked. Making a detour through the kitchen, we picked up a basinful of mince, a slice or two of steak, and a couple of bones. There was a mortice lock on the door of the next hot-house.

"Thin brown fingers clutching the key, my uncle swore me to secrecy. I made some feeble joke, but pandered to his whims. Even then, before opening the door, he delivered a mini-lecture of his current obsession—the thin line between plant and animal life. The man-eating vine was a commonplace of horror stories—well, there *was* an area where fantasy fiction merged with fantastic fact.

"The plants nearest the door were almost commonplace—if giant fly-traps and sundews can be counted as commonplace. We fed these with pinches of mince. I was even allowed the treat of sprinkling meat onto waiting flowers. I admit I found their reaction grimly fascinating, with some blooms snapping shut on dinner, and others curling tendrils over their morsels of protein. Uncle enjoyed himself almost as much as the plants.

"The larger specimens were more impressive. They were approached with a certain reverence. You have to accord respect to any vegetation that can make a meal of half a pound of steak. I wasn't allowed to feed these. Nor did I wish to. I felt that, unless approached with care, one of them might snap off a finger as an hors d'oeuvre.

"Something crawled towards my neck, and I put a cautious hand up to it. It was no more than a trickle of sweat. The temperature and humidity in the glasshouse were uncomfortably high. Uncle grinned as he noticed the gesture, but he didn't comment. Instead he continued his exposition on South American discoveries, coupled with research into hybrids, grafting, cross-fertilisation, and so on, all mixed up with a poly-syllabic jargon that bemused me completely.

"Although I couldn't understand what he was talking about, I could see what he was doing. We ended by confronting an unhealthy-looking mass with blotched saucer-like leaves—or were they blooms? By this time most of the meat had been consumed, the other plants devoted to the process of digestion. Uncle had only bloody bones left in his tuck box. Were they for this mottled monster? Of course they were.

"I believe the thing was quivering with expectation. It practically grabbed at the hunks of skin and bone, my uncle musing meanwhile on whether the thing was capable of consuming a man. Not whole, he concluded, answering his own queries. A man would have to be chopped up first, and that hardly counted. However, his researches were continuing. He had entered an area of delicate and fascinating speculation. Was the question now one of cultivation or of breeding? Was conception the dividing line between animal and vegetable? Could that line be crossed?

"One of the saucers opened with a plop and a nauseating reek of gas. I'll swear it burped. Uncle suggested that I had seen enough for one day. I agreed with him—my shirt was sticking to my back, and my soggy condition had nothing to do with either the temperature or the humidity.

"Outside in the sunshine Elaine was tanning prettily. She purred contentedly as I rubbed oil between her shoulder blades. But Uncle's references to breeding had touched me on a sore spot. The fact is—Elaine and I had experienced some difficulty in that department. It seemed that I couldn't and she didn't want to. At least, not often. I don't know whether I couldn't because she didn't want to, or whether she didn't want to because I couldn't. As a sex-symbol, Elaine was all symbol and no sex. None of which had escaped Uncle's beady eye.

"In fact at meal times—the only occasions on which the three of us seemed to come together—he would slip into the conversation occasional innuendos or half-jokes, meant to be funny because accompanied by a wrinkled grimace, but which I considered in rather poor taste. Naturally I didn't wince as I felt inclined, because a poor relation learns to laugh at the right time. Well, I suppose the old devil eventually did us a good turn.

"After a particularly good dinner—I can't recall what we ate, but the claret was remarkable—Uncle had been holding forth on his monomania. As a dutiful nephew I displayed some interest, and Elaine bestowed the occasional slow, sweet smile. Elaine has never been a great wit—being too involved with her private thoughts to follow much conversation—but her smile has warmed the cockles of many a monologuist's heart. She and I toyed relaxedly with our brandy snifters, content to let Uncle sparkle like the soda-water in his glass.

"On this occasion the bubbles must have gone to his head, because he prattled of his great experiment. At first I took this to mean the bone-crunching monster locked up in the hot-house but gradually came to realise that he was referring to some holy of holies. Apparently under the house lay unsuspected cellars, and he was offering to show us all. Elaine and I floated after him on an alcoholic cloud of euphoria.

"The cellar door was a cunningly devised panel in the kitchen. At the bottom of the stairs were doors to right and left. Behind the right-hand door lay the wine racks in an electronically controlled atmosphere at exactly the right temperature and humidity to keep their precious contents in condition.

"The same principle applied to the room behind the left-hand door, except that here conditions were equatorial. Within minutes of the door being shut behind us, our pores had opened like faucets, sweat running into our eyes. Even with vision somewhat blurred, though, we could not miss the vine that half-filled the cellar. The plant was supported by a frame of hausers, to which it clung with rope-like tendrils.

"As Uncle lectured on instinctive reactions in plants he held out a finger, and a green thread obligingly curled around it. A pretty demonstration. While we were admiring this performance I leaned unsteadily against the frame, whereupon something gripped me around the waist in a wrestler's hold, jerking me off my feet and among the dripping leaves.

"Uncle gently unwound the slippery bonds, clucking words like 'naughty, naughty'; though I could not be sure whether they applied to me, or the vine.

"Cautiously standing back, we were invited to admire the buds that festooned the branches—green fingers varying in size, with the largest a handspan in length and over an inch in diameter. Streaks of red showed through a tracery of cracks near the top of one bud that was ready to open.

"Subdued excitement gripped Uncle. He knew what to expect. He stared at the bud, biting his lip and breathing heavily. On cue, while we watched, the bud burst open. Later I wondered if the fact that we were there may have had something to do with this prompt exhibition. After all the movement of the tendrils had shown that the plant reacted to our presence. Even if we had been obliged to wait, though, we would have been rewarded by the display. The flower was remarkable.

"A bright, shining red, it parodied my inefficient reproductive equipment—the main difference being its rampant vigour compared with my habitual ineptitude. No wonder it had been kept behind locked doors: its appearance in a shop window might have exposed a florist to prosecution under the Obscene Publications Act.

"Elaine has a delicate mind. Easily offended by schoolboy smut, she switches off completely at an off-colour remark. I glanced sideways, expecting blushes at one of Nature's jokes. In that heat a blush was difficult to detect, but her eyes had opened very wide and her mouth hung open. For the space of a few heartbeats nothing existed in her world but that flower. She looked so peculiarly vulnerable that something stirred deep inside me—a chemical reaction with pity and jealousy fizzing together. I wanted to take her in my arms and console her for what she had been missing—at the same time realising, almost with fury, that in her present mood she would be easy game for anyone offering as much.

"The show was not yet over. My uncle giggled as he tapped the stem of the flower. It bounced backwards and forwards suggestively; and before quivering to a stop, it exuded a few drops of viscous honey-dew with a heady perfume.

"I can't describe the scent, only its effect—more potent than any combination of claret and brandy. Elaine felt it too: the melting ice-maiden turned to me moist-lipped. Her hair was streaming. Perspiration and the atmosphere had drenched her clothes until they clung to every curve. She was making little animal noises.

"Dizzy with perfume, I grabbed her and she clung to me. Murmuring incoherent excuses to my uncle we lunged from the cellar. I dimly remember him holding the cellar door open for us, and his laughter cackling behind us. We left a trail of scattered garments all the way up the stairs to our bedroom. From then on we threshed about in an ecstatic frenzy until first light, when sheer exhaustion brought us down to earth and we crashed into sleep."

Harry fell silent, savouring his drink and perhaps the memory. We could hear the midwife purposefully busy. Harry gestured vaguely in her direction with his glass, as though emphasising the link between the drama in the next room and the bedroom farce some nine months ago.

"Good for Uncle's potted plants," I murmured, quickly refilling my glass before the bottle was quite empty. Between the glow of the fire, the sighing of the wind, and

Harry's reminiscent drawl, I was losing a battle against lethargy.

Another cry from Elaine. I sat up with an expletive, and with one stride Harry was over to the door. It opened as he reached it. The freckled midwife, firm of bosom and bicep, shook her head.

"Early yet," she hooted. "Back to your bottle and dinna' fash yourself. I promise ye'll be the first tae ken when the bairn appears."

She disappeared, shutting the bedroom door with the speed and efficiency of a cuckoo returning to its clock.

Harry ambled back to his chair, nursed his empty glass for a minute, then began to talk again. It passed the time.

"That wasn't the only occasion," he went on. "She'd come panting to bed, eager as a wild colt for a gallop, and I'd know it had been blossom-time again. Luckily some of that perfume seemed to cling to her. Her fingers would be covered with red pollen. One sniff, and I'd be bucking like a bronco. At first, after these bouts we'd go back to our old sterile ways, but gradually we began to grow towards each other. Nothing madly shattering, of course, but at least giving us a new interest in life. I'm more grateful to Uncle for that than for his thousands."

More silence from Harry.

"A sudden bereavement?" I hazarded.

He sighed, as Adam might have sighed, looking back on lost Paradise.

"It was the onion seller," he said simply.

I waited for what must follow.

"Uncle was undisturbable down in the cellar, and Elaine was soaking up the ultra-violet, when the onion seller appeared at the kitchen door. He was a slight man, kippered by wind and sun. Little black eyes had taken in every item of kitchen equipment between his question and my reply. In point of fact, he only seemed to know one word, which was 'onions'—an easy one, because it's almost the same in French as in English. I replied, 'Non'—

showing off a bit—waving a hand at the deep-freeze, the micro-wave oven, and the washing-up machine, conveying the information that food in these parts was practically untouched by human hand. We just didn't need such items as old-fashioned onions. So off he trundled, bundles of onions swinging from his shoulders.

"He had a poor sense of direction because, instead of turning towards the front gate, he headed for the green-houses. I had to swivel him round and point him in the direction he ought to go. He paused before going on to his next customer, and looked back at the house—not casually as one does at a gate, but intently as though searching for something which ought to have been there that he'd missed.

"I remember telling myself that the poor bastard wasn't going to do much business in this area, with at least two miles between us and the next house. Then I went on to consider he must have been pretty stupid, because even an unlettered clod must have seen there were no other houses down this lane, and no houses meant no sales. Finally I recalled that I hadn't seen an onion seller for years. He was an anachronism, like a muffin man ringing his bell around Earl's Court.

"By way of pleasantry I mentioned this to Uncle half-way through dinner that evening. He didn't find my joke very funny. In fact, it put him off his food. He set down his knife and fork very precisely, cogitated for a count of forty, then fired a stream of questions at me like an interrogating commissar.

"He wanted to be told exactly what the man had looked like, exactly what he had said, every detail of time, place, and scenario until he knew as much about the encounter as if he'd been there. When all that information had been gathered in, he pushed abruptly from the table, and whisked from the room without waiting for coffee, muttering something that sounded like 'Now, now, now.' He spent the rest of the night down in the cellar.

"He surfaced half-way through the following morning,

just as I was massaging sun-tan oil into that awkward spot half-way up Elaine's spine. He wanted her assistance with a tricky process below-stairs. Knowing Elaine's limitations whenever anything practical is involved, I offered my services but was brushed aside. Uncle wanted Elaine and Elaine alone. I fastened her halter top and retired gracefully.

"My meditations were interrupted by the return of the onion seller; this time without the pretence of onions. In the twenty-four hours since our last encounter his vocabulary had improved, remarkably. He still had a marked foreign accent but expressed himself forcefully. Making enquiries in the neighbourhood, he had been informed that an old gentleman lived alone on these premises. Encountering me yesterday, he had assumed he must have taken a wrong turn. However, a conversation last night with a taxi-driver convinced him that he had been right first time. He wanted my uncle. What's more, the expression on his face and the tone of his voice did not encourage me to call for the old man.

"Fortunately the cellar door was closed, and the stranger's darting glances failed to spot the vital panel. However, my formal reply that Uncle was not at home to callers was clearly not believed. The bright black eyes came to rest almost lovingly on a gleaming butcher's cleaver hanging with other equipment on the kitchen wall. I don't know why it was there: I'd never seen it in action. The foreigner, though, was obviously considering a use for it.

"Suddenly he changed his tactics. With a smile, intended to be warm and friendly, he promised m'sieur that if m'sieur knew everything m'sieur would understand everything, and if the worse came to worst, perhaps even forgive everything. It was a long story, but I did not interrupt because while the chap was talking; he was not molesting Uncle. My main fear was that Uncle himself might come popping out in the middle of the narrative. Luckily he didn't.

"It seemed that, in his own village, the onion seller

once had a son—black hair, black eyes, and a lithe body brown as a nut. In the boy's thirteenth year an old man had come to live nearby. This old man was rich enough to indulge his hobby of raising peculiar plants. Some of these could only have been conceived by the Devil, but the boy was fascinated. As months passed, he began to spend all his spare time in the hellish gardens created by the Englishman. He was occasionally paid for doing odd jobs—not overpaid, because the very rich understand the value of money, but money changed hands.

"Because of the money rumours started, but there was no truth in those stories. Truly those two were not interested in each other but only in the loathsome specimens. The boy was warned to stay away, but he defied authority, even enduring beatings.

"There came a time when the boy did not come home at all. His father went up to the house of the crazy plants, intent on a reckoning. The old man had suddenly decamped. The boy was there, though.

"The stranger's voice was flat and unemotional as he described how the young body had been found tangled with a vine. Quite dead, of course. What else could have been expected? After being impaled. Did m'sieur understand? A great shoot of the plant had been thrust up inside the victim. Tendrils of the vine had held him fast while he perished in agonies—that Thing inside him.

"The man could spin a yarn. I slumped back on the kitchen stool as he helped himself to the cleaver. After that I was quick to take evasive action, putting the length of a table between myself and that shining steelware. I fancy I babbled something about not being responsible for my relation's misdeeds. However, the cleaver was not required for immediate bloodletting. Only for breaking the windows of accursed greenhouses.

"I didn't try to stop him. After all, glass is replaceable—I am not. A minute or so later I heard a crashing and tinkling like a mad comedy act.

"My next inclination was to brief Uncle on these developments. It says something for the intruder's narrative powers that, until I opened the cellar door, all my attention had been focussed on the poor devil's sufferings. Only when I stood at the top of the stairs did I begin to put two and two together. I didn't like the total. Uncle was down there with Elaine—and the vine. I was soon down there too. Quicker than I had intended, because I missed my footing and bounced half the way. But I didn't even feel the bruises. Scrambling to my feet I crashed open the double door. Thank heavens, the old devil had been so sure of my behaving myself he hadn't troubled to lock it.

"The first thing to hit me was the perfume, now so concentrated it had passed beyond sweetness into a stink. The vine, covered with red blooms, might have been dripping blood. Elaine was spread-eagled over it, tendrils binding her body in a Saint Andrew's cross. Her head drooped. She was unconscious.

"I hurtled over to her and tried to pull her free. Uncle did his feeble best to stop me, but I sent him spinning with a well-aimed if unsporting kick to the groin. He needn't have bothered because, before I realised what was happening, the vine had got me too and I was struggling with a thick green coil around my middle.

"Uncle and I screamed obscenities at each other. I won that round on points, because in barbed phrases I described what was happening upstairs to the rest of his collection. He howled like a creature possessed and fled, leaving me to wrestle on.

"The plant had an unfair advantage. I had only two arms and two legs, whereas it seemed to produce fresh thongs at will. My resistance grew weaker as it bound me firmly to itself. Was all that an inbuilt natural reaction, or did it have a mind of its own?

"I lost count of time but eventually felt a cool draught on my face and realised that the heavy scent was drifting away. In his hurry Uncle had left both doors open. The grip of one of the tendrils relaxed and I was able to free a hand. Slowly I disengaged myself. I don't know whether the sudden drop in temperature was affecting the plant, or whether, having done what it was intended to do, it would have died anyway.

"Once I had disentangled myself, I released Elaine. As I lowered her to the cellar floor, her eyelids fluttered. At least she was still alive.

"Filled with hot fury against the monsters that had treated her with this indignity, I fell upon the vine, tearing great bunches of flowers from it. By now it was a defenseless object, visibly wilting, and eventually I realised that I would be better employed in rending my uncle limb from limb.

"It says something for the incoherence of my reasoning that I left Elaine lying there while I surfaced, calling down damnation on that gibbering little ape.

"I found parts of him in the ruins of the carnivores' hot-house. The onion seller had fed the rest to various plants. On seeing me, the boy's father smiled, bowed, and walked away. The police caught up with him on the outskirts of Poole. Indisputably insane, he was never brought to trial.

"None of the plants survived. A chap from the botanical gardens at Kew was quite cut up about that. Not as cut up as Uncle, of course. Fortunately there was enough left of him for identification and a respectable funeral . . ."

Silence again, except for the wind and the snow.

"Is that all?" I asked after a while.

"I don't know," replied Harry. "You see, when I'd calmed down somewhat, and had Elaine properly sedated and tucked up in bed, something was found."

"Something?" I prompted after another long silence.

"Where Elaine had been lying. A long, limp, dirty-brown object. Rather like a flabby bean pod, only it had never had beans in it."

''What was it?''

Harry took a deep breath and was about to answer when he stopped.

In the next room the midwife had started to scream.

Roger Zelazny is one of the nicest people in the fantasy and science-fiction field as well as being one of its most talented. His multiple Hugo and Nebula Awards speak for themselves. His Amber series is already a classic and the series' first book often commands over two hundred dollars in its first edition despite its having been published only in 1970. Zelazny does not often venture purely on the fantasy side of the genre, especially with short fiction, but the following is one of those pleasant exceptions to the rule.

THE HORSES OF LIR

by Roger Zelazny

The moonlight was muted and scattered by the mist above the loch. A chill breeze stirred the white tendrils to a sliding, skating motion upon the water's surface. Staring into the dark depths, Randy smoothed his jacket several times, then stepped forward. He pursed his lips to begin and discovered that his throat was dry.

Sighing, almost with relief, he turned and walked back several paces. The night was especially soundless about him. He seated himself upon a rock, drew his pipe from his pocket and began to fill it.

What am I doing here? he asked himself. How can I . . . ?

As he shielded his flame against the breeze, his gaze fell upon the heavy bronze ring with the Celtic design that he wore upon his forefinger.

It's real enough, he thought, and it had been *his*, and *he* could do it. But this . . .

He dropped his hand. He did not want to think about the body lying in a shallow depression ten or twelve paces up the hillside behind him.

His Uncle Stephen had taken care of him for almost two years after the deaths of his parents, back in Philadelphia. He remembered the day he had come over—on that interminable plane flight—when the old man had met him at the airport in Glasgow. He had seemed shorter than Randy remembered, partly because he was a bit stooped now he supposed. His hair was pure white and his skin had the weathered appearance of a man's who had spent his life out-of-doors. Randy never learned his age.

Uncle Stephen had not embraced him. He had simply taken his hand, and his gray eyes had fixed upon his own for a moment as if searching for something. He had nodded then and looked away. It might have been then that Randy first noticed the ring.

"You'll have a home with me, lad," he had said. "Let's get your bags."

There was a brief splashing noise out in the loch. Randy searched its mist-ridden surface but saw nothing.

They know: Somehow they know, he decided. What now?

During the ride to his home, his uncle had quickly learned that Randy's knowledge of Gaelic was limited. He had determined to remedy the situation by speaking it with him almost exclusively. At first, this had annoyed Randy, who saw no use to it in a modern world. But the rudiments were there, words and phrases returned to him, and after several months he began to see a certain beauty in the Old Tongue. Now he cherished this knowledge—another thing he owed the old man.

He toyed with a small stone, cast it out over the waters, listened to it strike. Moments later, a much greater splash echoed it. Randy shuddered.

He had worked at his uncle's boat rental business all that summer. He had cleaned and caulked, painted and mended, spliced . . . He had taken out charters more and more often as the old man withdrew from this end of things.

"As Mary—rest her soul—never gave me children, it will be yours one day, Randy," he said. "Learn it well, and it will keep you for life. You will need something near here."

"Why?" he had asked.

"One of us has always lived here."

"Why should that be?"

Stephen had smiled.

"You will understand," he said, "in time."

But that time was slow in coming, and there were other things to puzzle him. About once a month, his uncle rose and departed before daybreak. He never mentioned his destination or responded to questions concerning it. He never returned before sundown, and Randy's strongest suspicion did not survive because he never smelled of whisky when he came in.

Naturally, one day Randy followed him. He had never been forbidden to do it, though he strongly suspected it would meet with disapproval. So he was careful. Dressing hastily, he kept the old man in sight through the window as he headed off toward a stand of trees. He put out the Closed sign and moved through the chill pre-dawn in that direction. He caught sight of him once again, briefly, and then Stephen vanished near a rocky area and Randy could find no trace of him after that. Half an hour later, he took the sign down and had breakfast.

Twice again, he tried following him, and he lost him on both occasions. It irritated him that the old man could baffle him so thoroughly, and perhaps it bothered him even more that there was this piece of his life which he chose to keep closed to him—for as he worked with him and grew to know him better he felt an increasing fondness for his father's older brother.

Then, one morning, Stephen roused him early.

"Get dressed," he said. "I want you to come with me."

That morning his uncle hung the Closed sign himself and Randy followed him through the trees, down among the rocks, past a cleverly disguised baffle, and down a long tunnel. Randy heard lapping sounds of water, and even before his uncle put a light to a lantern he knew from the echoes that he was in a fair-sized cave.

His eyes did not adjust immediately when the light spread. When they did, he realized that he was regarding an underground harbor. Nevertheless, it took longer for the possibility to occur to him that the peculiar object to his left might be some sort of boat in a kind of drydock. He moved nearer and examined it while his uncle filled and lit another lantern.

It was flat-bottomed and U-shaped. What he had taken to be some sort of cart beneath it, though, proved a part of the thing itself. It had a wheel on either side. Great metal rings hung loosely on both sides and on the forward end. The vehicle was tilted, resting upon its curved edge. These structural matters, however, aroused but a superficial curiosity, for all other things were overwhelmed within him by a kind of awe at its beauty.

Its gunwales, or sides—depending on exactly what the thing was—were faced with thin bronze plates of amazing design. They looped and swirled in patterns vaguely reminiscent of some of the more abstract figures in the *Book of Kells*, embossed here and there with large studs. The open areas looked to be enameled—green and red in the flickering light.

He turned as his uncle approached.

"Beautiful, isn't it?" he said, smiling.

"It—it belongs in a museum!"

"No. It belongs right here."

"What is it?"

Stephen produced a cloth and began to polish the plates.

"A chariot."

"It doesn't look exactly like any chariot I've seen pictures of. For one thing, it's awfully big."

Stephen chuckled.

"Ought to be. 'Tis the property of a god."

Randy looked at him to see whether he was joking. From the lack of expression on his face, he knew that he was not.

"Whose—is it?" he asked.

"Lir, Lord of the Great Ocean. He sleeps now with the other Old Ones—most of the time."

"What is it doing here?"

His uncle laughed again.

"Has to park it someplace now, doesn't he?"

Randy ran his hand over the cold, smooth design on the side.

"I could almost believe you," he said. "But what is your connection with it?"

"I go over it once a month, to clean it, polish it, keep it serviceable."

"Why?"

"He may have need of it one day."

"I mean, why you?"

He looked at his uncle again and saw that he was smiling.

"A member of our family has always done it," he said, "since times before men wrote down history. It is part of my duty."

Randy looked at the chariot again.

"It would take an elephant to pull something that size."

"An elephant is a land creature."

"Then what . . . ?"

His uncle held up his hand beside the lantern, displaying the ring.

"I am the Keeper of the Horses of Lir, Randy. This is my emblem of office, though they would know me without it after all these years."

Randy looked closely at the ring. Its designs were similar to those of the chariot.

"The Horses of Lir?" he asked.

His uncle nodded.

"Before he went to sleep with the other Old Ones, he put them to pasture here in the loch. It was given to an early ancestor of ours to have charge of them, to see that they do not forget."

Randy's head swam. He leaned against the chariot for support.

"Then all those stories, of—things—in the loch . . . ?"

"Are true." Stephen finished. "There's a whole family, a herd of them out there." He gestured toward the water. "I call them periodically and talk to them and sing to them in the Old Tongue, to remind them."

"Why did you bring me here, Uncle? Why tell me all these secret things?" Randy asked.

"I need help with the chariot. My hands are getting stiff," he replied. "And there's none else but you."

Randy worked that day, polishing the vehicle, oiling enormous and peculiarly contrived harnesses that hung upon the wall. And his uncle's last words bothered him more than a little.

The fog had thickened. There seemed to be shapes moving within it now—great slow shadows sliding by in the distance. He knew they were not a trick of the moonlight, for there had been another night such as this . . .

"Would you get your pullover, lad?" his uncle had said. "I'd like us to take a walk."

"All right."

He put down the book he had been reading and glanced at his watch. It was late. They were often in bed by this hour. Randy had only stayed up because his uncle had kept busy, undertaking a number of one-man jobs about the small cottage.

It was damp outside and somewhat chill. It had been

raining that day. Now the fogs stirred about them, rolling in off the water.

As they made their way down the footpath toward the shore, Randy knew it was no idle stroll that his uncle had in mind. He followed his light to the left past the docking area, toward a secluded rocky point where the land fell away sharply to deep water. He found himself suddenly eager, anxious to learn something more of his uncle's strange commitment to the place. He had grown steadily fonder of the old man in the time they had been together, and he found himself wanting to share more of his life.

They reached the point—darkness and mist and lapping water all about them—and Stephen placed his light upon the ground and seated himself on a stony ledge. He motioned for Randy to sit near him.

"Now, I don't want you to leave my side, no matter what happens," his uncle said.

"Okay."

"And if you must talk, speak the Old Tongue."

"I will."

"I am going to call the Horses now."

Randy stiffened. His uncle placed his hand upon his arm.

"You will be afraid, but remember that you will not be harmed so long as you stay with me and do whatever I tell you. You must be introduced. I am going to call them."

Randy nodded in the pale light.

"Go ahead."

He listened to the strange trilling noises his uncle made, and to the song that followed them. After a time, he heard a splashing, then he saw the advancing shadow . . . Big. Whatever it was, the thing was huge. Large enough to draw the chariot, he suddenly realized. If a person dare harness it . . .

The thing moved nearer. It had a long, thin neck atop its bulky form, he saw, as it suddenly raised its head high above the water, to sway there, regarding them through the shifting mist.

Randy gripped the ledge. He wanted to run but found that he could not move. It was not courage that kept him there. It was a fear so strong it paralyzed him, raising the hair on the back of his neck.

He looked at the Horse, hardly aware that his uncle was speaking softly in Erse now.

The figure continued to move before them, its head occasionally dipping partway toward them. He almost laughed as a wild vision of a snake-charming act passed through his head. The creature's eyes were enormous, with glints of their small light reflected palely within them. Its head moved forward, then back. Forward . . .

The great head descended until it was so close that it was almost touching his uncle, who reached out and stroked it, continuing to speak softly all the while.

He realized abruptly that his uncle was speaking to him. For how long he had been, he did not know.

". . . This one is Scafflech," he was saying, "and the one beside him is Finntag . . ."

Randy had not realized until then that another of the beasts had arrived. Now, with a mighty effort, he drew his eyes from the great reptilian head which had turned toward him. Looking past it, he saw that a second of the creatures had come up and that it, also, was beginning to lean forward. And beyond it there were more splashing sounds, more gliding shadows parting the mists like the prows of Viking ships.

". . . And that one is Garwal. Talk to them, so they'll know the sound of your voice."

Randy felt that he could easily begin laughing hysterically. Instead, he found himself talking, as he would to a large, strange dog.

"That's a good boy . . . Come on now . . . How are you? Good old fellow . . ."

Slowly he raised his hand and touched the leathery

muzzle. Stephen had not asked him to. Why he had done it he was not certain, except that it had always seemed a part of the dog-talk he was using and his hand had moved almost as if by reflex when he began it.

The first creature's head moved even nearer to his own. He felt its breath upon his face.

"Randy's my name, Scafflech," he heard himself telling it. "Randy . . ."

That night he was introduced to eight of them, of various sizes and dispositions. After his uncle had dismissed them and they had departed, he simply sat there staring out over the water. The fear had gone with them. Now he felt only a kind of numbness.

Stephen stood, stopped, retrieved the light.

"Let's go," he said.

Randy nodded, rose slowly, and stumbled after him. He was certain that he would get no sleep that night, but when he got home and threw himself into bed the world went away almost immediately. He slept later than usual. He had no dreams that he could recall.

They were out there again now, waiting. He had seen them several times since but never alone. His uncle had taught him the songs, the guide-words and phrases, but he had never been called upon to use them this way. Now, on this night so like the first, he was back, alone, and the fear was back, too. He looked down at the ring that he wore. Did they actually recognize it? Did it really hold some bit of the Old Magic? Or was it only a psychological crutch for the wearer?

One of the huge forms—Scafflech, perhaps—drew nearer and then hastily retreated. They had come without being called. They were waiting for his orders, and he clutched his pipe, which had long since gone out, and sat shaking.

Stephen had been ill much of the past month and had finally taken to his bed. At first, Randy had thought it to be influenza. But the old man's condition had steadily worsened. Finally he had determined to get him a doctor.

But Stephen had refused, and Randy had gone along with it until just that morning, when his uncle had taken a turn for the worse.

"No way, lad. This is it," he had finally told him. "A man sometimes has a way of knowing, and *we* always do. It is going to happen today, and it is very important that there be no doctor, that no one know for a time . . ."

"What do you mean?" Randy had said.

"With a doctor there would be a death certificate, maybe an autopsy, a burial. I can't have that. You see, there is a special place set aside for me, for all the Keepers . . . I want to join my fathers, in the place where the Old Ones sleep . . . It was promised—long ago . . ."

"Where? Where is this place?" he had asked.

"The Isles of the Blessed, out in the open sea . . . You must take me there . . ."

"Uncle," he said, taking his hand, "I studied geography in school. There's no such place. So how can I . . .?"

"It troubled me once, too," he said, "but I've been there . . . I took my own father, years ago . . . The Horses know the way . . ."

"The Horses! How could I—How could they—"

"The chariot . . . You must harness Scafflech and Finntag to the chariot and place my body within it. Bathe me first, and dress me in the clothes you'll find in that chest . . ." He nodded toward an old seachest in the corner. "Then mount to the driver's stand, take up the reins, and tell them to take you to the Isles . . ."

Randy began to weep, a thing he had not done since his parents' deaths—how long ago?

"Uncle, I can't," he said. "I'm afraid of them. They're so big—"

"You must. I need this thing to know my rest. —And set one of the boats adrift. Later, tell the people that I took it out . . ."

He wiped his uncle's face with a towel. He listened to his deepening breathing.

"I'm scared," he said.

"I know," Stephen whispered. "But you'll do it."

"I—I'll try."

"And here . . ." His uncle handed him the ring. "You'll need this—to show them you're the new Keeper . . ."

Randy took the ring.

"Put it on."

He did.

Stephen had placed his hand upon his head as he had leaned forward.

"I pass this duty to you," he said, "that you be Keeper of the Horses of Lir."

Then his hand slipped away and he breathed deeply once again. He awakened twice after that, but not for long enough to converse at length. Finally, at sundown, he had died. Randy bathed him and clothed him as he had desired, weeping the while and not knowing whether it was for his sadness or his fear.

He had gone down to the cave to prepare the chariot. By lantern light he had taken down the great harnesses and affixed them to the rings in the manner his uncle had shown him. Now he had but to summon the Horses to this pool through the wide tunnel that twisted in from the loch, and there place the harnesses upon them . . .

He tried not to think about this part of things as he worked, adjusting the long leads, pushing the surprisingly light vehicle into position beside the water. Least of all did he wish to think of aquaplaning across the waves, drawn by those beasts, heading toward some mythical isle, his uncle's body at his back.

He departed the cave and went to the docking area, where he rigged a small boat, unmoored it and towed it out some distance over the loch before releasing it. The mists were already rising by then. In the moonlight, the ring gleamed upon his finger.

He returned to the cottage for his uncle and bore him down to a cove near the water entrance to the cave. Then his nerve had failed, he had seated himself with his pipe and had not stirred since.

The splashing continued. The Horses were waiting. Then he thought of his uncle, who had given him a home, who had left him this strange duty . . .

He rose to his feet and approached the water. He held up his hand with the ring upon it.

"All right," he said. "The time has come, Scafflech! Finntag! To the cave! To the place of the chariot! Now!"

Two forms drifted near, heads raised high upon their great necks.

I should have known it would not be that easy, he thought.

They swayed, looking down at him. He began addressing them as he had the first night. Slowly, their heads lowered. He waved the ring before them. Finally, when they were near enough, he reached out and stroked their necks. Then he repeated the instruction.

They withdrew quickly, turned, and headed off toward the tunnel. He moved away then, making for the land entrance to the place.

Inside, he found them waiting in the pool. He discovered then that he had to unfasten most of the harnessing from the chariot in order to fit it over them, and then secure it once again. It meant clambering up onto their backs. He removed his boots to do it. Their skin was strangely soft and slick beneath his feet, and they were docile now, as if bred to this business. He talked to them as he went about the work, rubbing their necks, humming the refrain to one of the old tunes.

He worked for the better part of an hour before everything was secure and he mounted the chariot and took up the reins.

"Out now," he said. "Carefully. Slowly. Back to the cove."

The wheels turned as the creatures moved away. He felt the reins jerk in his hands. The chariot advanced to the edge of the pool and continued on into the water. It floated. It drifted behind them toward the first bend and around it.

They moved through pitch blackness, but the beasts went carefully. The chariot never touched the rocky walls.

At length, they emerged into moonlight and mist over black water, and he guided them to the cove and halted them there.

"Wait now," he said. "Right here."

He climbed down and waded ashore. The water was cold, but he hardly noticed it. He mounted the slope to the place where his uncle lay and gathered him into his arms. Gently, he bore him down to the water's edge and out again. He took hold of the reins with a surer grip.

"Off now," he said. "You know the way! To the Isles of the Blessed! Take us there!"

They moved, slowly at first, through a long, sweeping turn that bore them out onto the misty breast of the loch. He heard splashings at either hand, and turning his head saw that the other Horses were accompanying them.

They picked up speed. The beasts did seem to have a definite direction in mind. The mists swept by like a ghostly forest. For a moment, he almost felt as if he rode through some silent, mystical wood in times long out of mind.

The mists towered and thickened. The waters sparkled. He gave the creatures their head. Even if he had known the way, it would have done him little good, for he could not see where they were going. He had assumed that they were heading for the Caledonian Canal, to cut across to the sea. But now he wondered. If the Keepers, down through the ages, had been transported to some strange island, how had it been accomplished in earlier times? The Canal, as he recalled, had only been dug sometime in the nineteenth century.

But as the moonlit mists swirled about him and the great beasts plunged ahead, he could almost believe that there was another way—a way that perhaps only the Horses knew. Was he being borne, somehow, to a place that only impinged occasionally upon normal existence?

How long they rode across the ghostly seascape, he could not tell. Hours, possibly. The moon had long since set, but now the sky paled and a bonfire-like sunrise began somewhere to the right. The mists dispersed and the chariot coursed the waves beneath a clear blue sky with no trace of land anywhere in sight.

The unharnessed Horses played about him as Scafflech and Finntag drew him steadily ahead. His legs and shoulders began to ache and the wind came hard upon him now, but still he gripped the reins, blinking against the drenching spray.

Finally, something appeared ahead. At first he could not be certain, but as they continued on it resolved itself into a clear image. It was an island, green trees upon its hills, white rocks along its wave-swept shores.

As they drew nearer, he saw that the island was but one among many, and they were passing this one by.

Two more islands slipped past before the Horses turned and made their way toward a stone quay at the back of a long inlet at the foot of a high green slope. Giant trees dotted the hillside and there were several near the harbor. As they drew up beside the quay, he could hear birds singing within them.

As he took hold of the stone wall, he saw that there were three men standing beneath the nearest tree, dressed in green and blue and gray. They moved toward him, halting only when they had come alongside. He felt disinclined to look into their faces.

"Pass up our brother Keeper," one of them said in the Old Tongue.

Painfully, he raised his uncle's soaked form and felt them lift it from his arms.

"Now come ashore yourself, for you are weary. Your steeds will be tended."

He told the Horses to wait. He climbed out and followed the three figures along a flagged walk. One of them took him aside and led him into a small stone cottage while the others proceeded on, bearing his uncle's form.

"Your garments are wet," said the man. "Have this one," and he passed him a light green-blue robe of the sort he himself had on, of the sort in which Randy had dressed his uncle for the journey. "Eat now. There is food upon the table," the man continued, "and then there is the bed." He gestured. "Sleep."

Randy stripped and donned the garment he had been given. When he looked about again, he saw that he was alone. He went to the table, suddenly realizing that his appetite was enormous. Afterward, he slept.

It was dark when he awoke, and still. He got up and went to the door of the cottage. The moon had already risen, and the night had more stars in it than he could remember ever having seen before. A fragrant breeze came to him from off the sea.

"Good evening."

One of the men was seated upon a stone bench beneath a nearby tree. He rose.

"Good evening."

"Your Horses are harnessed. The chariot is ready to bear you back now."

"My uncle . . . ?"

"He has come home. Your duty is discharged. I will walk with you to the sea."

They moved back to the path, headed down to the quay. Randy saw the chariot, near to where he had left it, two of the Horses in harness before it. He realized with a start that he was able to tell that they were not Scafflech and Finntag. Other forms moved in the water nearby.

"It is good that two of the others travel the route in harness," the man said, as if reading his mind, "and give the older ones a rest."

Randy nodded. He did not feel it appropriate to offer to shake hands. He climbed down into the chariot and untwisted the reins from the crossbar.

"Thank you," he said, "for—everything. Take good care of him. Goodbye."

"A man who dines and sleeps in the Isles of the Blessed always returns," the other said. "Good night."

Randy shook the reins and the Horses began to move. Soon they were in open water. The new Horses were fresh and spirited. Suddenly Randy found himself singing to them.

They sped east along the path of the moon.

"Woodland Burial" is one of Frank Belknap Long's infrequent journeys back to the short story form he excelled at for Weird Tales. *Those were the years he was Howard Phillips Lovecraft's best friend and the first to add to HPL's famed Cthulhu Mythos. Despite the wealth of horror fiction Long has created, it must be remembered that his literary hoard also includes much excellent poetry and science fiction. The year 1978 saw Frank Belknap Long win the World Fantasy Award for Life Achievement; it seemed more appropriate than at any other time in the history of these awards that the trophy was a bust of Howard Phillips Lovecraft.*

WOODLAND BURIAL

by Frank Belknap Long

Some small animal of the night was making a rustling sound out on the front porch. Will Gage arose from the dinner table and crossed to the window, to see whether or not the squirrel he'd given some nuts to at sundown had come back for more. It had looked thin and bedraggled and he'd felt sorry for it, if only because it had reminded him so much of the woman he'd covered with freshly turned earth and raked-over leaves eight weeks previously.

He'd felt sorry for her, too, right up to the time she'd taken the last sip—quite possibly the fatal one—of the arsenic-laced tea.

It was the same squirrel and he had to admit that it reminded him a little of himself as well, particularly when his face stared back at him in the bathroom mirror upstairs, the shaving cream making his cheeks seem more puffed out than they actually were.

He wasn't cut out to be a lean man, he told himself, whether from worrying about Molly Tanner's extravagance and his fear of losing her, or just from not getting enough expensive steaks and good table wine to make every moment when Molly wasn't coiled up in bed at his side seem worth paying the toll.

She's late, he thought, and this separate cottage business has got to stop. Who's going to give a hoot now whether she stays here night and day? Not Sheriff Merril. Everyone knows he's keeping two women in separate cottages down at the Point, and he's been re-elected three times.

Do your job and do it well, and people look the other way. Nowadays, with the Bomb and the rising crime rate, it's twice as true as ever before. It's on everybody's mind that maybe tomorrow or the next day you won't be around to mind your neighbor's business—or your own. Higgety pop and whoosh—you're gone.

He suddenly became irritated with the squirrel for wanting two helpings of nuts in less than three hours. Going out on the porch, he picked up a rock and hurled it at the scrawny little beast, the stone smashing into it as it made a dive for the nearest tree.

He saw her then, emerging from the double row of pines on the opposite side of the clearing, the moonlight glimmering on the silver-textured scarf she had wrapped around her shoulders, more out of vanity, he was quite sure, than as a protection against the October night's increasing chilliness.

There had been times in the past when great vanity in a woman had not been entirely to his liking. But it mattered not at all with Molly, for she was shaped to perfection and had that certain added something—

Twenty years fell from Gage's shoulders, coiled up at his feet and died. He was a boy of twenty again and Molly was seventeen. Except that no seventeen-year-old Molly could have pleased him quite as much as the Molly he'd come to know.

A moment later she was in his arms. "Well . . ." he murmured. "Well . . ."

"I bet if we were together all day you wouldn't grab hold of me like that," she said. "Do you still love me? How much?"

"What kind of question is that?" he asked.

"The kind a woman always asks."

"Sure, I know. And the guy spreads his arms wide and gets off some spiel about how big the ocean is, and that's how it is with him. But not me. I'm not that kind of sentimental kook."

"Couldn't you be that kind of a kook . . . just once."

"Come off it, Molly. You know damn well that every time I wrap my arms around you, tight like this, I can't think of anything to say. Maybe later . . ."

"You never say anything later either. You're such a strange, silent man."

"Who'd want to do any talking when—"

"You'd be surprised."

"What's that supposed to mean? I'm not a jealous man, but you'd better be careful. Don't run the number up too high."

"Have I ever?"

"I wouldn't put talking about it beyond you. But you're sensible enough to know it doesn't take more than a carelessly dropped hint or two in that direction to set a man off."

"How do *you* know I wouldn't *like* you to rough me up a little?"

"Stop talking nonsense. I've never struck a woman in my life."

Gage was amused, despite himself, by how true that was. Basically he was a kind and gentle man. He'd even wanted to go down on his knees, stroke his wife's hair and beg her to forgive him for putting a little too much arsenic in her tea.

"Let's go inside," Molly said. "It's getting chillier by the minute out here."

"I'll mix you a bourbon and soda," Gage said. "I went into town today and bought some new blankets. The soft, baby-wool kind—nice to cuddle under. You'll like them."

"What color are they?"

"Did you ever see a robin's egg?"

"Oh, that *is* nice," she said. "Robin's egg blue. That's my favorite color."

They went inside, and Gage hummed a few lines from the Little Sonata in C Minor while he mixed her a drink and carried it to her on a tray, jarring it a little to make the ice cubes clink, a sound he always enjoyed.

"I don't like to drink even the first one alone," Molly said. "You forget so many little things a woman treasures. But I'll forgive you this time if you fix yourself a stiff one quick and bring it over here before the chill settles into my very bones."

"That was my idea," Gage said, grinning. "You said it was cold outside. Why don't you gulp that down and let it warm you. Then we'll have the rest together and go on from there."

"You're not such a silent man after all," Molly said, patting his cheek. "Get one for yourself. I'll wait."

They had several drinks together as the evening wore on and the grandfather clock said it was ten minutes to eleven.

"I'm getting sleepy," Gage said, at last.

"So am I," Molly said. "There seems to be a strong bond of empathy between us."

A half hour later Gage was telling himself that if there were nights to remember this was certainly one of them. Molly knew how to please a man in so many different ways that he had the feeling at times that he was holding in his arms some phantom woman who might at any moment vanish in the night, if it had not been impossible for him to doubt her flesh-and-blood reality. There were delights in lovemaking which Molly alone had mastered to perfection, and there were times when her kisses seemed to burn their way through his lips into his brain. She moved away from him at last with a still rapturous sigh, and he was content to let her physical closeness recede, since no man could remain forever raised high above the earth amid revolving beams of loin-dissolving fire.

How long he slept he had no way of knowing. He could only be sure that the night had passed and that the darkness had been replaced by the first bright flush of dawn.

He had never been a light sleeper and few men were more beholden to sleep for long hours of blissful forgetfulness, untroubled by dreams of any kind. But he was also quick to awaken, with little of the drowsy feeling of unreality that can make familiar objects seem to blur and run together for a considerable period of time.

His hand had gone out for an instant to feel around under the sheets until it encountered a motionless form that was ice-cold to his touch. But a full realization of what that coldness could have implied occurred almost simultaneously with so acute a sharpening of his faculties that his head jerked backward and he sat bolt upright, tossing the sheets aside. The robin's-egg blue blanket went as well, it being as crumpled as the sheets and just as dark with stains, as if it had been carried outside and trampled in rain-splashed earth before being returned to the bed. Strangulation, if it has been slowly and not too violently applied, does not always distort the human countenance into a hideously grimacing mask. But Molly Tanner's face had been spared nothing in that respect. Her eyes bulged from their sockets and stared sightlessly up at him and her mouth was so twisted and convulsed that it was impossible to think of it as having been normally formed at any time in the past.

The long, matted strands of ash-blond hair that had been used as a noose had been drawn so tightly about Molly Tanner's throat that most of them were embedded in her flesh. But enough remained visible to make it impossible for Gage to doubt that it was the exact shade of the hair that he had gone on admiring in his wife when the rest of her attractiveness had dwindled to the vanishing point.

There are horrors too ghastly to be sanely endured, or, at the very least, as sanity-endangering as a cobra poised to strike with all avenues of escape blocked off, the great head with its swollen, pulsating hood weaving back and forth. Gage knew that there were only two courses open to him. He could leap from the bed and stagger about, his terror finding vent in shriek after shriek. Or he could hold the horror at bay just long enough to escape from the cottage and go plunging through the woods, to seek immediate confirmation—absolute proof—that his mind and the evidence of his eyes had conspired to betray him in some way. It was precisely that latter course he chose.

Despite a violent trembling he managed to get dressed, struggling into the dungarees and flannel shirt he'd thrown across a chair in his haste to get undressed when there had still been a living Molly to make haste meaningful. In another moment he was crossing to the porch in the heavy boots he'd dragged out from under the bed, turning back just once to glance again at her lifeless form in the wildly irrational way some people have of inflicting needless torment on themselves.

Outside the cottage the dawnlight could hardly have been brighter, but it had rained during the night and he had to slosh through a wide pool of water to get to the tool shed at the edge of the forest, and the heavy shovel and small trowel he felt he might be needing. The trowel he thrust into the hip pocket of his dungarees as he might have done with a pistol, but he had in mind a far more sinister use for it than merely killing someone. Prepared now, he headed off. He knew exactly where to go, even though a gloom enveloped the forest against the brightness of the dawn, and no visible path remained from his journey of eight weeks ago with his limp and not-very-heavy burden. It angered him still, despite the black horror that continued to clutch at his throat, that his wife had allowed herself to become so thin and unattractive in the months following their marriage. It was almost as if she had done it to spite him because of their numerous quarrels and her ungovernable temper. It was no way to treat a man who was by nature thoughtful and tender-minded.

It took him less than five minutes to traverse the distance from the cottage to where he had deposited her. The instant the site came into view all of the horror he'd experienced on awakening swept over him again.

The site itself looked very much as he'd thought it might. Eight weeks can bring about many changes. Carefully raked over leaves and branches are certain to be displaced to some extent by the scampering feet of small forest animals. Small mounds of earth may be born as a result of torrential rains and subsequent channels carrying off the water. These small modifications, though, were not what made him stand transfixed at the far end of the site. His momentary paralysis came from the immediate recognition of an object that protruded from a small mound of dirt. It was twisted and mud-spattered and had lost all of the silver-textured beauty which it had possessed last night when it had been wrapped around Molly Tanner's shoulders. Still, it was the same scarf, beyond any possibility of doubt.

He thought he knew why an attempt had been made to carry it down into the charnel darkness of the pit where what had once been a woman lay mouldering. It had been to her a token, a trophy, a symbol of triumph over a rival and of retribution against the man who had once been her beloved husband. For a moment longer Gage remained transfixed, unable to move or cry out in protest at the monstrous injustice that had been done to him. Then he stepped back, raised the shovel, and started digging.

He was still digging furiously, throwing up great clods of earth, when Sheriff Merril stepped out from between the trees where the shadows clustered thickly. He was accompanied by Lou Evans, who acted as his deputy when he wasn't clerking at Tilman's hardware store.

"What are you doing here, Will?" Merril asked, advancing swiftly. "It's quite a surprise, I must say, although we were about to pay you a visit before we got sidetracked."

Gage straightened, letting the shovel remain buried in the earth and looking at the sheriff in so wildly distraught a way that Merril seemed to feel it might be wiser to go right on talking.

"We were on our way just now to ask you a few more questions about your wife's disappearance when something rather astounding happened."

"Something—" Gage seemed almost unaware that he had spoken, for his gaze was riveted on the sheriff's face with a close to manic intensity.

"Astounding, yes. There was a persistent chattering sound overhead, almost a calling to us. When Evans looked up he saw that a squirrel was moving swiftly about on one of the lower branches. It almost purposefully dropped something to us that it had been gnawing on. Let Will see it, Lou. I'm sure it will be of interest to him."

Evans spoke then, for the first time. "After the squirrel dropped its burden, it ran to this clearing. And once you see what it dropped, you'll know why we postponed our call and started searching in the woods for the spot it must have come from. Funny thing, though. If Mr. Gage has to dig so deeply to unearth what's buried here, it's hard to see how a squirrel could have gotten to it. Maybe that squirrel found it somewhere else . . . but that's crazy—"

"You can say that again," Merril grunted. "Just show him what the squirrel dropped."

Gage's hand went out automatically to receive the object Evans placed on his palm.

It was an almost fleshless human finger, one with just enough sinew left to hold it together. On it, just below the bony knuckle joint, was a golden wedding ring Gage knew well.

The trembling of *his* hand was the last and only motion Gage made before he crashed to the ground in a dead faint.

Merril shook his head, and his hand darted to his hip. "I never saw a wife killer look quite so peaceful," he said, after a moment of tight-lipped silence. "But I guess I'd better put the cuffs on him, just to be on the safe side."

*Karl Edward Wagner has taken over the helm of DAW's
Year's Best Horror series from Gerald W. Page. This is most
disconcerting to me because it means Karl's own stories
cannot appear in that book! Physician Wagner has put his
medical practice on a back burner in order to devote his
full time to writing, editing, and publishing. Medicine's
loss is the genre's gain. In a very few years, Karl has
already garnered a lifetime of honors to include a Year's
Best Story ("Sticks" from* Whispers *magazine #3) as well
as winning or sharing the honors for six World Fantasy
Awards. His antihero Kane has garnered for him a large
and faithful following. When he was called upon to re-
create Robert E. Howard's Conan (*The Road of Kings,
1979*), he easily came through with the best novel in the
series. The following story is a staggeringly original venture that reads on several different levels. It needs concentration and atmosphere, so close the blinds, let the shadows
gather, and ignore those things going bump in the night.*

THE RIVER OF
NIGHT'S DREAMING

by Karl Edward Wagner

Everywhere: grayness and rain.

The activities bus with its uniformed occupants. The wet
pavement that crawled along the crest of the high bluff.
The storm-fretted waters of the bay far below. The night
itself, gauzy with gray mist and traceries of rain, feebly
probed by the wan headlights of the bus.

Grayness and rain merged in a slither of skidding rubber and a protesting bawl of brakes and tearing metal.

For an instant the activities bus paused upon the broken guardrail, hung half-swallowed by the grayness and rain upon the edge of the precipice. Then, with thirty voices swelling a chorus to the screams of rubber and steel, the bus plunged over the edge.

Halfway down it struck glancingly against the limestone face, shearing off wheels amidst a shower of glass and bits of metal, its plunge unchecked. Another carom, and the bus began to break apart, tearing open before its final impact onto the wave-frothed jumble of boulders far below. Water and sound surged upward into the night, as metal crumpled and split open, scattering bits of humanity like seeds flung from a bursting melon.

Briefly, those trapped within the submerging bus made despairing noises—in the night they were no more than the cries of kittens, tied in a sack and thrown into the river. Then the waters closed over the tangle of wreckage, and grayness and rain silenced the torrent of sound.

She struggled to the surface and dragged air into her lungs in a shuddering spasm. Treading water, she stared about her—her actions still automatic, for the crushing impact into the dark waters had all but knocked her unconscious. Perhaps for a moment she *had* lost consciousness; she was too dazed to remember anything very clearly. Anything.

Fragments of memory returned. The rain and the night, the activities bus carrying them back to their prison. Then the plunge into darkness, the terror of her companions, metal bursting apart. Alone in another instant, flung helplessly into the night, and the stunning embrace of the waves.

Her thoughts were clearing now. She worked her feet out of her tennis shoes and tugged damp hair away from her face, trying to see where she was. The body of the bus

had torn open, she vaguely realized, and she had been
thrown out of the wreckage and into the bay. She could
see the darker bulk of the cliff looming out of the grayness
not far from her, and dimly came the moans and cries of
other survivors. She could not see them, but she could
imagine their presence, huddled upon the rocks between
the water and the vertical bluff.

Soon the failure of the activities bus to return would
cause alarm. The gap in the guardrail would be noticed.
Rescuers would come, with lights and ropes and stretch-
ers, to pluck them off the rocks and hurry them away in
ambulances to the prison's medical ward.

She stopped herself. Without thought, she had begun to
swim toward the other survivors. But why? She took
stock of her situation. As well as she could judge, she had
escaped injury. She could easily join the others where they
clung to the rocks, await rescue—and once the doctors
were satisfied she was whole and hearty, she would be
back on her locked ward again. A prisoner, perhaps until
the end of her days.

Far across the bay, she could barely make out the
phantom glimmering of the lights of the city. The distance
was great—in miles, two? three? more?—for the prison
was a long drive beyond the outskirts of the city and
around the sparsely settled shore of the bay. But she was
athletically trim and a strong swimmer—she exercised
regularly to help pass the long days. How many days, she
could not remember. She only knew she would not let
them take her back to that place.

The rescue workers would soon be here. Once they'd
taken care of those who clung to the shoreline, they'd send
divers to raise the bus—and when they didn't find her
body among those in the wreckage, they'd assume she was
drowned, her body washed away. There would surely be
others who were missing, others whose bodies even now
drifted beneath the bay. Divers and boatmen with drag
hooks would search for them. Some they might never find.

Her they would never find.

She turned her back to the cliff and began to swim out into the bay. Slow, patient strokes—she must conserve her strength. This was a dangerous act, she knew, but then they would be all the slower to suspect when they discovered she was missing. The rashness of her decision only meant that the chances of escape were all the better. Certainly, they would search along the shoreline close by the wreck—perhaps use dogs to hunt down any who might have tried to escape along the desolate stretch of high cliffs. But they would not believe that one of their prisoners would attempt to swim across to the distant city—and once she reached the city, no bloodhounds could seek her out there.

The black rise of rock vanished into the gray rain behind her, and with it dwindled the sobbing wails of her fellow prisoners. No longer her fellows. She had turned her back on that existence. Beyond, where lights smeared the distant grayness, she would find a new existence for herself.

For a while she swam a breaststroke, switching to a backstroke whenever she began to tire. The rain fell heavily onto her upturned face; choppy waves spilled into her mouth, forcing her to abandon the backstroke each time before she was fully rested. Just take it slow, take your time, she told herself. Only the distant lights gave any direction to the grayness now. If she tried to turn back, she might swim aimlessly through the darkness, until . . .

Her dress, a drab prison smock, was weighting her down. She hesitated a moment—she would need clothing when she reached the shore, but so encumbered she would never reach the city. She could not waste strength in agonizing over her dilemma. There was no choice. She tugged at the buttons. A quick struggle, and she was able to wrench the wet dress over her head and pull it free. She flung the shapeless garment away from her, and it sank into the night. Another struggle, and her socks followed.

She struck out again for the faraway lights. Her bra and

panties were no more drag than a swimsuit, and she moved
through the water cleanly—berating herself for not having
done this earlier. In the rain and the darkness it was
impossible to judge how far she had swum. At least half-
way, she fervently hoped. The adrenaline that had coursed
through her earlier with its glib assurances of strength was
beginning to fade, and she became increasingly aware of
bruises and wrenched muscles suffered in the wreck.

The lights never appeared to come any closer, and by
now she had lost track of time as well. She wondered
whether the flow of the current might not be carrying her
away from her destination whenever she rested, and that
fear sent new power into her strokes. The brassiere straps
chafed her shoulders, but this irritation was scarcely noticed against the gnawing ache of fatigue. She fought
down her growing panic, concentrating her entire being
upon the phantom lights in the distance.

The lights seemed no closer than the stars might have
been—only the stars were already lost in the grayness and
rain. At times the city lights vanished as well, blotted out
as she labored through a swell. She was cut off from
everything in those moments, cut off from space and from
time and from reality. There was only the grayness and the
rain, pressing her deeper against the dark water. Memories
of her past faded—she had always heard that a drowning
victim's life flashes before her, but she could scarcely
remember any fragment of her life before they had shut her
away. Perhaps that memory would return when at last her
straining muscles failed, and the water closed over her face
in an unrelinquished kiss.

But then the lights *were* closer—she was certain of it
this time. True, the lights were fewer than she had remembered, but she knew it must be far into the night after her
seemingly endless swim. Hope sped renewed energy into
limbs that had moved like a mechanical toy, slowly wind-
ing down. There was a current here, she sensed, seeking to

drive her away from the lights and back into the limitless expanse she had struggled to escape.

As she fought against the current, she found she could at last make out the shoreline before her. Now she felt a new rush of fear. Sheer walls of stone awaited her. The city had been built along a bluff. She might reach the shore, but she could never climb its rock face.

She had fought too hard to surrender to despair now. Grimly she attacked the current, working her way along the shoreline. It was all but impossible to see anything—only the looming wall of blackness that cruelly barred her from the city invisible upon its heights. Then, beyond her in the night, the blackness seemed to recede somewhat. Scarcely daring to hope, she swam toward this break in the wall. The current steadily increased. Her muscles stabbed with fatigue, but now she had to swim all the harder to keep from being swept away.

The bluff was indeed lower here, but as a defense against the floods, they had built a wall where the natural barrier fell away. She clutched at the mossy stones in desperation—her clawing fingers finding no purchase. The current dragged her back, denying her a moment's respite.

She sobbed a curse. The heavy rains had driven the water to highest levels, leaving no rim of shoreline beneath cliff or dike. But since there was no escape for her along the direction she had come, she forced her aching limbs to fight on against the current. The line of the dike seemed to be curving inward, and she thought surely she could see a break in the barrier of blackness not far ahead.

She made painful progress against the increasing current, and at length was able to understand where she was. The seawall rose above a river that flowed through the city and into the bay. The city's storm sewers swelling its stream, the river rushed in full flood against the manmade bulwark. Its force was almost more than she could swim against now. Again and again she clutched at the slippery face of the wall, striving to gain a hold. Each time the current dragged her back again.

Storm sewers, some of them submerged now, poured into the river from the wall—their cross currents creating whirling eddies that shielded her one moment, tore at her the next, but allowed her to make desperate headway against the river itself. Bits of debris, caught up by the flood, struck at her invisibly. Rats, swimming frenziedly from the flooded sewers, struggled past her, sought to crawl onto her shoulders and face. She hit out at them, heedless of their bites, too intent on fighting the current herself to feel new horror.

A sudden eddy spun her against a recess in the seawall, and in the next instant her legs bruised against a submerged ledge. She half-swam, half-crawled forward, her fingers clawing slime-carpeted steps. Her breath sobbing in relief, she dragged herself out of the water and onto a flight of stone steps set out from the face of the wall.

For a long while she was content to press herself against the wet stone, her aching limbs no longer straining to keep her afloat, her chest hammering in exhaustion. The flood washed against her feet, its level still rising, and a sodden rat clawed onto her leg—finding refuge as she had done. She crawled higher onto the steps, becoming aware of her surroundings once more.

So. She had made it. She smiled shakily and looked back toward the direction she had come. Rain and darkness and distance made an impenetrable barrier, but she imagined the rescue workers must be checking off the names of those they had found. There would be no checkmark beside her name.

She hugged her bare ribs. The night was chilly, and she had no protection from the rain. She remembered now that she was almost naked. What would anyone think who saw her like this? Perhaps in the darkness her panties and bra would pass for a bikini—but what would a bather be doing out at this hour and in this place? She might explain that she had been sunbathing, had fallen asleep, taken refuge from the storm, and had then been forced to flee from the rising waters. But when news of the bus wreck spread, anyone who saw her would remember.

She must find shelter and clothing—somewhere. Her chance to escape had been born of the moment; she had not had time yet to think matters through. She only knew she could not let them recapture her now. Whatever the odds against her, she would face them.

She stood up, leaning against the face of the wall until she felt her legs would hold her upright. The flight of steps ran diagonally down from the top of the seawall. There was no railing on the outward face, and the stone was treacherous with slime and streaming water. Painfully she edged her way upward, trying not to think about the rushing waters below her. If she slipped, there was no way she could check her fall; she would tumble down into the black torrent, and this time there would be no escape.

The climb seemed as difficult as had her long swim, and her aching muscles seemed to rebel against the task of bearing her up the slippery steps, but at length she gained the upper landing and stumbled onto the storm-washed pavement atop the seawall. She blinked her eyes uncertainly, drawing a long breath. The rain pressed her black hair to her neck and shoulders, sluiced away the muck and filth from her skin.

There were no lights to be seen along here. A balustrade guarded the edge of the seawall, with a gap to give access to the stairs. A street, barren of any traffic at this hour, ran along the top of the wall, and, across the empty street, rows of brick buildings made a second barrier. Evidently she had come upon a district of warehouses and such—and, from all appearances, this section was considerably run-down. There were no streetlights here, but even in the darkness she could sense the disused aspect of the row of buildings with their boarded-over windows and filthy fronts, the brick street with its humped and broken paving.

She shivered. It was doubly fortunate that none were here to mark her sudden appearance. In a section like this, and dressed as she was, it was unlikely that anyone she might encounter would be of good Samaritan inclinations.

Clothing. She had to find clothing. Any sort of clothing. She darted across the uneven paving and into the deeper shadow of the building fronts. Her best bet would be to find a shop: perhaps some sordid second-hand place such as this street might well harbor, a place without elaborate burglar alarms, if possible. She could break in, or at worst find a window display and try her luck at smash and grab. Just a simple raincoat would make her far less vulnerable. Eventually she would need money, shelter, and food, until she could leave the city for someplace faraway.

As she crept along the deserted street, she found herself wondering whether she could find anything at all here. Doorways were padlocked and boarded over; behind rusted gratings, windows showed rotting planks and dirty shards of glass. The waterfront street seemed to be completely abandoned—a deserted row of ancient buildings enclosing forgotten wares, cheaper to let rot than to haul away, even as it was cheaper to let these brick hulks stand than to pull them down. Even the expected winos and derelicts seemed to have deserted this section of the city. She began to wish she might encounter at least a passing car.

The street had not been deserted by the rats. Probably they had been driven into the night by the rising waters. Once she began to notice them, she realized there were more and more of them—creeping boldly along the street. Huge, knowing brutes; some of them large as cats. They didn't seem afraid of her, and at times she thought they might be gathering in a pack to follow her. She had heard of rats attacking children and invalids, but surely . . . She wished she were out of this district.

The street plunged on atop the riverside, and still there were no lights or signs of human activity. The rain continued to pour down from the drowned night skies. She began to think about crawling into one of the dark warehouses to wait for morning, then thought of being alone in a dark, abandoned building with a closing pack of rats. She walked faster.

Some of the empty buildings showed signs of former grandeur, and she hoped she was coming toward a better section of the riverfront. Elaborate entranceways of fluted columns and marble steps gave onto the street. Grotesque Victorian façades and misshapen statuary presented imposing fronts to buildings filled with the same musty decay as the brick warehouses. She must be reaching the old merchants' district of the city, although these structures as well appeared long abandoned, waiting only for the wrecking ball of urban renewal. She wished she could escape this street, for there seemed to be more rats in the darkness behind her than she could safely ignore.

Perhaps she might find an alleyway between buildings that would let her flee this waterfront section and enter some inhabited neighborhood—for it became increasingly evident that this street had long been derelict. She peered closely at each building, but never could she find a gap between them. Without a light, she dared not enter blindly and try to find her way through some ramshackle building.

She paused for a moment and listened. For some while she had heard a scramble of wet claws and fretful squealings from the darkness behind her. Now she heard only the rain. Were the rats silently closing about her?

She stood before a columned portico—a bank or church? —and gazed into the darker shadow, wondering whether she might seek shelter. A statue—she supposed it was of an angel or some symbolic figure—stood before one of the marble columns. She could discern little of its features, only that it must have been malformed—presumably by vandalism—for it was hunched over and appeared to be supported against the column by thick cables or ropes. She could not see its face.

Not liking the silence, she hurried on again. Once past

the portico, she turned quickly and looked back—to see if the rats were creeping after her. She saw no rats. She could see the row of columns. The misshapen figure was no longer there.

She began to run then. Blindly, not thinking where her panic drove her.

To her right, there was only the balustrade, marking the edge of the wall, and the rushing waters below. To her left, the unbroken row of derelict buildings. Behind her, the night and the rain, and something whose presence had driven away the pursuing rats. And ahead of her—she was close enough to see it now—the street made a deadend against a rock wall.

Stumbling toward it, for she dared not turn back the way she had run, she saw that the wall was not unbroken—that a stairway climbed steeply to a terrace up above. Here the bluff rose high against the river once again, so that the seawall ended against the rising stone. There were buildings crowded against the height, fronted upon the terrace a level above. In one of the windows, a light shone through the rain.

Her breath shook in ragged gasps and her legs were rubbery, but she forced herself to half-run, half-clamber up the rain-slick steps to the terrace above. Here, again a level of brick paving and a balustrade to guard the edge. Boarded windows and desolate façades greeted her from a row of decrepit houses, shouldered together on the rise. The light had been to her right, out above the river.

She could see it clearly now. It beckoned from the last house on the terrace—a looming Victorian pile built over the bluff. A casement window, level with the far end of the terrace, opened out onto a neglected garden. She climbed over the low wall that separated the house from the terrace, and crouched outside the curtained window.

Inside, a comfortable-looking sitting room with old-fashioned appointments. An older woman was crocheting, while in a chair beside her a young woman, dressed in a maid's costume, was reading aloud from a book. Across the corner room, another casement window looked out over the black water far below.

Had her fear and exhaustion been less consuming, she might have taken a less reckless course, might have paused to consider what effect her appearance would make. But she remembered a certain shuffling sound she had heard as she scrambled up onto the terrace, and the way the darkness had seemed to gather upon the top of the stairway when she glanced back a moment gone. With no thought but to escape the night, she tapped her knuckles sharply against the casement window.

At the tapping at the window, the older woman looked up from her work, the maid let the yellow-bound volume drop onto her white apron. They stared at the casement, not so much frightened as if uncertain of what they had heard. The curtain inside veiled her presence from them.

Please! she prayed, without voice to cry out. She tapped more insistently, pressing herself against the glass. They would see that she was only a girl, see her distress.

They were standing now, the older woman speaking too quickly for her to catch the words. The maid darted to the window, fumbled with its latch. Another second, and the casement swung open, and she tumbled into the room.

She knelt in a huddle on the floor, too exhausted to move any farther. Her body shook and water dripped from her bare flesh. She felt like some half-drowned kitten, plucked from the storm to shelter. Vaguely she could hear their startled queries, the protective clash as the casement latch closed out the rain and the curtain swept across the night.

The maid had brought a coverlet and was furiously towelling her dry. Her attentions reminded her that she must offer some sort of account of herself—before her benefactors summoned the police, whose investigation would put a quick end to her freedom.

"I'm all right now," she told them shakily. "Just let me get my breath back, get warm."

"What's your name, child?" the older woman inquired solicitously. "Camilla, bring some hot tea."

She groped for a name to tell them. "Cassilda." The maid's name had put this in mind, and it was suited to her surroundings. "Cassilda Archer." Dr. Archer would indeed be interested in *that* appropriation.

"You poor child! How did you come here? Were you . . . attacked?"

Her thoughts worked quickly. Satisfy their curiosity, but don't make them suspicious. Justify your predicament, but don't alarm them.

"I was hitch-hiking." She spoke in uncertain bursts. "A man picked me up. He took me to a deserted section near the river. He made me take off my clothes. He was going to . . ." She didn't need to feign her shudder.

"Here's the tea, Mrs. Castaigne. I've added a touch of brandy."

"Thank you, Camilla. Drink some of this, dear."

She used the interruption to collect her thoughts. The two women were alone here, or else any others would have been summoned.

"When he started to pull down his trousers . . . I hurt him. Then I jumped out and ran as hard as I could. I don't think he came after me, but then I was wandering lost in the rain. I couldn't find anyone to help me. I didn't have anything with me except my underwear. I think a tramp was following me. Then I saw your light and ran toward it.

"Please, don't call the police!" She forestalled their obvious next move. "I'm not hurt. I know I couldn't face the shame of a rape investigation. Besides, they'd never be able to catch that man by now."

"But surely you must want me to contact someone for you."

"There's no one who would care. I'm on my own. That

man has my pack and the few bucks in my handbag. If you could please let me stay here for the rest of the night, lend me some clothes just for tomorrow, and in the morning I'll phone a friend who can wire me some money.''

Mrs. Castaigne hugged her protectively. ''You poor child! What you've been through! Of course you'll stay with us for the night—and don't fret about having to relive your terrible ordeal for a lot of leering policemen! Tomorrow there'll be plenty of time for you to decide what you'd like to do.

''Camilla, draw a nice hot bath for Cassilda. She's to sleep in Constance's room, so see that there's a warm comforter, and lay out a gown for her. And you, Cassilda, must drink another cup of this tea. As badly chilled as you are, child, you'll be fortunate indeed to escape your death of pneumonia!''

Over the rim of her cup, the girl examined the room and its occupants more closely. The sitting room was distinctly old-fashioned—furnished like a parlor in an old photograph, or like a set from some movie that was supposed to be taking place at the turn of the century. Even the lights were either gas or kerosene. Probably this house hadn't changed much since years ago before the neighborhood had begun to decay. Anyone would have to be a little eccentric to keep staying on here, although probably this place was all Mrs. Castaigne had, and Mr. Castaigne wasn't in evidence. The house and property couldn't be worth much in this neighborhood, although the furnishings might fetch a little money as antiques—she was no judge of that, but everything looked to be carefully preserved.

Mrs. Castaigne seemed well fitted to this room and its furnishings. Hers was a face that might belong to a woman of forty or of sixty—well featured but too stern for a younger woman, yet without the lines and age marks of an elderly lady. Her figure was still very good, and she wore a tight-waisted ankle-length dress that seemed to belong to the period of the house. The hands that stroked her bare shoulders were strong and white and unblemished, and the hair she wore piled atop her head was as black as the girl's own.

It occurred to her that Mrs. Castaigne must surely be too young for this house. Probably she was a daughter or more likely a granddaughter of its original owners—a widow who lived alone with her young maid. And who might Constance be, whose room she was to sleep in?

"Your bath is ready now, Miss Archer." Camilla reappeared. Wrapped in the coverlet, the girl followed her. Mrs. Castaigne helped support her, for her legs had barely strength to stand, and she felt ready to pass out from fatigue.

The bathroom was spacious—steamy from the vast claw-footed tub and smelling of bath salts. Its plumbing and fixtures were no more modern than the rest of the house. Camilla entered with her and, to her surprise, helped her remove her scant clothing and assisted her into the tub. She was too tired to feel ill at ease at this unaccustomed show of attention, and when the maid began to rub her back with scented soap, she sighed at the luxury.

"Who else lives here?" she asked casually.

"Only Mrs. Castaigne and myself, Miss Archer."

"Mrs. Castaigne mentioned someone—Constance?—whose room I am to have."

"Miss Castaigne is no longer with us, Miss Archer."

"Please call me Cassilda. I don't like to be so formal."

"If that's what you wish to be called, of course . . . Cassilda."

Camilla couldn't be very far from her own age, she guessed. Despite the old-fashioned maid's outfit—black dress and stockings with frilled white apron and cap—the other girl was probably no more than in her early twenties. The maid wore her long blonde hair in an upswept topknot like her mistress, and she supposed she only followed Mrs. Castaigne's preferences. Camilla's figure was full—much more buxom than her own boyish slenderness—and her cinch-waisted costume accented this. Her eyes were a bright blue, shining above a straight nose and wide-mouthed face.

"You've hurt yourself." Camilla ran her fingers tenderly along the bruises that marred her ribs and legs.

"There was a struggle. And I fell in the darkness—I don't know how many times."

"And you've cut yourself." Camilla lifted the other girl's black hair away from her neck. "Here on your shoulders and throat. But I don't believe it's anything to worry about." Her fingers carefully touched the livid scrapes.

"Are you certain there isn't someone whom we should let know of your safe whereabouts?"

"There is no one who would care. I am alone."

"Poor Cassilda."

"All I want is to sleep," she murmured. The warm bath was easing the ache from her flesh, leaving her deliciously sleepy.

Camilla left her to return with large towels. The maid helped her from the tub, wrapping her in one towel as she dried her with another. She felt faint with drowsiness, allowed herself to relax against the blonde girl. Camilla was very strong, supporting her easily as she towelled her small breasts. Her fingers found the parting of her thighs, lingered, then returned again in a less than casual touch.

Her dark eyes were wide as she stared into Camilla's luminous blue gaze, but she felt too pleasurably relaxed to object when the maid's touch became more intimate. Her breath caught, and heid.

"You're very warm, Cassilda."

"Hurry, Camilla." Mrs. Castaigne spoke from the doorway. "The poor child is about to drop. Help her into her nightdress."

Past wondering, she lifted her arms to let Camilla drape the beribboned lawn nightdress over her head and to her ankles. In another moment she was being ushered into a bedroom, furnished in the fashion of the rest of the house, and to an ornate brass bed whose mattress swallowed her up like a wave of foam. She felt the quilts drawn over her, sensed their presence hovering over her, and then she slipped into a deep sleep of utter exhaustion.

"Is there no one?"

"Nothing at all."

"Of course. How else could she be here? She is ours."

Her dreams were troubled by formless fears—deeply disturbing as experienced, yet their substance was already forgotten when she awoke at length on the echo of her outcry. She stared about her anxiously, uncertain where she was. Her disorientation was the same as when she awakened after receiving shock, only this place wasn't a ward, and the woman who entered the room wasn't one of her wardens.

"Good morning, Cassilda." The maid drew back the curtains to let long shadows streak across the room. "I should say, good evening, as it's almost that time. You've slept throughout the day, poor dear."

Cassilda? Yes, that was she. Memory came tumbling back in a confused jumble. She raised herself from her pillows and looked about the bedchamber she had been too tired to examine before. It was distinctly a woman's room—a young woman's—and she remembered that it had been Mrs. Castaigne's daughter's room. It scarcely seemed to have been unused for very long: the brass bed was brightly polished, the walnut of the wardrobe, the chests of drawers and the dressing table made a rich glow, and the gay pastels of the curtains and wallpaper offset the gravity of the high tinned ceiling and parquetry floor. Small oriental rugs and pillows upon the chairs and chaise longue made bright points of color. Again she thought of a movie set, for the room was altogether lacking in anything modern. She knew very little about antiques, but she guessed that the style of furnishings must go back before the First World War.

Camilla was arranging a single red rose in a crystal bud vase upon the dressing table. She caught her gaze in the mirror. "Did you sleep well, Cassilda? I thought I heard you cry out, just as I knocked."

"A bad dream, I suppose. But I slept well. I don't, usually." They had made her take pills to sleep.

"Are you awake, Cassilda? I thought I heard your voices." Mrs. Castaigne smiled from the doorway and crossed to her bed. She was dressed much the same as the night before.

"I didn't mean to sleep so long," she apologized.

"Poor child! I shouldn't wonder that you slept so, after your dreadful ordeal. Do you feel strong enough to take a little soup?"

"I really must be going. I can't impose any further."

"I won't hear any more of that, my dear. Of course you'll stay with us, until you're feeling stronger." Mrs. Castaigne sat beside her on the bed, placed a cold hand against her brow. "Why, Cassilda, your face is simply aglow. I do hope you haven't taken a fever. Look, your hands are positively trembling!"

"I feel all right." In fact, she did not. She did feel as if she were running a fever, and her muscles were so sore that she wasn't sure she could walk. The trembling didn't concern her: the injections they gave her every two weeks made her shake, so they gave her little pills to stop the shaking. Now she didn't have those pills, but since it was time again for another shot, the injection and its side effects would soon wear off.

"I'm going to bring you some tonic, dear. And Camilla will bring you some good nourishing soup, which you must try to take. Poor Cassilda, if we don't nurse you carefully, I'm afraid you may fall dangerously ill."

"But I can't be such a nuisance to you," she protested as a matter of form. "I really must be going."

"Where to, dear child?" Mrs. Castaigne held her hands gravely. "Have you someplace else to go? Is there someone you wish us to inform of your safety?"

"No," she admitted, trying to make everything sound right. "I've no place to go; there's no one who matters. I was on my way down the coast, hoping to find a job during the resort season. I know one or two old girlfriends who could put me up until I get settled."

"See there. Then there's no earthly reason why you can't just stay here until you're feeling strong again. Why, perhaps I might find a position for you myself. But we shall discuss these things later when you're feeling well. For the moment, just settle back on your pillow and let us help you get well."

Mrs. Castaigne bent over her, kissed her on the forehead. Her lips were cool. "How lovely you are, Cassilda," she smiled, patting her hand.

She smiled back, and returned the other woman's firm grip. She'd seen no sign of a TV or radio here, and an old eccentric like Mrs. Castaigne probably didn't even read the papers. Even if Mrs. Castaigne had heard about the bus wreck, she plainly was too overjoyed at having a visitor to break her lonely routine to concern herself with a possible escapee—assuming they hadn't just listed her as drowned. She couldn't have hoped for a better place to hide out until things cooled off.

The tonic had a bitter licorice taste and made her drowsy, so that she fell asleep not long after Camilla carried away her tray. Despite her long sleep throughout that day, fever and exhaustion drew her back down again—although her previous sleep robbed this one of restful oblivion. Again came troubled dreams, this time cutting more harshly into her consciousness.

She dreamed of Dr. Archer—her stern face and mannish shoulders craning over her bed. Her wrists and ankles were fixed to each corner of the bed by padded leather cuffs. Dr. Archer was speaking to her in a scolding tone, while her wardens were pulling up her skirt, dragging down her panties. A syringe gleamed in Dr. Archer's hand, and there was a sharp stinging in her buttock.

She was struggling again, but to no avail. Dr. Archer was shouting at her, and a stout nurse was tightening the last few buckles of the straitjacket that bound her arms to her chest in a loveless hug. The straps were so tight she could hardly draw breath, and while she could not understand what Dr. Archer was saying, she recognized the spurting needle that Dr. Archer thrust into her.

She was strapped tightly to the narrow bed, her eyes staring at the gray ceiling as they wheeled her through the corridors to Dr. Archer's special room. Then they stopped; they were there, and Dr. Archer was bending over her again. Then came the sting in her arm as they penetrated her veins, the helpless headlong rush of the drug—and Dr. Archer smiles and turns to her machine, and the current blasts into her tightly strapped skull and her body arches and strains against the restraints and her scream strangles against the rubber gag clenched in her teeth.

But the face that looks into hers now is not Dr. Archer's, and the hands that shake her are not cruel.

"Cassilda! Cassilda! Wake up! It's only a nightmare!"

Camilla's blonde and blue face finally focused into her awakening vision.

"Only a nightmare," Camilla reassured her. "Poor darling." The hands that held her shoulders lifted to smooth her black hair from her eyes, to cup her face. Camilla bent over her, kissed her gently on her dry lips.

"What is it?" Mrs. Castaigne, wearing her nightdress and carrying a candle, came anxiously into the room.

"Poor Cassilda has had bad dreams," Camilla told her. "And her face feels ever so warm."

"Dear child!" Mrs. Castaigne set down her candlestick. "She must take some more tonic at once. Perhaps you should sit with her, Camilla, to see that her sleep is untroubled."

"Certainly, madame. I'll just fetch the tonic."

"Please, don't bother . . ." But the room became a vertiginous blur as she tried to sit up. She slumped back and closed her eyes tightly for a moment. Her body *did* feel feverish, her mouth dry, and the trembling when she moved her hand to take the medicine glass was so obvious that Camilla shook her head and held the glass to her lips herself. She swallowed dutifully, wondering how much of this was a reaction to the Prolixin still in her flesh. The injection would soon be wearing off, she knew, for when she smiled back at her nurses, the sharp edges of color were beginning to show once again through the haze the medication drew over her perception.

"I'll be all right soon," she promised them.

"Then do try to sleep, darling." Mrs. Castaigne patted her arm. "You must regain your strength. Camilla will be here to watch over you.

"Be certain that the curtains are drawn against any night vapors," she directed her maid. "Call me, if necessary."

"Of course, madame. I'll not leave her side."

She was dreaming again—or dreaming still.

Darkness surrounded her like a black leather mask, and her body shook with uncontrollable spasms. Her naked flesh was slick with chill sweat, although her mouth was burning dry. She moaned and tossed—striving to awaken order from out of the damp blackness, but the blackness only embraced her with smothering tenacity.

Cold lips were crushing her own, thrusting a cold tongue into her feverish mouth, bruising the skin of her throat. Fingers, slender and strong, caressed her breasts, held her nipples to hungry lips. Her hands thrashed about, touched smooth flesh. It came to her that her eyes were indeed wide open, that the darkness was so profound she could no more than sense the presence of other shapes close beside her.

Her own movements were languid, dreamlike. Through

the spasms that racked her flesh, she became aware of a perverse thrill of ecstasy. Her fingers brushed somnolently against the cool flesh that crouched over her, with no more purpose or strength than the drifting limbs of a drowning victim.

A compelling lassitude bound her, even as the blackness blinded her. She seemed to be drifting away, apart from her body, apart from her dream, into deeper ever deeper darkness. The sensual arousal that lashed her lost reality against the lethargy and fever that held her physically, and rising out of the eroticism of her delirium shrilled whispers of underlying revulsion and terror.

One pair of lips imprisoned her mouth and throat now, sucking at her breath, while other lips crept down across her breasts, hovered upon her navel, then pounced upon the opening of her thighs. Her breath caught in a shudder, was sucked away by the lips that held her mouth, as the coldness began to creep into her burning flesh.

She felt herself smothering, unable to draw breath, so that her body arched in panic, her limbs thrashed aimlessly. Her efforts to break away were as ineffectual as was her struggle to awaken. The lips that stole her breath released her, but only for a moment. In the darkness she felt other flesh pinion her tossing body, move against her with cool strength. Chill fire tormented her loins, and as she opened her mouth to cry out, or to sigh, smooth thighs pressed down onto her cheeks and the coldness gripped her breath. Mutely, she obeyed the needs that commanded her, that overwhelmed her, and through the darkness blindly flowed her silent scream of ecstasy and of horror.

Cassilda awoke.

Sunlight spiked into her room—the colored panes creating a false prism effect. Camilla, who had been adjusting the curtains, turned and smiled at the sound of her movement.

"Good morning, Cassilda. Are you feeling better this morning?"

"A great deal better." Cassilda returned her smile. "I feel as if I'd slept for days." She frowned slightly, suddenly uncertain.

Camilla touched her forehead. "Your fever has left you; Mrs. Castaigne will be delighted to learn that. You've slept away most of yesterday and all through last night. Shall I bring your breakfast tray now?"

"Please—I'm famished. But I really think I should be getting up."

"After breakfast, if you wish. And now I'll inform madame that you're feeling much better."

Mrs. Castaigne appeared as the maid was clearing away the breakfast things. "How very much better you look today, Cassilda. Camilla tells me you feel well enough to sit up."

"I really can't play the invalid and continue to impose upon your hospitality any longer. Would it be possible that you might lend me some clothing? My own garments . . ." Cassilda frowned, trying to remember why she had burst in upon her benefactress virtually naked.

"Certainly, my dear." Mrs. Castaigne squeezed her shoulder. "You must see if some of my daughter's garments won't fit you. You cannot be very far from Constance, I'm certain. Camilla will assist you."

She was lightheaded when first she tried to stand, but Cassilda clung to the brass bedposts until her legs felt strong enough to hold her. The maid was busying herself at the chest of drawers, removing items of clothing from beneath neat coverings of tissue paper. A faint odor of dried rose petals drifted from a sachet beneath the folded garments.

"I do hope you'll overlook it if these are not of the latest mode," Mrs. Castaigne was saying. "It has been some time since Constance was with us here."

"Your daughter is . . . ?"

"Away."

Cassilda declined to intrude further. There was a dressing screen behind which she retired, while Mrs. Castaigne waited upon the chaise longue. Trailing a scent of dried roses from the garments she carried, Camilla joined her behind the screen and helped her out of her nightdress.

There were undergarments of fine silk, airy lace, and gauzy pastels. Cassilda found herself puzzled, both from their unfamiliarity and at the same time their familiarity, and while her thoughts struggled with the mystery, her hands seemed to dress her body with practiced movements. First the chemise, knee-length and trimmed with light lace and ribbons. Seated upon a chair, she drew on pale stockings of patterned silk, held at mid-thigh by beribboned garters. Then silk knickers, open front and back and tied at the waist, trimmed with lace and ruching where they flared below her stocking tops. A frilled petticoat fell almost to her ankles.

"I won't need that," Cassilda protested. Camilla had presented her with a boned corset of white and sky broché.

"Nonsense, my dear," Mrs. Castaigne directed, coming around the dressing screen to oversee. "You may think of me as old-fashioned, but I insist that you not ruin your figure."

Cassilda submitted, suddenly wondering why she had thought anything out of the ordinary about it. She hooked the straight busk together in front, while Camilla gathered the laces at the back. The maid tugged sharply at the laces, squeezing out her breath. Cassilda bent forward and steadied herself against the back of the chair, as Camilla braced a knee against the small of her back, pulling the laces as tight as possible before tying them. Once her corset was secured, she drew over it a camisole of white cotton lace and trimmed with ribbon, matching her petticoat. Somewhat dizzy, Cassilda sat stiffly before the dressing table, while the maid brushed out her long black hair and gathered it in a loose knot atop her head, pinning it in place with tortoise-shell combs. Opening the wardrobe, Camilla found her a pair of shoes, with high heels that mushroomed outward at the bottom, which fit her easily.

"How lovely, Cassilda!" Mrs. Castaigne approved. "One would scarcely recognize you as the poor drowned thing that came out of the night!"

Cassilda stood up and examined herself in the full-length dressing mirror. It was as if she looked upon a stranger, and yet she knew she looked upon herself. The corset constricted her waist and forced her slight figure into an "S" curve—hips back, bust forward—imparting an unexpected opulence, further enhanced by the gauzy profusion of lace and silk. Her face, dark-eyed and finely boned, returned her gaze watchfully from beneath a lustrous pile of black hair. She touched herself, almost in wonder, almost believing that the reflection in the mirror was a photograph of someone else.

Camilla selected for her a long-sleeved linen shirtwaist, buttoned at the cuffs and all the way to her throat, then helped her into a skirt of some darker material that fell away from her cinched waist to her ankles. Cassilda studied herself in the mirror, while the maid fussed about her.

I look like someone in an old illustration—a Gibson girl, she thought, then puzzled at her thought.

Through the open window she could hear the vague noises of the city, and for the first time she realized that intermingled with these familiar sounds was the clatter of horses' hooves upon the brick pavement.

"You simply must not say anything more about leaving us, Cassilda," Mrs. Castaigne insisted, laying a hand upon the girl's knee as she leaned toward her confidentially.

Beside her on the settee, Cassilda felt the pressure of her touch through the rustling layers of petticoat. It haunted her, this flowing whisper of sound that came with her every movement, for it seemed at once strange and again familiar—a shivery sigh of silk against silk, like the whisk of dry snow sliding across stone. She smiled, holding her teacup with automatic poise, and wondered that such little, commonplace sensations should seem at all out of the ordinary to her. Even the rigid embrace of her corset seemed quite familiar to her now, so that she sat gracefully at ease, listening to her benefactress, while a part of her thoughts stirred in uneasy wonder.

"You have said yourself that you have no immediate prospects," Mrs. Castaigne continued. "I shouldn't have to remind you of the dangers the city holds for unattached young women. You were extremely fortunate in your escape from those white slavers who had abducted you. Without family or friends to question your disappearance—well, I shan't suggest what horrible fate awaited you."

Cassilda shivered at the memory of her escape—a memory as formless and uncertain, beyond her *need* to escape, as that of her life prior to her abduction. She had made only vague replies to Mrs. Castaigne's gentle questioning, nor was she at all certain which fragments of her story were half-truths or lies.

Of one thing she was certain beyond all doubt: the danger from which she had fled awaited her beyond the shelter of this house.

"It has been so lonely here since Constance went away," Mrs. Castaigne was saying. "Camilla is a great comfort to me, but nonetheless she has her household duties to occupy her, and I have often considered engaging a companion. I should be only too happy if you would consent to remain with us in this position—at least for the present time."

"You're much too kind! Of course I'll stay."

"I promise you that your duties shall be no more onerous than to provide amusements for a rather old-fashioned lady of retiring disposition. I hope it won't prove too dull for you, my dear."

"It suits my own temperament perfectly," Cassilda assured her. "I am thoroughly content to follow quiet pursuits within doors."

"Wonderful!" Mrs. Castaigne took her hands. "Then it's settled. I know Camilla will be delighted to have another young spirit about the place. And you may relieve her of some of her tasks."

"What shall I do?" Cassilda begged her, overjoyed at her good fortune.

"Would you read to me, please, my dear? I find it so relaxing to the body and so stimulating to the mind. I've taken up far too much of Camilla's time from her chores, having her read to me for hours on end."

"Of course." Cassilda returned Camilla's smile as she entered the sitting room to collect the tea things. From her delight, it was evident that the maid had been listening from the hallway. "What would you like for me to read to you?"

"That book over there beneath the lamp." Mrs. Castaigne indicated a volume bound in yellow cloth. "It is a recent drama—and a most curious work, as you shall quickly see. Camilla was reading it to me on the night you came to us."

Taking up the book, Cassilda again experienced a strange sense of unaccountable *déjà vu*, and she wondered where she might previously have read *The King in Yellow*, if indeed she ever had.

"I believe we are ready to begin the second act," Mrs. Castaigne told her.

Cassilda was reading in bed when Camilla knocked tentatively at her door. She set aside her book with an almost furtive movement. *"Entrez vous."*

"I was afraid you might already be asleep," the maid explained, "but then I saw light beneath your door. I'd forgotten to bring you your tonic before retiring."

Camilla, *en déshabillé*, carried in the medicine glass on a silver tray. Her fluttering lace and pastels seemed a pretty contrast to the black maid's uniform she ordinarily wore.

"I wasn't able to go to sleep just yet," Cassilda confessed, sitting up in bed. "I was reading."

Camilla handed her the tonic. "Let me see. Ah, yes. What a thoroughly wicked book to be reading in bed!"

"Have you read *The King in Yellow*?"

"I have read it through aloud to madame, and more than once. It is a favorite of hers."

"It is sinful and more than sinful to imbue such decadence with so compelling a fascination. I cannot imagine that anyone could have allowed it to be published. The author must have been mad to pen such thoughts."

"And yet, you read it."

Cassilda made a place for her on the edge of the bed. "Its fascination is too great a temptation to resist. I wanted to read further after Mrs. Castaigne bade me good night."

"It was Constance's book." Camilla huddled close beside her against the pillows. "Perhaps that is why madame cherishes it so."

Cassilda opened the yellow-bound volume to the page she had been reading. Camilla craned her blonde head over her shoulder to read with her. She had removed her corset, and her ample figure swelled against her beribboned chemise. Cassilda in her nightdress felt almost scrawny as she compared her own small bosom to the other girl's.

"Is it not strange?" she remarked. "Here in this decadent drama we read of Cassilda and Camilla."

"I wonder if we two are very much like them," Camilla laughed.

"They are such very dear friends."

"And so are we, are we not?"

"I do so want us to be."

"But you haven't read beyond the second act, dear Cassilda. How can you know what may their fate be?"

"Oh, Camilla!" Cassilda leaned her face back against Camilla's perfumed breasts. "Don't tease me so!"

The blond girl hugged her fiercely, stroking her back.
''Poor, lost Cassilda.''

Cassilda nestled against her, listening to the heartbeat
beneath her cheek. She was feeling warm and sleepy, for
all that the book had disturbed her. The tonic always
carried her to dreamy oblivion, and it was pleasant to drift
to sleep in Camilla's soft embrace.

''Were you and Constance friends?'' she wondered.

''We were the very dearest of friends.''

''You must miss her very much.''

''No longer.''

Cassilda sat at the escritoire in her room, writing in the
journal she had found there. Her petticoats crowded against
the legs of the writing table as she leaned forward to reach
the inkwell. From time to time she paused to stare pen-
sively past the open curtains of her window, upon the
deepening blue of the evening sky as it met the angled
rooftops of the buildings along the waterfront below.

''I think I should feel content here,'' she wrote. ''Mrs.
Castaigne is strict in her demands, but I am certain she
takes a sincere interest in my own well-being, and that she
has only the kindliest regard for me. My duties during the
day are of the lightest nature and consist primarily of
reading to Mrs. Castaigne or of singing at the piano while
she occupies herself with her needlework, and in all other
ways making myself companionable to her in our simple
amusements.

''I have offered to assist Camilla at her chores, but Mrs.
Castaigne will not have it that I perform other than the
lightest household tasks. Camilla is a very dear friend to
me, and her sweet attentions easily distract me from what
might otherwise become a tedium of sitting about the
house day to day. Nonetheless, I have no desire to leave
my situation here, nor to adventure into the streets outside
the house. We are not in an especially attractive section of
the city here, being at some remove from the shops and in

a district given over to waterfront warehouses and commercial establishments. We receive no visitors, other than the tradesmen who supply our needs, nor is Mrs. Castaigne of a disposition to wish to seek out the society of others.

"Withal, my instincts suggest that Mrs. Castaigne has sought the existence of a recluse out of some very great emotional distress which has robbed life of its interests for her. It is evident from the attention and instruction she has bestowed upon me that she sees in me a reflection of her daughter, and I am convinced that it is in the loss of Constance where lies the dark secret of her self-imposed withdrawal from the world. I am sensible of the pain Mrs. Castaigne harbors within her breast, for the subject of her daughter's absence is never brought into our conversations, and for this reason I have felt loath to question her, although I am certain that this is the key to the mystery that holds us in this house."

Cassilda concluded her entry with the date: June 7th, 189—

She frowned in an instant's consternation. What *was* the date? How silly. She referred to a previous day's entry, then completed the date. For a moment she turned idly back through her journal, smiling faintly at the many pages of entries that filled the diary, each progressively dated, each penned in the same neat hand as the entry she had just completed.

Cassilda sat at her dressing table in her room. It was night, and she had removed her outer clothing preparatory to retiring. She gazed at her reflection—the gauzy paleness of her chemise, stockings, and knickers was framed against Camilla's black maid's uniform, as the blonde girl stood behind her, brushing out her dark hair.

Upon the dressing table she had spread out the contents of a tin box she had found in one of the drawers, and she and Camilla had been looking over them as she prepared for bed. There were paper dolls, valentines, and greeting cards, illustrations clipped from magazines, a lovely cut-out of a swan. She also found a crystal ball that rested upon an ebony cradle. Within the crystal sphere was a tiny house, covered with snow, with trees and a frozen lake and a young girl playing. When Cassilda picked it up, the snow stirred faintly in the transparent fluid that filled the globe. She turned the crystal sphere upside down for a moment, then quickly righted it, and a snowstorm drifted down about the tiny house.

"How wonderful it would be to dwell forever in a crystal fairyland just like the people in this little house," Cassilda remarked, peering into the crystal ball.

Something else seemed to stir within the swirling snow-flakes, she thought; but when the snow had settled once more, the tableau was unchanged. No: there was a small mound, there beside the child at play, that she was certain she had not seen before. Cassilda overturned the crystal globe once again, and peered more closely. There it was. Another tiny figure spinning amidst the snowflakes. A second girl. She must have broken loose from the tableau. The tiny figure drifted to rest upon the frozen lake, and the snowflakes once more covered her from view.

"Where is Constance Castaigne?" Cassilda asked.

"Constance . . . became quite ill," Camilla told her carefully. "She was always subject to nervous attacks. One night she suffered one of her fits, and she . . ."

"Camilla!" Mrs. Castaigne's voice from the doorway was stern. "You know how I despise gossip—especially idle gossip concerning another's misfortunes."

The maid's face was downcast. "I'm very sorry, madame. I meant no mischief."

The older woman scowled as she crossed the room. Cassilda wondered if she meant to strike the maid. "Being sorry does not pardon the offense of a wagging tongue. Perhaps a lesson in behavior will improve your manners in the future. Go at once to your room."

"Please, madame . . ."

"Your insolence begins to annoy me, Camilla."

"Please, don't be harsh with her!" Cassilda begged, as the maid hurried from the room. "She was only answering my question."

Standing behind the seated girl, Mrs. Castaigne placed her hands upon her shoulders and smiled down at her. "An innocent question, my dear. However, the subject is extremely painful to me, and Camilla well knows the distress it causes me to hear it brought up. I shall tell you this now, and that shall end the matter. My daughter suffered a severe attack of brain fever. She is confined in a mental sanatorium."

Cassilda crossed her arms over her breasts to place her hands upon the older woman's wrists. "I'm terribly sorry."

"I'm certain you can appreciate how sorely this subject distresses me." Mrs. Castaigne smiled, meeting her eyes in the mirror.

"I shan't mention it again."

"Of course not. And now, my dear, you must hurry and make yourself ready for bed. Too much exertion so soon after your illness will certainly bring about a relapse. Hurry along now, while I fetch your tonic."

"I'm sure I don't need any more medicine. Sometimes I think it must bring on evil dreams."

"Now don't argue, Cassilda dear." The fingers on her shoulders tightened their grip. "You must do as you're told. You can't very well perform your duties as companion if you lie about ill all day, now can you? And you *do* want to stay."

"Certainly!" Cassilda thought this last had not been voiced as a question. "I want to do whatever you ask."

"I know you do, Cassilda. And I only want to make you into a perfect young lady. Now let me help you into your night things."

Cassilda opened her eyes into complete darkness that swirled about her in an invisible current. She sat upright in her bed, fighting back the vertigo that she had decided must come from the tonic they gave her nightly. Something had wakened her. Another bad dream? She knew she often suffered them, even though the next morning she was unable to recall them. Was she about to be sick? She was certain that the tonic made her feel drugged.

Her wide eyes stared sleeplessly at the darkness. She knew sleep would not return easily, for she feared to lapse again into the wicked dreams that disturbed her rest and left her lethargic throughout the next day. She could not even be certain that this now might not be another of those dreams.

In the absolute silence of the house, she could hear her heart pulse, her breath stir anxiously.

There was another sound, more distant, and of almost the same monotonous regularity. She thought she heard a woman's muffled sobbing.

Mrs. Castaigne, she thought. The talk of her daughter had upset her terribly. Underscoring the sobbing came a sharp, rhythmic crack, as if a rocker sounded against a loose board.

Cassilda felt upon the nightstand beside her bed. Her fingers found matches. Striking one, she lit the candle that was there—her actions entirely automatic. Stepping down out of her bed, she caught up the candlestick and moved cautiously out of her room.

In the hallway, she listened for the direction of the sound. Her candle forced a small nimbus of light against the enveloping darkness of the old house. Cassilda shivered and drew her nightdress closer about her throat; its gauzy lace and ribbons were no barrier to the cold darkness that swirled about her island of candlelight.

The sobbing seemed no louder as she crept down the hallway toward Mrs. Castaigne's bedroom. There, the bedroom door was open, and within was only silent darkness.

"Mrs. Castaigne?" Cassilda called softly, without answer. The sound of muffled sobbing continued, and now seemed to come from overhead. Cassilda followed its sound to the end of the hallway, where a flight of stairs led to the maid's quarters in the attic. Cassilda paused fearfully at the foot of the stairway, thrusting her candle without effect against the darkness above. She could still hear the sobbing, but the other sharp sound had ceased. Her head seemed to float in the darkness as she listened, but despite her dreamlike lethargy, she knew her thoughts raced too wildly now for sleep. Catching up the hem of her nightdress, Cassilda cautiously ascended the stairs.

Once she gained the landing above, she could see the blade of yellow light that shone beneath the door to Camilla's room, and from within came the sounds that had summoned her. Quickly Cassilda crossed to the maid's room and knocked softly upon the door.

"Camilla? It's Cassilda. Are you all right?"

Again no answer, although she sensed movement within. The muffled sobs continued.

Cassilda tried the doorknob, found it was not locked. She pushed the door open and stepped inside, dazzled a moment by the bright glare of the oil lamp.

Camilla, dressed only in her corset and undergarments, stood bent over the foot of her bed. Her ankles were lashed to the base of either post, her wrists tied together and stretched forward by a rope fixed to the headboard. Exposed by the open-style knickers, her buttocks were crisscrossed with red welts. She turned her head to look at Cassilda and the other girl saw that Camilla's cries were gagged by a complicated leather bridle strapped about her head.

"Come in, Cassilda, since you wish to join us," said Mrs. Castaigne from behind her. Cassilda heard her close the door and lock it, before the girl had courage enough to turn around. Mrs. Castaigne wore no more clothing than did Camilla, and she switched her riding crop anticipatorily. Looking from mistress to maid, Cassilda saw that both pairs of eyes glowed alike with the lusts of unholy pleasure.

* * *

For a long interval Cassilda resisted awakening, hovering in a languor of unformed dreaming despite the rising awareness that she still slept. When she opened her eyes at last, she stared at the candlestick on her nightstand, observing without comprehension that the candle had burned down to a misshapen nub of cold wax. Confused memories came to her, slipping away again as her mind sought to grasp them. She had dreamed . . .

Her mouth seemed bruised and sour with a chemical taste that was not the usual anisette aftertaste of the tonic, and her limbs ached as if sore from too strenuous exercise the day before. Cassilda hoped she was not going to have a relapse of the fever that had stricken her after she had fled the convent that stormy night so many weeks ago.

She struggled for a moment with that memory. The sisters in black robes and white aprons had intended to wall her up alive in her cell because she had yielded to the temptation of certain unspeakable desires . . . The memory clouded and eluded her, like a fragment of some incompletely remembered book.

There were too many elusive memories, memories that died unheard . . . Had she not read that? *The King in Yellow* lay open upon her nightstand. Had she been reading, then fallen asleep to such dreams of depravity? But dreams, like memories, faded mirage-like whenever she touched them, leaving only tempting images to beguile her.

Forcing her cramped muscles to obey her, Cassilda climbed from her bed. Camilla was late with her tray this morning, and she might as well get dressed to make herself forget the dreams. As she slipped out of her nightdress, she looked at her reflection in the full-length dressing mirror.

The marks were beginning to fade now, but the still painful welts made red streaks across the white flesh of her shoulders, back, and thighs. Fragments of repressed nightmare returned as she stared in growing fear. She reached out her hands, touching the reflection in wonder. There were bruises on her wrists, and unbidden came a memory of her weight straining against the cords that bound her wrists to a hook from an attic rafter.

Behind her, in the mirror, Mrs. Castaigne ran the tip of her tongue along her smiling lips.

"Up and about already, Cassilda? I hope you've made up your mind to be a better young lady today. You were most unruly last night."

Her brain reeling under the onrush of memories, Cassilda stared mutely. Camilla, obsequious in her maid's costume, her smile a cynical sneer, entered carrying a complex leather harness of many straps and buckles.

"I think we must do something more to improve your posture, Cassilda," Mrs. Castaigne purred. "You may think me a bit old-fashioned, but I insist that a young lady's figure must be properly trained if she is to look her best."

"What are you doing to me?" Cassilda wondered, feeling panic.

"Only giving you the instruction a young lady must have if she is to serve as my companion. And you *do* want to be a proper young lady, don't you, Cassilda."

"I'm leaving this house. Right now."

"We both know why you can't. Besides, you don't really want to go. You quite enjoy our cozy little *ménage à trois*."

"You're deranged."

"And you're one to talk, dear Cassilda." Mrs. Castaigne's smile was far more menacing than any threatened blow. "I think, Camilla, the scold's bridle will teach this silly girl to mind that wicked tongue."

A crash of thunder broke her out of her stupor. Out of reflex, she tried to dislodge the hard rubber ball that filled her mouth, choked on saliva when she failed. Half-strangled

by the gag strapped over her face, she strained in panic to
sit up. Her wrists and ankles were held fast, and, as her
eyes dilated in unreasoning fear, a flash of lightning beyond
the window rippled down upon her spreadeagled body,
held to the brass bedposts by padded leather cuffs.

Images, too chaotic and incomprehensible to form co-
herent memory, exploded in bright shards from her shattered mind.

She was being forced into a straitjacket, flung into a
padded cell, and they were bricking up the door . . . no, it
was some bizarre corset device, forcing her neck back,
crushing her abdomen, arms laced painfully into a single
glove at her back . . . Camilla was helping her into a
gown of satin and velvet and lace, and then into a hood of
padded leather that they buckled over her head as they led
her to the gallows . . . and the nurses held her down while
Dr. Archer penetrated her with a grotesque syringe of vile
poison, and Mrs. Castaigne forced the yellow tonic down
her throat as she pinned her face between her thighs . . .
and Camilla's lips dripped blood as she rose from her kiss,
and her fangs were hypodermic needles, injecting poison,
sucking life . . . they were wheeling her into the torture
chamber, where Dr. Archer awaited her ("It's only a
frontal lobotomy, just to relieve the pressure on these two
diseased lobes.") and plunges the bloody scalpel deep
between her thighs . . . and they were strapping her into
the metal chair in the death cell, shoving the rubber gag
between her teeth and blinding her with the leather hood,
and Dr. Archer grasps the thick black handle of the switch
and pulls it down and sends the current ripping through her
nerves . . . she stands naked in shackles before the
blackmasked judges, and Dr. Archer gloatingly exposes
the giant needle ("Just an injection of my elixir, and she's
quite safe for two more weeks.") . . . and the nurses in
rubber aprons hold her writhing upon the altar, while Dr.
Archer adjusts the hangman's mask and thrusts the electrodes into her breast . . . ("Just a shot of my Prolixin,

and she's quite sane for two more weeks.") . . . then the judge in wig and mask and black robe smacks down the braided whip and screams, "She must be locked away forever!" . . . she tears away the mask and Dr. Archer screams, "She must be locked inside forever!" . . . she tears away the mask and Mrs. Castaigne screams, "She must be locked in here forever!" . . . she tears away the mask and her own face screams, "She must be locked in you forever!" . . . then Camilla and Mrs. Castaigne lead her back into her cell, and they strap her to her bed and force the rubber gag between her teeth, and Mrs. Castaigne adjusts her surgeon's mask while Camilla clamps the electrodes to her nipples, and the current rips into her and her brain screams and screams unheard . . . "I think she no longer needs to be drugged." Mrs. Castaigne smiles and her lips are bright with blood. "She's one of us now. She always has been one of us" . . . and they leave her alone in darkness on the promise, "We'll begin again tomorrow," and the echo, "She'll be good for two more weeks."

She moaned and writhed upon the soiled sheets, struggling to escape the images that spurted like foetid purulence from her tortured brain. With the next explosive burst of lightning, her naked body lifted in a convulsive arc from the mattress, and her scream against the gag was like the first agonized outcry of the newborn.

The spasm passed. She dropped back limply onto the sodden mattress. Slippery with sweat and blood, her relaxed hand slid the rest of the way out of the padded cuff. Quietly in the darkness, she considered her free hand—suddenly calm, for she knew she had slipped wrist restraints any number of times before this.

Beneath the press of the storm, the huge house lay in darkness and silence. With her free hand she unbuckled the other wrist cuff, then the straps that held the gag in place, and the restraints that pinned her ankles. Her tread no louder than a phantom's, she glided from bed and crossed the room. A flicker of lightning revealed shabby furnishings and a disordered array of fetishist garments and paraphernalia, but she threw open the window and looked down upon the black waters of the lake and saw the cloud waves breaking upon the base of the cliff, and when she turned away from that vision her eyes knew what they beheld and her smile was that of a lamia.

Wraith-like she drifted through the dark house, passing along the silent rooms and hallways and stairs, and when she reached the kitchen she found what she knew was the key to unlock the dark mystery that bound her here. She closed her hand upon it, and her fingers remembered its feel.

Camilla's face was tight with sudden fear as she awakened at the clasp of fingers closed upon her lips, but she made no struggle as she stared at the carving knife that almost touched her eyes.

"What happened to Constance?" The fingers relaxed to let her whisper, but the knife did not waver.

"She had a secret lover. One night she crept through the sitting room window and ran away with him. Mrs. Castaigne showed her no mercy."

"Sleep now," she told Camilla, and kissed her tenderly as she freed her with a swift motion that her hand remembered.

In the darkness of Mrs. Castaigne's room she paused beside the motionless figure on the bed.

"Mother?"

"Yes, Constance?"

"I've come home."

"You're dead."

"I remembered the way back."

And she showed her the key and opened the way.

It only remained for her to go. She could no longer find shelter in this house. She must leave as she had entered.

She left the knife. That key had served its purpose. Through the hallways she returned, in the darkness her bare feet sometimes treading upon rich carpets, sometimes dust and fallen plaster. Her naked flesh tingled with the blood that had freed her soul.

She reached the sitting room and looked upon the storm that lashed the night beyond. For one gleam of lightning the room seemed festooned with torn wallpaper; empty wine bottles littered the floor and dingy furnishings. The flickering mirage passed, and she saw that the room was exactly as she remembered. She must leave by the window.

There was a tapping at the window.

She started, then recoiled in horror as another repressed memory escaped into consciousness.

The figure that had pursued her through the darkness on that night she had sought refuge here. It waited for her now at the window. Half-glimpsed before, she saw it now fully revealed in the glare of the lightning.

Moisture glistened darkly upon its rippling and exaggerated musculature. Its uncouth head and shoulders hunched forward bullishly; its face was distorted with insensate lust and drooling madness. A grotesque phallus swung between its misshapen legs—serpentine, possessed of its own life and volition. Like an obscene worm, it stretched blindly toward her, blood oozing from its toothless maw.

She raised her hands to ward it off, and the monstrosity pawed at the window, mocking her every terrified movement as it waited there on the other side of the rain-slick glass.

The horror was beyond enduring. There was another casement window to the corner sitting room, the one that overlooked the waters of the river. She spun about and lunged toward it—noticing from the corner of her eye that the creature outside also whirled about, sensing her intent, flung itself toward the far window to forestall her.

The glass of the casement shattered, even as its blubbery hands stretched out toward her. There was no pain in that release, only a dream-like vertigo as she plunged into the grayness and the rain. Then the water and the darkness received her falling body, and she set out again into the night, letting the current carry her, she knew not where.

"A few personal effects remain to be officially disposed of, Dr. Archer—since there's no one to claim them. It's been long enough now since the bus accident, and we'd like to be able to close the files on this catastrophe."

"Let's have a look." The psychiatrist opened the box of personal belongings. There wasn't much; there never was in such cases, and had there been anything worth stealing, it was already unofficially disposed of.

"They still haven't found a body," the ward superintendent wondered, "do you suppose . . . ?"

"Callous as it sounds, I rather hope not," Dr. Archer confided. "This patient was a paranoid schizophrenic—and dangerous."

"Seemed quiet enough on the ward."

"Thanks to a lot of ECT—and to depot phenothiazines. Without regular therapy, the delusional system would quickly regain control, and the patient would become frankly murderous."

There were a few toiletry items and some articles of clothing, a brassiere and pantyhose. "I guess send this over to Social Services. These shouldn't be allowed on a locked ward," the psychiatrist pointed to the nylons, "nor these smut magazines."

"They always find some way to smuggle the stuff in," the ward superintendent sighed, "and I've been working here at Coastal State since back before the War. What about these other books?"

Dr. Archer considered the stack of dog-eared gothic romance novels. "Just return these to the Patients' Library. What's this one?"

Beneath the paperbacks lay a small hardcover volume, bound in yellow cloth, somewhat soiled from age.

"Out of the Patients' Library too, I suppose. People have donated all sorts of books over the years, and if the patients don't tear them up, they just stay on the shelves forever."

"*The King in Yellow*," Dr. Archer read from the spine, opening the book. On the flyleaf a name was penned in a graceful script: *Constance Castaigne*.

"Perhaps the name of a patient who left it here," the superintendent suggested. "Around the turn of the century this was a private sanatorium. Somehow, though, the name seems to ring a distant bell."

"Let's just be sure this isn't vintage porno."

"I can't be sure—maybe something the old-timers talked about when I first started here. I seem to remember there was some famous scandal involving one of the wealthy families in the city. A murderess, was it? And something about a suicide, or was it an escape? I can't recall . . ."

"Harmless nineteenth-century romantic nonsense," Dr. Archer concluded. "Send it on back to the library."

The psychiatrist glanced at a last few lines before closing the book:

Cassilda. I tell you, I am lost! Utterly lost!
Camilla (terrified herself). You have seen the King . . . ?
Cassilda. And he has taken from me the power to direct or to escape my dreams.

Charles E. Fritch currently edits Mike Shayne's Mystery Magazine *and is sneaky enough to slip an occasional horror story in among the whodunnits. The following work of black humor steals its title from* The Shadow *and its kidnapped princess from the fairy tales, but the treatment is deliciously original.*

WHO NOSE WHAT EVIL

by Charles E. Fritch

To hear another voice, any voice, at any time, in that small, drab, lonely, ordinarily voiceless room, would have been a surprise and a treat. But to hear a plaintive, totally unfamiliar female voice crying out in the small hours of the still-dark morning was nothing short of miraculous.

"Help!" the voice had cried, waking him from a restless slumber. "Help me, please!"

Billy sat upright in the narrow bed, instantly and fully awake, his wide-pupiled eyes eagerly probing the dimness. Sometime during the night his allergy medicine had worn off, and now he could hardly breathe. But never mind that—the female voice was enough to take his breath away. She was a beautiful creature, he could tell that, beautiful and helpless, and she was here with him in his bachelor bedroom pleading for help.

"Where are you?" he asked the empty room.

"I'm here," the female voice jubilated at his response. "I'm being held prisoner inside your nose."

An ordinary man might have laughed, scoffed at the absurdity of such a claim. But not Billy Horton. Billy had been through even more absurd experiences during his thirty-four years of living, loving, and hating. Yet a woman held prisoner inside his nose? On the face of it, an absurd notion—or so an ordinary man might consider it. Billy, however, was no ordinary man. He was special, he knew that. People in the outside world would call him crazy if he told them now about the voice and what the voice had told him. But of course he wasn't going to tell them about it.

Without considering the consequences of such an automatic action, Billy sniffed, trying to breathe.

"Oh!" the girl cried.

"I'm sorry," Billy said quickly, alarmed. "Did I hurt you?"

"No, I was just startled, that's all. It was like a sudden gust of wind, almost a gale."

Billy held his breath; he tried not to exhale or inhale or at least to do it so gently it could not be noticed.

It was an untenable situation. The delicate membranes webbing his tortured nostrils had once again swollen, clogging the air passages. Logic proclaimed there was no room in there for a woman. At least not the kind of woman Billy saw in the street where he loitered, and in the store where he worked, and in the magazines he collected, and in the delightful dreams he occasionally dreamed.

"You probably think you're dreaming," the girl said, as though sensing his thoughts.

"Not necessarily dreaming," Billy told her. "Maybe just imagining."

"Don't think that," the female voice pleaded. "You're awake, and I'm very real."

He had been accused many times of—well, of having an overactive imagination, which is why he seldom told anyone his thoughts any more. People never believed him, and of course they wouldn't now, even if the girl were as real as she claimed.

Still, he had no proof and, after all, a woman held prisoner in a person's nose *was* kind of unusual. He said, "Come on. I'm thirty-four years old. A grown man. Where are you—really!"

"I told you where I am," the female voice insisted. "I'm a Beautiful Princess from a Far Away Country. An Evil Wizard kidnapped me and is holding me prisoner in here."

Billy really did believe her. After all, he was hearing her voice, wasn't he—and what better judge of reality than his own senses?

Still, he placed an experimental finger along the outside of his nose and pressed gently.

"Get your hand away from there," a male voice gruffed.

Startled, Billy jerked his hand away. "Are you in there too?" he marveled.

"Of course I am. Where else would I be? I must guard my prisoner to make sure no one rescues her."

"And you're the Evil Wizard, I suppose, who's kidnapped the Beautiful Princess and is holding her prisoner inside my nose."

"I suppose you could put it that way, although it does make me out the villain. I must tell you my side of the story."

"Not necessarily," Billy contradicted. He'd already made up his mind. "I have enough trouble breathing with my allergy, so you'll have to get out of there, both of you. There *are* only two of you in there, I hope?"

"Only two," the Evil Wizard admitted. "You haven't got the biggest nose in the world, you know. I mean, it's not a condominium of a nose; more like a bachelor apartment nose."

"Well, I like his nose," the Beautiful Princess said. "It's cute."

"As I was saying," the Evil Wizard went on, "there's not much room in here, but it was the best I could do under the circumstances. I was in a hurry, what with the King after me with all his Knights and those barking dogs chasing us through the Enchanted Forest. I had to whip up a spell in a hurry and escape from our own land—and here's where I wound up, crawling around inside a stranger's nose."

"And you can crawl right back out and find somebody else's nose," Billy Horton said determinedly.

He wanted desperately now to see the Beautiful Princess and see if she really resembled the image he'd gotten of her. After that, she could live inside his nose or any other part of him forever and ever.

"Not possible," the Wizard said. "Your nose is very handy."

"I've always thought so," Billy agreed, trying to stifle a sniffle so as not to inconvenience his female guest.

Damn! Not only did he have trouble breathing, an itch was developing inside his left nostril. Automatically, he reached for the plastic container of nose spray on the nightstand.

"What are you doing?"

"I'm going to clear up my nose."

"Not with nose drops! That stuff could be deadly to us."

"Just a light spray."

The Wizard's groan was loud in his nose. "That's even worse. A lingering death!"

"Well, *I've* got to breathe," Billy insisted.

"And *I've* got to live," the Evil Wizard insisted right back at him.

"Not necessarily," Billy said, placing the plastic nozzle of the nose spray into his left nostril. "Nobody's *got* to live, especially wicked mothers and bad sisters and evil wizards."

The Beautiful Princess started crying, and Billy paused,

listening to her with a suddenly heavy heart, visualizing crystal tears cascading down alabaster cheeks, sensing her well-formed body shaking as she sobbed in despair.

Billy eased the sprayer from his nostril. "I'm sorry," he said softly. "I didn't mean to frighten you."

"That's all right," she said between racking sobs. "I understand, Billy. You've got your own life to live. Never mind about me. I have nothing to go back to in my father's kingdom anyway."

"But you're a Beautiful Princess," Billy protested wonderingly. "Dozens of boyfriends must be after you."

"Fa!" she said. "They're ugly creatures, in spirit if not in body and, what's worse, they're bores. I don't want any of them. I want someone like you to love, Billy. Have you ever been in love?"

After a moment's thought, Billy said, "I think so. I loved my mother before she was killed, and my sister before she died."

"And now you're all alone in the world?"

Billy nodded. "All alone. Just me."

"With nobody to look after you and take care of you?"

"Nobody," Billy said.

"Poor Billy," the Beautiful Princess purred. "I wish I could take care of you. But of course there's no way. No way at all."

"Not necessarily no way," Billy told her. "Maybe I can rescue you."

"Oh, do you think you can. I'd be ever so grateful."

"I can try. Is the Wizard still there?"

"He's asleep. Our conversation bored him. Evil Wizards don't take much interest in love and romance."

Billy's heart gazelled. *Love and romance.* She'd said it herself. *Love and romance.* Billy had never had a girl of his own. He'd always wanted one, but he could never seem to communicate with girls. When he tried, they screamed and their fathers threatened to call the police.

The Princess seemed to be through with her crying. "Tell me about yourself, Billy," she said.

Billy told her about his childhood on the farm, where the accident had killed his father. Then the move to the city, where his mother was killed. And then his sister, whom he loved very much, had died on him.

"How sad," the Beautiful Princess said. "Everything you love seems to die, Billy."

"Not necessarily everything," Billy said, adding impulsively, "I have *you* now."

He blushed self-consciously as he said that, but her answering laughter made him feel at ease. Hers wasn't the mocking laughter he'd known from some people. It was the laughter of happiness, of discovery, of hope and love. Perhaps, he thought wildly, he could keep the Princess in his nose forever, and talk to her when he was lonely, which was quite often. She was temporarily in his nose, but she would be in his heart forever.

He liked the sound of that phrase, so he repeated it to himself, silently: "She'll be in my heart forever."

"You know something wonderful, Billy," she said in a voice bursting with mist and flowers and moonlight and rainbows and sunshine rippling a wood-fringed lake, "I'm falling in love with you."

Billy could hardly believe his ears. "In love? With me?"

"You're the man I've always wanted," she said. "If you want me, Billy, I'm yours."

The words caught in Billy's throat. "If I want you—"

"What's going on here? What's happening?" the Evil Wizard sputtered, waking up. "Are you two planning something?"

"We were just talking," the Princess told him.

"You were not just talking. You were planning to escape. Well, there is no escape, believe me. We're secure here."

"Not necessarily secure," Billy muttered.

"Huh? What's that? Well, never mind. That nap did me a lot of good," the Wizard said, chuckling.

There was the rustle of clothing.

"What are you doing?" the Princess said in alarm.

"What good is holding a Beautiful Princess prisoner if you don't do terrible things to her while she's helpless," the Evil Wizard said.

"What sort of things?" the Princess said, her voice suddenly faint and indicating she was not at all sure she really wanted to know.

"Well, first—"

Billy Horton listened in increasing horror as the Evil Wizard spelled out in no uncertain terms, using vile language Billy had often heard but seldom used himself, exactly what he had in store for the Beautiful Princess who was utterly helpless and unable to do anything to prevent him from doing whatever he wanted to do with her.

Billy was in love. It had been love at first—well, not sight exactly, since he hadn't directly seen the object of his affection and desire. But he could see her in his mind's eye, and she was every bit as beautiful as he'd imagined her.

"No, don't touch me," her terrified voice cried.

She screamed.

The scream tore at Billy's heart. His fists hammered at the sides of his nose. "Leave her alone, damn you!" he shouted. "Leave her alone!"

"Mind your own business," the Evil Wizard snarled. "I'll do what I want, and there's nobody or anything that can stop me."

"Not necessarily nobody or anything," Billy said determinedly.

Leaping from the bed, he rushed into the kitchen, where he yanked open a cabinet drawer and pulled out a long, gleaming-sharp butcher knife.

The Wizard was laughing triumphantly and the Princess

was screaming hopelessly as Billy desperately, savagely sliced the edge of the blade into the top of his nose and rammed it down, severing that bump of flesh completely, though not neatly, from his face.

He hadn't stopped to consider how dangerous this action might be to the Princess he loved, or to his nose, or to his life. He only knew that he wanted to, had to, save her from the monstrous madman who held her captive.

Though growing faint with weakness, he searched the blood and bits of flesh decorating his kitchen floor. She had disappeared, and so had the Evil Wizard, who perhaps had whisked them back to the Magic Kingdom from which they'd come.

At least, he thought with some pride and satisfaction, she would be home, where her father the King and all his Knights might rescue her from the Evil Wizard.

"I can die happy, knowing she loved me," Billy muttered.

Well, of course, Billy didn't die. And of course he didn't tell the authorities about the girl or that he'd been the one attacking his nose. He blamed it on a mythical burglar whom he'd surprised in the middle of the night, who'd seized the knife from a drawer and slashed out wildly at him.

While he was in the hospital, psychiatrists came to question him, but Billy was wise to their tricks. He'd been questioned by psychiatrists before, and he knew what answers they wanted to hear so they could send him to the mental institution like before. He wasn't permitting that. He stuck to his story, because he wanted to be free. It was a dim hope, but he thought he might see the Beautiful Princess again. He was sure she loved him as much as he loved her and would find some magical way to return to him.

A month later he lay in his bachelor bed at night, dozing, dreaming of the Beautiful Princess, when a voice said, "Hello, Billy."

He sat up in bed, fully awake. "Princess?"

"It's me, Billy, your Beautiful Princess," the voice laughed.

It was her, it really was. She was back.

He was almost afraid to ask. "Are you alone?"

"Of course I'm alone," the Evil Wizard's voice came.

Billy was silent for a long moment. "I don't understand," he said finally.

The Beautiful Princess's laugh trilled with delight. "Of course you don't understand, Billy. That's because you're dumb. And you're crazy, too, Billy, did you know that? You're crazy, crazy, crazy!"

Billy shook his head and covered his ears with his hands, but the voice was inside him. That was what his mother had said to him, and his sister, before he had made them stop saying things to hurt him.

He started to cry.

"I am the Beautiful Princess, Billy," the Evil Wizard said.

"And I am the Evil Wizard," the Beautiful Princess said.

"One and the same." Billy's voice was bitter. "You lied to me."

"The truth then, at last, Billy," the voice of the Beautiful Princess said. "I'm a sexless witch-wizard from a place far, far away, and I wanted to see how crazy I could make you, Billy—crazy enough to mutilate your own face."

"Then you never loved me?" Billy said sadly.

"Loved you?" the Evil Wizard shrieked. "Who could love a thing like you? You want to see how beautiful your Princess is, Billy. Open up your mind. Take a look."

Concentrating, Billy opened his mind and looked. The Beautiful Princess was not human. She was a blob of something that writhed obscenely, making his stomach churn at the sight of her. He closed his eyes tightly and tried to keep from vomiting.

*   *   *

"Where you've always wanted me to be," she taunted, shrilling mocking laughter. "I'm here, forever, in your heart!"

With her laughter ringing in his mind, Billy Horton stumbled from the bedroom into the kitchen.

"Not necessarily forever," he said, smiling, reaching for the knife again.

COMB MY HAIR, PLEASE COMB MY HAIR

by Jean Darling

Margaret Becker stood on the steps waiting for her daughter to come home from school. Jeanie was only a few minutes later than usual but, ever since the accident, Margaret lived in fear that this child too would be taken from her. After Jeanie left to catch the school bus at eight, Margaret cleaned house. Not that there was much to do any more, they used only the front part of the cottage now, but she needed to be busy, keep her mind occupied, feel useful to somebody. So, with the radio on full blast, each chore was done slowly, methodically. Routine was all she had to cling to, routine and Jeanie.

The only oasis in the long lonely week was Saturday and Sunday when the two of them went into the City Centre for a meal and to see a movie. They didn't own a television set, Jeff wouldn't have one of the "time wasters," as he called them, in the house. Somehow, respecting his

192

wishes in even this small matter made him seem less dead. Margaret wondered what her husband would think if he could see her now, thin, angular; face lined with worry, blonde hair greying. She glanced at her watch, where could the child be? From the moment Jeanie left in the morning until she came bounding up the hill at a quarter to five, anxiety was held tightly in check. Peace and security returned with Jeanie, the lovely replica of herself before tragedy had struck. As time ticked on towards five-thirty, horrid thoughts flashed in her mind like a tourist's color slides: CLICK—Jeanie run down by a car. CLICK—Jeanie at poolside being given artificial respiration. CLICK—the school bus smashed, Jeanie sprawled bleeding on the cement. "Oh God!" Margaret said, out loud. "Not again!" It couldn't happen again. Once more in her imagination she heard the screech of brakes, felt the impact of anguished metal. Then came the silence, ear-numbing, mind-blowing silence; the warm wetness soft against her flesh. Warm wetness that had been a melding of husband and son trickling life away into a garnet pool.

Suddenly, the woman was wrapped in a bear hug, a schoolbag bumping painfully against her back. "You never even saw me wave or heard me whistle!" Jeanie said, laughing. "You were day-dreaming, Mommy."

"Jeanie, I was worried half out of my—" a haphazard kiss that landed between ear and chin hushed the admonishments clustered at Margaret's lips, why scold, the child was home safe.

"Sorry I'm late, Mommy." Jeanie whirled away, her pleated uniform skirt billowing. "But it was the good deed. Good deeds always seem to take so long. I'm starving."

"Well, as soon as you're changed we'll eat." The girl swooped into the house. Margaret followed her inside wondering where the child got all the energy. She didn't remember being that full of life when she had been twelve years old. "Don't forget to wash your hands," she called.

"Mommy, my best friend Mary's having pu—"

"Don't shout from one room to another, dear." A moment later Jeanie burst into the kitchen metamorphosed from demure school girl into denimed tomboy.

"She's having puppies!" she said.

"Who? Mary?" Margaret asked, ladling soup into bowls.

"No, silly. Her collie and she said I could have one. Can I, Mommy, please?"

"Well—we'll see." Perhaps a dog would be company when Jeanie was in school. "Tell me about your good deed."

"Oh, well, you see I got bored coming home from the bus stop the same old way every day. It rhymes!" She laughed. "Let me see, home every day, the same old way. That's better. See, Mommy, maybe I'll grow up to be a poet, wouldn't you be proud?"

"Right now I'll be proud if you sit down and eat your soup while it's hot."

For a while they ate in silence, the woman gaining nourishment more from watching her daughter than from food. "Aren't you going to tell me what happened?" She needed the sound of Jeanie's voice to make her feel alive.

"Okay. Well, I got bored. You know how dull it is, not even a house or a dog or anything and I noticed this little path going off between two bushes, you have to squat down and wiggle your way through. You know where I mean. Right next to the yellow flowers near the bus stop."

"I can't place it. Eat your liver and onions before it gets cold. Goodness, I don't know why I cook it in the first place."

"You do know where it is, Mommy. Those yellow

flowers next to the geraniums.'' The child was impatient, her mouth drawn down into a pout.

''Yes, I remember now,'' Margaret said.

''Well, anyway—there's this tiny little path after you squeeze through the bushes and it leads up the hill getting steeper and steeper but it didn't bother me.'' Jeanie bragged, ''You know me, second cousin to a mountain goat.''

''Mountain goats don't wear shoes.'' Jeanie stuck her feet to one side. Guilt shadowed her face on seeing the scuffed dullness.

''Never mind,'' Margaret said hastily to restore joy. ''A dab of polish and a little elbow grease, they'll be as good as new.''

''I'll do them later, Mommy. Okay?'' Margaret nodded and the girl continued only slightly subdued. ''At the top of the path I found a narrow dirt road. It was all deserted like nobody had used it for years and years and it winds like a corkscrew, but you know what a wonderful sense of direction Daddy says I—'' her voice trailed off. She looked away from the sadness in her mother's eyes. Silence lay palpably between them until the urge to comfort Margaret unblocked the dam. Jeanie went on, ''So, I just decided which way was home, turned off the old road and cut through the trees. It was awful scary.'' She giggled nervously at the delicious tingle evoked by the word ''scary.'' She repeated it, ''Scary, so scary.''

''You want some ice cream?''

''Um-hum. You should see it, Mommy, the trees meet overhead, it's like being in a long green tunnel and that was when I heard the little voice.'' Jeanie paused for effect. ''At first I thought it was just my imagination but it wasn't, and as I went on it grew louder. Oh, I forgot to tell you, I went back and followed the road. Oh, Mommy, you haven't heard a word I said.'' The child sulked, the spoon snipping bits off the ice cream to be tucked between pouting lips.

'' 'I went back and followed the road.' See, I was

listening," Margaret said, not entirely truthfully. She had been listening to the sound of the high sweet voice, not paying too much attention to the words it said. "Go on, dear, what happened then?"

"At first I thought the voice belonged to some baby animal, then as it grew louder I decided it must be a little lost child. Oh, Mommy, it sounded so hopeless, so forlorn."

"You found it then? Everything is all right?"

"You're spoiling the whole thing." Why couldn't her mother let her tell it her way? "Yes, you're right, I found her and everything is all right." Without another word, Jeanie went into the large front room that served as both living and sleeping quarters. "I'm finished," she said, closing the door behind her. "I'll make a fire," came muffled through the wood panel.

Puzzled at the unusual sulkiness, Margaret washed up so everything would be ready for morning. She thought of making popcorn as a peace offering or fudge, but first there was a pile of socks to mend. "Thank goodness the dishes are done. I swear someday I'll just get paper plates and that will be that," she said on entering the room.

"We could use them to light the fire." Jeanie grinned and Margaret knew she had been forgiven.

"You were telling me about the little voice." Her hands found the sewing basket.

"Umm, so I kept going until I came to this clearing and right in the middle was a little house all dripping red ivy and green shutters and ringed with a white picket fence—"

"It sounds like something out of a fairy tale." Margaret looked up from her mending.

"Well, it wasn't a fairy tale, it was for real and, guess what, the voice didn't belong to a child at all."

"It didn't?" Margaret asked, wondering how long the dreary story could go on.

"Nope. There on the porch in a funny curly chair,

bentwood, I think it's called—well, there on the porch sat an old, old lady, a hundred if she was a day—''

"That must have been a disappointment, you disliking old people the way you do."

"Umm, you're right, I don't like old people much, but she's different. She's so cute with a little wrinkled-up face and big gentle eyes. Guess what the poor little thing wanted."

"I can't imagine."

"Her hair combed! That was what she had been saying all along: 'Comb my hair, please comb my hair.' '' Jeanie moved around the room as she spoke. "Anyway, she wanted someone to comb her hair." She sprawled full length in front of the fire, suddenly angry. Margaret regarded the yellow head, a frown between her brows at the child's bad temper.

"Sorry, Mommy." Jeanie rolled over onto her back. "I don't know what's got into me tonight." She sat up resting her head against her mother's knee. "Am I forgiven?"

"Silly, there's nothing to forgive." Margaret stroked the shining blonde curls.

"You wouldn't believe the hair the old lady wanted combed. It was about six feet long and lay on the floor fine as cobwebs and so thin her scalp showed as plain as if she were bald. And you should see the comb she held in her little claws, all tortoise shell and silver."

"If she's so old," Margaret leaned forward, "as old as you say, how can she care for herself, eating, bathing, and—you know?"

"Oh, she can get around just fine, especially after I'd combed her hair. You wouldn't believe how much better she felt, even her hair looked stronger, not so thin. She even went in the house to get me a biscuit. Oh yes, I almost forgot." Jeanie jumped up, ran over to her school-bag and dumped it out on the floor. "Here, she gave me one for you. Eat it, it's very good." Obediently, Margaret unwrapped the tissue and took a small bite in much the same way as when the baby Jeanie had offered a hand-melted, grubby chocolate.

"Umm, you're right, it's delicious." Margaret looked down at the biscuit. "It's full of holes." Small black bugs moved on the surface. Suddenly Margaret flung it in the fire. "Ugh! Was yours full of bugs like that?"

"Oh, for goodness sakes, they're only weevils!" Disgust turned down the pink mouth.

"Did you know the biscuit was full of bugs when you ate it?"

"Of course I did, it would have hurt her feelings if I'd behaved like you just did." How could her mother be so unreasonable?

"One of them bit me." Margaret looked down at her hand, wondering if weevils did bite.

"Weevils don't bite," the child stated, looking at the spots on Margaret's hand. "You pricked yourself with the needle."

"But you have bites too." She grabbed the child's hand. The thumb on her right hand bore two small red lumps exactly like the two she had on her palm. Jeanie wrenched away.

"Thorns." She said, "I'm sorry you hurt yourself on the needle, Mother. You did prick your hand with the needle, didn't you, Mother?—Mother?—Say it." The eyes locked. "Say it!"

"Yes, dear, I pricked my hand with the needle," Margaret said.

"I'm glad you admit it. Anyway, I promised to comb her hair every day after school." Margaret's hand rose as though to ward off a blow, then fell back to her lap where, automatically, it found the darning ball. She began to mend. A warning not to anger Jeanie flashed in her mind.

"But your exams are coming up, dear, you won't have much time." That's the right note, appeal to her reasonable side, Margaret thought.

"I'll find time. I promised." The eyes were cold above a squared jaw.

"You're right, you can't break a promise but promise *me* something, don't eat stuff like that. What if you got sick? Oh, Jeanie, I don't know what I'd do if anything happened to you." All at once the child's face crumpled. Tears spilled down her cheeks. This was the little girl Margaret knew, not the other hard-faced creature.

"Please, Mommy, I promised," the child said.

"Darling, I know you promised the little old woman, but if she's really as old as you say, she'll have forgotten all about it by now. The person who takes care of her has come home from shopping or whatever and she's not lonely any more." A burning sensation drew attention to her hand. "I never knew a needle prick could burn so," she said, rubbing her palm. "Anyway, Jeanie, it doesn't make sense for you to see the woman again and—" Margaret glanced down at the offending hand. The lumps were swelling as she watched. Swelling, darkening, spinning round, fire ringed, flames long and longer; eyes now in the dark centers, two luminous eyes, tiny pinpricks far away, growing, growing until they bored deep into hers.

Resolution faltered, perhaps the old lady did need Jeanie to visit her, perhaps she was being unkind not to let her go to the cottage. After all, what harm could it do, a few minutes a day. "After all, what harm could it do, dear, a few minutes a day," Margaret said. "Yes, dear, it wouldn't do to disappoint the old lady since you've promised." Margaret's voice seemed to come from a great distance through her unmoving lips.

The following day when Jeanie came home from school she was subdued, uncommunicative. Her mother's inquiries as to whether she had visited the old lady were met with evasion. "Everything's fine, Mommy, it's just I have lots of homework." The rest of the evening was spent hidden in school books until the girl dragged herself off to bed. In the morning she awoke unrefreshed, her eyes were purple smudged, she was noticeably thinner, her hair was lank and dull, almost colorless. The child looked so ill that Margaret suggested she spend the day in bed.

"Are you daft or something? It's the school picnic. I can't miss the Annual Picnic," Jeanie said in her new insolent manner, her feverish eyes draining all strength of will from her mother.

As in a dream Margaret sent the child off with a bulging picnic basket bumping awkwardly against fleshless legs. She stood, unable to move, feet riveted to the spot, watching as the child stumbled and fell. She tried to call, lips forming words without sound. How ill the girl looked, how slowly she picked herself up. Basket in hand, Jeanie drifted down the hill out of sight.

Released now, Margaret ran to the place where half the contents of the basket lay. "She didn't even notice," she said out loud while gathering foil-wrapped sandwiches, two bananas, and an apple. "She didn't even notice anything had fallen out." She carried the food into the kitchen. "Well, one thing's for sure, my girl, you're going to see Dr. Benson whether you like it or not." Suiting action to thought, Margaret Becker dialed his office and made an appointment for five o'clock that afternoon. "And that will take care of you," she said after hanging up the phone. "I'll pick you up at school and there'll be no back chat this time."

Nothing seemed to go right that morning, the handle came off a cup that was getting washed, the filler went dry in the ball-point before a letter was half-written; the book she was reading had hidden itself somewhere. As a last resort she decided to turn up a hem in an old brown skirt but found her hand had begun to burn again. She rubbed it on the stuff of the chair in which she was sitting. And then she heard Jeanie whistle, a high sweet sound repeating the same two notes. "Yes, dear, I'm coming," Margaret said, pushing a hairpin into place. The whistle sounded again, louder this time. "I'm coming," she called, hurrying out the front door.

Standing on the steps, hand shading her eyes from the brilliant sun, she peered down the hill. "Jeanie, where are you?" she queried the breeze-rippled sea of knee-high grass. "Please, baby, don't play games," Margaret called in a loud clear voice. "Jeanie, where are you?" she cried and then saw Jeanie a hundred yards away. The child was running towards her laughing. She looked so unlike the girl who barely had been able to carry her own weight just a few hours before. Suddenly the child wheeled around, ephemeral, shimmering as she danced ahead of the woman now hurtling headlong down the hill in pursuit of the illusory child.

"Jeanie, wait!" Margaret cried, feet scattering the gravel on the drive that slashed across the hill. "Please, Jeanie, wait!" she called again, pace never slackening until the avenue below was reached.

"Did you see where the child went?" Margaret asked the group at the bus stop. The women stared back at her flat-eyed. Drunk, they thought as one, turning away from the wild creature with hairpin-thorned-bun adrift. "Please, did you see where a blonde girl went—long blonde hair?" Margaret inquired of the clamped-shut faces, then she caught a flash of yellow and crouched at their very feet to follow it between two low bushes.

Once on the other side, Margaret clawed and scrambled up the embankment, breaking nails and bruising sandaled feet, until she found herself gasping for breath on the road above. "Jeanie—Jeanie, where are you?" she called to the tree-lined empty road. As her breathing eased, an impossible weight of silence spun itself around the woman drawing her to the left away from sun-dappled ground into the shade. Trees towered linking arms overhead to drive back the sweet fresh air. Ferns sprang up, moss carpeted the road. Chill pricked her skin with damp, piercing the flesh to wrap icy fingers around her heart.

"Oh, God, help me!" she cried into the sudden gust that whipped the skirt about her legs. But it was a silent wind that carried the song of a distant singer, a delicate, fragile sound coming from the direction in which Margaret found herself drifting. The tune was unfamiliar, a haunting melody from out of the past evoking powdered wigs bowing and satin gowns rustling in measured movement. Onward, onward Margaret floated until, at last, she came to the clearing where, suddenly, movement ceased.

Before her was the cottage, small, white, and red ivy draped just as Jeanie had said. It was ringed by a picket fence and on the porch the singer rocked contentedly. But this woman wasn't more than ten years Margaret's senior. Surely, she couldn't be Jeanie's old lady. A friend, perhaps, or the old woman's daughter. An aged creature such as Jeanie had described would have someone to care for her. Or perhaps Jeanie had simply overestimated age as children do. But this woman's hair was pale, not white, a silvery mass that cascaded to the floor. It was then that Margaret noticed the quaint cut of the woman's dress, tight-bodiced with a fichu of delicate lace above a voluminous skirt. An exquisite comb fashioned of tortoise shell and silver rested in the velvet folds. The sight of the comb gleaming in a truant sunbeam sent panic crawling up Margaret's spine. Somehow it was the comb that epitomized evil, not the smooth-faced woman who held it on her lap.

Love, overcoming terror, unloosed Margaret's tongue, "Jeanie!" she called, stepping forward firmly, "Jeanie, I know you're there." At the sound of her voice the woman's eyes flew open to fix upon Margaret a glittering brown gaze of indescribable malevolence. Clinging fast to her slender strength Jeanie's mother forceably averted her eyes and, moving nearer, she called, "Jeanie, come here this instant!"

Slowly the door opened to reveal a stoop-shouldered,

white-haired creature who shuffled out onto the porch. "Yes, Mommy?" it said.

"Come here, darling! Now!" Command was firm in her voice despite the shock of Jeanie's voice, hoarse, faint, yet still Jeanie's, that spoke from thin juiceless lips. Oh, God, Margaret prayed, let me get her away while there's still hope. Don't ask, command, she told herself. "Jeanie, come here!" she repeated to the thing that must be Jeanie.

Jeanie stood in an agony of indecision, head turning from one woman to the other, a snake weaving to a piper's silent tune. Once more the mother called. In response the ancient child looked towards her.

"Yes, Mommy, I'll just get the picnic—"

"Leave it! Come here, *now*!" Margaret's voice betrayed her, shrillness destroyed the calm note of command. Up until then the woman on the porch had remained immobile except for her eyes, which swept from Margaret to the child and back again. At last she spoke.

"Comb my hair, please comb my hair," she said.

Turning away from her mother, Jeanie took the comb, huge now in her skeletal fingers. Stroke, stroke, the comb moved through the luxuriant hair. Stroke, stroke, the silvery sheen glowed golden, deep and deeper. Stroke, stroke, the wizened child faltered.

"Comb my hair, please comb my hair," the woman said. An anguished cry escaped Margaret's lips as she stepped forward, determined to physically take her daughter away, only to be flung back by the impact of the woman's eyes. The bites on her hand burned, pulsing heat through her body, draining it of will or purpose. Helpless, Margaret watched as the woman bloomed under the clumsy ministrations of Jeanie. Stroke, stroke, the hair color grew deeper, the woman's cheek more rosy. Stroke, stroke, she was younger, more vibrant. Stroke, stroke, Jeanie held the comb in both hands, now making shorter and shorter strokes through the shimmering cascade of hair.

All this Margaret watched, unable to move, fixed as

though nailed to the spot. Gradually she relaxed, struggling no longer to reach Jeanie. And as she relaxed, the pain in her hand eased. She found herself admiring the beauty of the woman on the porch. She now realized that the expression in the woman's eyes had not been evil, just surprise. Margaret flushed with shame at the error, wishing with all her heart that she could do something to make amends for her stupidity, apologize to the lovely creature with the full pink lips. But she found herself tongue-tied like a love-sick adolescent, shy, unsure.

Margaret marvelled at the woman's patience in tolerating the inept manner in which Jeanie was combing her hair, never complaining when the comb caught a few strands in its teeth. The girl was too slow-witted to appreciate being allowed to comb such lovely hair. Margaret's hands ached to feel the silk of it sliding through them, ached to plunge themselves into the red-gold mass which tumbled over the fichued shoulders down to the floor. Margaret's eyes narrowed. She was torn between jealousy of the girl and a passionate desire to be close to the voluptuous woman, smiling now, sweetly smiling an invitation.

Slower, slower, the comb rose and fell, shorter, shorter, became its arc. At last, Jeanie swayed, one hand fluttered away from the comb to her breast. Momentarily she seemed to hang in the air before crumpling to the floor. In an agony of yearning her mother awaited the summons to take the place of the thing that lay so still beside the chair, defiling the sea of glorious hair with its loathsome touch.

With wonderful eyes shining welcome, the woman leaned toward Margaret. "Comb my hair, please comb my hair," she said. Released at last, Jeanie's mother rushed forward, eagerness overcoming repugnance at having to touch the horrid creature which still clutched the comb with death's grasp.

Once in possession of the wondrous silver-backed bit of tortoise shell, Margaret shoved the limp body of the ancient defunct child to one side with her foot and began to comb the wealth of red-gold hair. Stroke, stroke, her arm rose and fell. Stroke, stroke, her life drained into the radiant woman who sang an unfamiliar, haunting melody from out of the past evoking powdered wigs bowing and satin gowns rustling in measured movement.

I believe Steve Sneyd's "A Fly One" was his first major sale in the field, but his work had previously appeared extensively in many of the genre's most prestigious amateur journals. This Englishman currently is a copy writer for the Manchester Evening News *and lives in Huddersfield, West Yorkshire. I did not publish the story for some time after its purchase, but Steve forgave me once it saw publication and Karl Edward Wagner selected it for* Year's Best Horror Series VIII.

A FLY ONE

by Steve Sneyd

Strange and rather horrible how Nature sometimes supplies just the right cliché to suit a situation, as if to say, "You little Men are so blind you need everything made simple." Like here. Her hair was not scarlet nor brown nor russet. It was a dull, lifeless red-brown. The colour of dried blood. Considering the terrible injuries that had brought about her death, she looked surprisingly intact on the slab. The face was not touched of course: that had a lot to do with it. The expression, under the unmarked smoothness like good soap, had a curious quality. There was a knowing slyness, as if long-held preconceptions were confirmed by the horror that had come on her. It was as if she was saying at the instant of her death, to parents, teachers, all elders, "You tried to tell me all along the world was sweet and good. But I knew: I knew what it was really like, and see, I'm right. I told you so." This odd knowingness, masking any terror there had been, somehow made the death more awful—as if, I thought, me a tough copper with years to crust over like old cave stone, I should somehow have changed the world to golden fragrance just to prove her horrible cynicism wrong. She had been fourteen a month ago: her parents said so. I hated them, for some reason, even more than the murderer, whoever he was—and finding that out was our job, of course: as if it would do her any good, or change her opinion of us all, an opinion unchanged, I knew, by the sheet the mortuary attendant had now thrown over her, all necessary inspection complete, and would doubtless survive even the closing of the coffin lid on what the autopsy left, and maybe, rot withstanding, I thought, shivering against all logic, would face Christ and all angels at the last judgement with the same prematurely wise contempt for the hypocrisy of all grownups.

Her father and mother, beneath a mask of cunningly choking tears, glittered, despite their obvious ingrained drabness, with the excited exultation of those to whom the role of witness, object of attention, focus of questions tempered with sympathy, had at last come. Years of watching the box tell them of real life, real stars, and now, by reaching out a strangling, devastating hand to one who had often sat next to them, the world had gifted them, as Premium Bonds or Pools transform the ordinary, with the survivors' sense of superiority over one till today sat next to them, who now is dead, and at one and the same time the joy of being the object of all the care the victim would have got had she lived, which foiled of her to spill on, must still go somewhere.

They made me sick.

Still, emotions were not my job. Finding out who had killed Elizabeth Joy Manvers, after considerable sexual interference, was. I had better get on with it.

The murder had puzzling features.

The body found by two tadpole-seeking schoolboys,

truants as one would expect in a working class area like
this, lay in the centre of a large area of waste growth. Rain
the night before had turned its low furze and ratty grass to
a sea of mud. Yet no footprints, aside from those of the
finders, not even the girl's own, could be found within a
hundred yards.

Still, as son of a mother who tended to pay the coalman
in kind behind the coalhouse door, the milkman likewise
behind the kitchen door, and the insurance man, in defer-
ence to his superior social standing, in the spare bedroom,
I am perhaps temperamentally less inclined to trust the
sanctity of family life than the average member of the
Great British Public.

So I decided to start by ignoring Forensic's boring air of
defeatism (no flesh or hair under the fingernails, and the
like)—and suspect in ever-widening rings as stones in a
stagnant pool: family first, then neighbours, schoolmates,
and so throughout the neighbourhood.

Shifty and ratlike as her father was, aside from the times
he tended to remember his role as Grieving Father and
grew walrusly pompous, tearful, and peevish at once, he
unfortunately had an alibi: having won the Full House at
the local Trades and Labour Club, and stayed to spend his
winnings, forcing his free drinks on unwilling cronies,
way past the period fixed for the girl's death. A loud-
speaker announcement interrupting Mabel on the Organ
had roused dozens of witnesses at the club, and noisy as
they now were in the waiting room, their stories tallied.

The girl's brother was another kettle of fish.

Tall, stupid, dressed in neo-Edwardian gear, blessed of
several trivial convictions and one Borstal do for thieving,
to say nothing of LOVE and HATE amateurishly tattooed
by a poor artist across his knuckles, and I LOVE MUM
and THE BOOT BOYS RULE in various frames of hearts,
flowers, and fists on his upper arm; he seemed promising.
Especially as he would not or could not say where he'd
been, taking refuge in "I was puddled. Anyway she was

only a kid . . . she did naught but laugh at me, why should I even notice her, the brat.''

I showed him the new smooth polish on the station steps, with an old and well-tempered sergeant's aid. Then rubbing his ribs as if they would go away, he talked. But all that came out was a dull confession of being involved in some childish affair of bashing an old man over the head with a bottle the same night, about the same time. I could hold him, and would, but knew with weary distaste that it was the truth. He lacked the imagination to make up such a story.

Sounds of a disturbance at the desk distracted the thoughts I was trying to clarify with the aid of too many cigarettes and a sheaf of illegible notes that tiredness converted to hieroglyphics before my very eyes, even though they were my own scrawl. It had been a long day, from news of the body's finding, to identification (*why* hadn't they reported her missing before she had been gone a night and a morning both?), to the beginning of the search, to now, when all Blackpool Sands seemed to be lying stranded in my eyes.

I rubbed them.

The row of shouting and brawling continued.

Just another drunk, probably some tedious incident any uniformed constable could make a perfect balls of with ease.

Normally, I would have ignored it. But, though it was hard to admit, with so terrible a case to face and deal with, I was bored. Yes, bored. Me, Vrczynski, that rare beast, a foreign-born high up in the Elmet Police Force, and high up because of my dedication to duty, never flagging, as they say. I was bored. The case seemed somehow point-less. No dreary words from some fried-up wigheaded judge, half-dead, half-senile, could bring the girl back to life, or cure the waste of her soft body.

Yet conscience would not let me go home. So I compromised. I kept a dog and barked myself, this time—what I always swore not to do. I went out to see what went on.

Chaos at the desk.

A tangle of uniformed constables, towering above them the desk sergeant, clasping and shaking a figure impossible to make out in the heaving, a vignette of shouts, gasps, groans, curses. What one of my University-and-Hendon-Police-College-trained-upstart-cleverdick-London colleagues would have doubtless compared to the statue of Laocoon and his children fighting the seamonster.

"Everybody freeze," I shouted.

There must be something peculiarly nasty about my voice, it worked the oracle. The constables leapt back and tried to look as if they were merely onlookers. The sergeant sheepishly deposited the struggling figure he held back on the floor, and even brushed him down a bit. The figure itself ceased writhing, kicking, and ineffectively gouging, and shrank into silence.

"What's this all about, sergeant?"

"He came in here, sir, and started a disturbance." The faintest trace of resentment in his voice at my interference.

"What about?"

"Something about how we must clear a way for him, he was anointed or something similar, sir. He was obviously drunk and disorderly and became violent when we tried to restrain him."

"What do you think about it, sergeant?"

"I don't know, sir." In my army days we called that tone of voice insolence, and that look that followed dumb insolence.

The man was little, wartish, wart-nosed even. He was weathered, dirty, smelly at even this distance. Hair greasy black with cheap dye, raincoat stained in contrasting layers that fought and overlapped. String tied-up trouser-bottoms. It took me a minute or two of staring at the snivelling figure now rubbing various afflicted portions, to realise

what should have been obvious at first, so salient was it
now that I noticed it.

A hunchback.

And the hump not just lumpy, but huge, camel-like.

The eyes were red as if crying or frenzy.

And suddenly I *knew* I had to interrogate him.

Doubtless your long-haired lefties'd say I found some
friendless and obviously subsocial to pin the Manvers job
on. I prefer to think that a sort of cross-logical instinct,
intuition, akin to perhaps what poets claim they feel,
allowing them to make sudden leaps that join apparently
disconnected information, had occurred. (One poet I knew,
I remembered irrelevantly, would have been, I'm sure, a
better detective by far than I had he not been so busy
abusing everybody on grounds his Art, the capital his own,
entitled him to do just what he liked and they kept trying
to stop him. I almost felt regret getting him sent down for
five for living on immoral earnings.) This character, this
horrid little Quasimodo, triggered off similar firerocket
processes in my mind: Guy Fawkes Day all over again.

"All right, I'll take care of this. Put him in Cell 15. I'll
see him when I've had a cup of tea. Oh, and get his tie,
belt, and laces."

"No tie, sir, and no laces," the sergeant's resentment
clearly redoubling as I continued interfering.

And then I knew what had hit me about this bubble-
back. No laces because no shoes. On his feet, shapeless
masses of what looked like pullovers in plastic bags.

No footprints this bird'd leave, no more than if he flew
in vulture-style from a great height. I was sure now. Now
to get the facts, or the confession, that proved it.

The canteen tea was vile, somehow dieselish. I scarcely
tasted it, mind busy with framing, then rejecting approaches
to the questioning.

In the cell, I sent the guardian constable, young and
obviously affected by the man's smell, out for cigarettes.
"I can deal with him, Constable—don't worry, I'm not

senile yet.'' A scared half-smile from the constable, and
he went. The door clanged.

Humpy looked at me oddly sideways, like a cat in a
rabbit trap, wondering if the farmer will have enough
sense to see, and free, what he'd caught. And I abandoned
right there my whole planned patient-wearing-down approach. This creature would only respond to directness, as
animals do.

''Why did you kill her?''

He looked up, there was a pause that perhaps made
fifteen seconds and felt like days. And then he spoke, and
every muscle in my body relaxed at once. I had won.

''I had to, I needed virgin blood, don't you see?'' As if
to an idiot.

''Why dirty her?''

His manner suddenly changed, becoming at once con-
fiding and condescending, like a lecturer in some Poly
winning over a class. ''It was a logical problem. I had to
be sure she was a virgin, but in the process I had to make
sure I didn't spoil her virginity else the blood'd've been
useless. I think I did very well. I must have done or it
wouldn't have worked.''

''What wouldn't?''

''The spell I found in the old book to cure me.''

''Cure you?''

''I said that because you're too stupid to understand. To
break the chrysalis and let me enter the next stage. In an
hour I'll be complete and free and no one'll ever laugh at
me again. That's why I wanted to be in here where there'd
be no fools to interfere while I was helpless.''

''Helpless?''

''Yes, soon, when the splitting begins. Can I trust you?
You keep guard. You have brain enough to realise what I
can mean to mankind''; he moved suddenly and I clenched
my fists, but all he did was tear off that horrid flasher's
raincoat, then, moved at a speed that seemed to accelerate
as I watched, a patched and leather-elbowed tweed jacket,

filthier still, a dirty shirt, and a string vest, and turned to show his hump. "Protect me and you'll see a miracle," he said, lying face down on the stone floor of the cell, and seemingly instantly then to go to sleep.

The hump was wrinkled, almost walnut-like. And seemed to be oddly cracked, as if by some unhealed scar. As I watched, what seemed small pustules of green ichor erupted, like a broken kneecap I had had once as a child, that swelled the more after the old school teacher made me run with it, calling me "Girl, crybaby" when I screamed with pain.

Things happened fast after that.

I'd like to think it was for the Manvers girl's sake I did what I did, and not for my career's. But who can ever be sure on such debatable points, and who beside me will ever know or care anyway. *He* is in an asylum for the criminally insane until this day, still cursing me for stopping Superman from becoming what *He* should be.

Some strange defiance made me hang the trophies on the wall of my den. They are curling now, brown and drooping, my choice of alcohol as a preservative, borrowed from Forensic, doubtless a bad one. Occasionally friends ask me where I got them, and what they are. I answer them, "You tell me," to the second question, and for the first say a curio stall down Portobello Road that was gone the next Saturday I went to question the proprietor further, furtive and brownly foreign among his plastic elephant tusks, Benares trays, and curious Victorian books of "Illustrated Correspondence Journals."

The stall *did* exist, mind you, but those dried, those horrid wings, are what I tore from the killer's back even as they began to sprout, still soft and unformed, out of what till then a lifetime had passed merely as a hump.

THE BUTTON MOLDER

by Fritz Leiber

I don't rightly know if I can call this figure I saw for a devastating ten seconds a ghost. And *heard* for about ten seconds just before that. These durations are of course to a degree subjective judgments. At the time they seemed to be lasting forever. Ten seconds can be long or short. A man can light a cigarette. A sprinter can travel a hundred yards, sound two miles, and light two million. A rocket can launch, or burn up inside. A city can fall down. It depends on what's happening.

The word "ghost," like "shade" or "wraith" or even "phantom," suggests human personality and identity, and what this figure had was in a way the antithesis of that. Perhaps "apparition" is better, because it ties it in with astronomy, which may conceivably be the case in a far-fetched way. Astronomers speak of apparitions of the planet Mercury, just as they talk of spurious stars (novas) and occultations by Venus and the moon. Astronomy talk can sound pretty eerie, even without the help of any of the witching and romantic lingo of astrology.

But I rather like "ghost," for it lets me bring in the theory of the Victorian scholar and folklorist Andrew Lang that a ghost is simply a short waking dream in the mind of the person who thinks he sees one. He tells about it in his book *Dreams and Ghosts*, published in 1897. It's a praise-worthily simple and sober notion (also a very polite one, typically English!—"I'd never suggest you were lying about that ghost, old boy. But perhaps you dreamed it, not knowing you were dreaming?") and a theory easy to believe, especially if the person who sees the ghost is fatigued and under stress and the ghost something seen in the shadows of a dark doorway or a storm-lashed window at night or in the flickering flames of a dying fire or in the glooms of a dim room with faded tapestries or obscurely patterned wallpaper. Not so easy to credit for a figure seen fully illuminated for a double handful of long seconds by someone untired and under no physical strain, yet I find it a reassuring theory in my case. In fact, there are times when it strikes me as vastly preferable to certain other possibilities.

The happening occurred rather soon after I moved from one six-storey apartment building to another in downtown San Francisco. There were a remarkable number of those put up in the decades following the quake and fire of 1906. A lot of them started as small hotels but transformed to apartments as the supply of cheap menial labor shrank. You can usually tell those by their queer second floors, which began as mezzanines. The apartment I was moving from had an obvious one of those, lobby-balcony to the front, manager's apartment and some other tiny ones to the rear.

I'd been thinking about moving for a long time, because

my one-room-and-bath was really too small for me and getting crammed to the ceiling with my files and books, yet I'd shrunk from the bother involved. But then an efficient, "savvy" manager was replaced by an ineffectual one, who had little English, or so pretended to save himself work, and the place rather rapidly got much too noisy. Hi-fi's thudded and thumped unrebuked until morning. Drunken parties overflowed into the halls and took to wandering about. Early on in the course of deterioration the unwritten slum rule seemed to come into effect of "If you won't call the owner (or the cops) on me, I won't call him on you." (Why did I comply with this rule? I hate rows and asserting myself.) There was a flurry of mailbox thefts and of stoned folk setting off the building's fire alarm out of curiosity, and of nodding acquaintances whose names you didn't know hitting you for small loans. Pets and stray animals multiplied—and left evidence of themselves, as did the drunks. There were more than the usual quota of overdosings and attempted suicides and incidents of breaking down doors (mostly by drunks who'd lost their keys) and series of fights that were, perhaps unfortunately, mostly racket and at least one rape. In the end the halls came to be preferred for every sort of socializing. And if the police were at last summoned, it was generally just in time to start things up again when they'd almost quieted down.

I don't mind a certain amount of stupid noise and even hubbub. After all, it's my business to observe the human condition and report on it imaginatively. But when it comes to spending my midnight hours listening to two elderly male lovers shouting horrendous threats at each other in prison argot, repeatedly slamming doors on each other and maddeningly whining for them to be reopened, and stumbling up and down stairs menacing each other with a dull breadknife which is periodically wrested in slow-motion from hand to hand, I draw the line. More important, I am even able to summon up the energy to get myself away from the offensive scene forever.

My new apartment building, which I found much more easily than I'd expected to once I started to hunt, was an earthly paradise by comparison. *The occupants stayed out of the halls* and when forced to venture into them traveled as swiftly as was compatible with maximum quiet. The walls were thick enough so that I hadn't the faintest idea of what they did at home. The manager was a tower of resourceful efficiency, yet unobtrusive and totally uninquisitive. Instead of the clanking and groaning monster I'd been used to, the small elevator (I lived on six in both places) was a wonder of silent reliability. Twice a week the halls roared softly and briefly with a large vacuum cleaner wielded by a small man with bowed shoulders who never seemed to speak.

Here the queer second-floor feature hinting at hotel-origins took the form of three private offices (an architect's, a doctor's and a CPA's), instead of front apartments, with a stairway of their own shut off from the rest of the building, while the entire first floor except for the main entrance and its hall was occupied by a large fabrics or yard-goods store, which had in its display window an item that intrigued me mightily. It was a trim lay figure, life-size, made of a ribbed white cotton material and stuffed. It had mitts instead of hands (no separate fingers or toes) and an absolutely blank face. Its position and attitude were altered rather frequently, as were the attractive materials displayed with it—it might be standing or reclining, sitting or kneeling. Sometimes it seemed to be pulling fabrics from a roller, or otherwise arranging them, things like that. I always thought of it as female, I can't say why; although there were the discreet suggestions of a bosom and a pubic bump, its hips were narrow; perhaps a woman would have thought of it as male. Or perhaps my reasons for thinking of it as feminine were as simple as its small life-size (about five feet tall) or (most obvious) its lack of any external sex organ. At any rate, it rather fascinated as well as amused me, and at first I fancied it as standing for the delightfully quiet, unobtrusive folk who were my new fellow tenants as opposed to the noisy and obstreperous quaints I had endured before. I even thought of it for a bit as the "faceless" and unindividualized proto-human being to which the Button Molder threatens to melt down Peer Gynt. (I'd just reread that classic of Ibsen's—really, Peer stands with Faust and Hamlet and Don Quixote and Don Juan as one of the great fundamental figures of western culture.) But then, I became aware of its extreme mute expressiveness. If a face is left blank, the imagination of the viewer always supplies an expression for it—an expression which may be more intense and "living" because there are no lifeless features for it to clash with.

(If I seem to be getting off on sidetracks, please bear with me. They really have a bearing. I haven't forgotten my ghost, or apparition, or those agonizing ten seconds I want to tell you about. No indeed.)

My own apartment in the new building was almost too good to be true. Although advertised as only a studio, it contained four rooms in line, each with a window facing east. They were, in order from north to south (which would be left to right as you entered the hall): bathroom, small bedroom (its door faced you as you entered from the outside hall), large living room, and (beyond a low arched doorway) dinette-kitchen. The bathroom window was frosted; the other three had venetian blinds. And besides two closets (one half the bedroom long) there were seventeen built-in cupboards with a total of thirty-one shelves—a treasure trove of ordered emptiness, and all, all, mine alone! To complete the pleasant picture, I had easy access to the roof—the manager assured me that a few of the tenants regularly used it for sunbathing. But I wasn't interested in the roof by day.

The time came soon enough when I eagerly supervised the transfer to my new place of my luggage, boxes, clothes, the few articles of furniture I owned (chiefly bookcases and filing cabinets), and the rather more extensive materials of my trade of fiction-writing and chief avocation of roof-top astronomy. That last is more important to me than one might guess. I like big cities, but I'd hate to have to live in one without having easy access to a flat roof. I'd had that at my old apartment, and it was one of the features that kept me there so long—I'd anticipated difficulties getting the same privilege elsewhere.

I have the theory, you see, that in this age of mechanized hive-dwelling and of getting so much input from necessarily conformist artificial media such as TV and newspapers, it's very important for a person to keep himself more directly oriented, in daily touch with the heavens or at least the sky, the yearly march of the sun across the stars, the changing daily revolution of the stars as the world turns, the crawl of the planets, the swift phases of the moon, things like that. After all, it's one of the great healing rhythms of nature like the seas and the winds, perhaps the greatest. Stars are a pattern of points upon infinity, elegant geometric art, with almost an erotic poignancy, but all, all nature. Some psychologists say that people stop dreaming if they don't look out over great distances each day, "see the horizon," as it were, and that dreams are the means by which the mind keeps its conscious and unconscious halves in balance, and I certainly agree with them. At any rate I'd deliberately built up the habit of rooftop observing, first by the unaided eye, then with the help of binoculars, and, finally, a small refracting telescope on an equatorial mounting.

Moreover—and especially in a foggy city like San Francisco!—if you get interested in the stars, you inevitably get interested in the weather if only because it so often thwarts you with its infinitely varied clouds and winds (which can make a telescope useless by setting it trembling), its freaks and whims and its own great all-over rhythms. And then it gives you a new slant on the city itself. You become absorbed into the fascinating world of roofs, a secret world above the city world, one mostly uninhabited and unknown. Even the blocky, slablike high-rises cease to be anonymous disfigurements, targets of protest. They become the markers whence certain stars appear or whither they trend, or which they graze with twinkling caress, and which the sun or moon touch or pass behind at certain times of the year or month, exactly like with the menhirs at Stonehenge which primitive man used similarly. And through the gaps and narrow chinks between the great high-rises, you can almost always glimpse bits and pieces of the far horizon. And always once in a while there will be some freakish sky or sky-related event that will completely mystify you and really challenge your imagination.

Of course, roof-watching, like writing itself, is a lonely occupation, but at least it tends to move outward from self, to involve more and more of otherness. And in any case, after having felt the world and its swarming people much too much with me for the past couple of years (and in an extremely noisy, sweaty way!) I was very much looking forward to living alone by myself for a good long while in a supremely quiet environment.

In view of that last, it was highly ironic that the first thing to startle me about my new place should have been *the noise*—noise of a very special sort, the swinish grunting and chomping of the huge garbage trucks that came rooting for refuse every morning (except Sunday) at 4 A.M. or a little earlier. My old apartment had looked out on a rear inner court in an alleyless block, and so their chuffing, grinding sound had been one I'd been mostly spared. While the east windows of my new place looked sidewise down on the street in front and also into a rather busy alley—there wasn't a building nearly as high as mine in that direction for a third of a block. Moreover, in moving the three blocks between the two apartments, I'd moved into a more closely supervised and protected district—that of the big hotels and theaters and expensive stores—with more police protection and enforced tidiness—which meant more garbage trucks. There were the yellow municipal ones and the green and gray ones of more than one private collection company, and once at three-thirty I saw a tiny white one draw up on the sidewalk beside an outdoor phone booth and the driver get out and spend ten minutes rendering it pristine with vacuum, sponge, and squeegee.

The first few nights when they waked me, I'd get up and move from window to window, and even go down the outside hall to the front fire escape with its beckoning red light, the better to observe the rackety monsters and their hurrying attendants—the wide maws into which the refuse was shaken from clattering cans, the great revolving steel drums that chewed it up, the huge beds that would groaningly tilt to empty the drums and shake down the shards. (My God, they were ponderous and cacophonous vehicles!)

But nothing could be wrong with my new place—even these sleep-shattering mechanical giant hogs fascinated me. It was an eerie and mysterious sight to see one of them draw up, say, at the big hotel across the street from me and an iron door in the sidewalk open upward without visible human agency and four great dully gleaming garbage cans slowly arise there as if from some dark hell. I found myself comparing them also (the trucks) to the Button Molder in *Peer Gynt*. Surely, I told myself, they each must have a special small compartment for discarded human souls that had failed to achieve significant individuality and were due to be melted down! Or perhaps they just mixed in the worn-out souls with all the other junk.

At one point I even thought of charting and timing the trucks' exact routes and schedules, just as I did with the planets and the moon, so that I'd be better able to keep tabs on them.

That was another reason I didn't mind being waked at four—it let me get in a little rooftop astronomy before the morning twilight began. At such times I'd usually just take my binoculars, though once I lugged up my telescope for an apparition of Mercury when he was at his greatest western elongation.

Once, peering down from the front fire escape into the dawn-dark street below, I thought I saw a coveralled attendant rudely toss my fabric-store manikin into the rear-end mouth of a dark green truck, and I almost shouted down a protesting inquiry . . . and ten minutes later felt sorry that I hadn't—sorry and somehow guilty. It bothered me so much that I got dressed and went down to check out the display window. For a moment I didn't see her, and I felt a crazy grief rising, but then I spotted her peeping up at me coyly from under a pile of yardage arranged so that she appeared to have pulled the colorful materials down on herself.

And once at four in the warm morning of a holiday I was for variety wakened by the shrill, argumentative cries of four slender hookers, two black, two white, arrayed in their uniform of high heels, hotpants, and long-sleeved lacy blouses, clustered beneath a streetlight on the far corner of the next intersection west and across from an all-hours nightclub named the Windjammer. They were preening and scouting about at intervals, but mostly they appeared to be discoursing, somewhat less raucously now, with the unseen drivers and passengers of a dashing red convertible and a slim white hardtop long as a yacht, which were drawn up near the curb at nonchalant angles across the corner. Their customers? Pimps more likely, from the glory of their equipages. After a bit the cars drifted away and the four lovebirds wandered off east in a loose formation, warbling together querulously.

After about ten days I stopped hearing the garbage trucks, just as the manager had told me would happen, though most mornings I continued to wake early enough for a little astronomy.

My first weeks in the new apartment were very happy ones. (No, I hadn't encountered my ghost yet, or even got hints of its approach, but I think the stage was setting itself and perhaps the materials were gathering.) My writing, which had been almost stalled at the old place, began to go well, and I finished three short stories. I spent my afternoons pleasantly setting out the stuff of my life to best advantage, being particularly careful to leave most surfaces clear and not to hang too many pictures, and in expeditions to make thoughtful purchases. I acquired a dark blue celestial globe I'd long wanted and several maps to fill the space above my filing cabinets: one of the world, a chart of the stars on the same Mercator projection, a big one of the moon, and two of San Francisco, the city and its downtown done in great detail. I didn't go to many shows during this time or see much of any of my friends—I didn't need them. But I got caught up on stacks of unanswered correspondence. And I remember expending considerable effort in removing the few blemishes I discovered on my new place: a couple of inconspicuous but unsightly stains, a slow drain that turned out to have been choked by a stopper-chain, a venetian blind made cranky by twisted cords, and the usual business of replacing low-wattage globes with brighter ones, particularly in the case of the entry light just inside the hall door. There the ceiling had been lowered a couple of feet, which gave the rest of the apartment a charmingly spacious appearance, as did the arched dinette doorway, but it meant that any illumination there had to come down from a fixture in the true ceiling through a frosted plate in the lowered one. I put in a 200-watter, reminding myself to use it sparingly. I even remember planning to get a thick rubber mat to put under my filing cabinets so they wouldn't indent and perhaps even cut the heavy carpeting too deeply, but I never got around to that.

Perhaps those first weeks were simply too happy, perhaps I just got to spinning along too blissfully, for after finishing the third short story, I suddenly found myself tempted by the idea of writing something that would be more than fiction and also more than a communication addressed to just one person, but rather a general statement of what I thought about life and other people and history and the universe and all, the roots of it, something like Descartes began when he wrote down, "I think, therefore I am." Oh, it wouldn't be formally and certainly not stuffily philosophical, but it would contain a lot of insights just the same, the fruits of one man's lifetime experience. It would be critical yet autobiographical, honestly rooted in me. At the very least it would be a testimonial to the smooth running of my life at a new place, a way of honoring my move here.

I'm ordinarily not much of a nonfiction writer. I've done a few articles about writing and about other writers I particularly admire, a lot of short book reviews, and for a dozen or so years before I took up full-time fiction, I edited a popular science magazine. And before that I'd worked on encyclopedias and books of knowledge.

But everything was so clear to me at the new place, my sensations were so exact, my universe was spread out around me so orderly, that I knew that now was the time to write such a piece if ever, so I decided to take a chance on the new idea, give it a whirl.

At the same time at a deeper level in my mind and feelings, I believe I was making a parallel decision running something like this: *Follow this lead. Let all the other stuff go, ease up, and see what happens*. Somewhere down there a control was being loosened.

An hour or so before dawn the next day I had a little experience that proved to be the pattern for several subsequent ones, including the final unexpected event. (You see, I haven't forgotten those ten seconds I mentioned. I'm keeping them in mind.)

I'd been on the roof in the cool predawn to observe a rather close conjunction (half a degree apart) of Mars and Jupiter in the east (they didn't rise until well after midnight), and while I was watching the reddish and golden planets without instrument (except for my glasses, of course) I twice thought I saw a shooting star out of the corner of my eye but didn't get my head around in time to be sure. I was intrigued because I hadn't noted in the handbook any particular meteor showers due at this time and also because most shooting stars are rather faint and the city's lights tend to dim down everything in the sky. The third time it happened I managed to catch the flash and for a long instant was astounded by the sight of what appeared to be three shooting stars traveling fast in triangular formation like three fighter planes before they whisked out of sight behind a building. Then I heard a faint bird-cry and realized they had been three gulls winging quite close and fast overhead, their white under-feathers illumined by the upward streaming streetlights. It was really a remarkable illusion, of the sort that has to be seen to be fully believed. You'd think your eye wouldn't make that sort of misidentification—three seabirds for three stars—but from the corner of your eye you don't see shape or color or even brightness much, only pale movement whipping past. And then you wouldn't think three birds would keep such a tight and exact triangular formation, very much like three planes performing at an air show.

I walked quietly back to my apartment in my bathrobe and slippers. The stairway from the roof was carpeted. My mind was full of the strange triple apparition I'd just seen. I thought of how another mind with other anticipations might have seen three UFOs. I silently opened the door to my apartment, which I'd left on the latch, and stepped inside.

I should explain here that I always switch off all the lights when I leave my apartment and am careful about how I turn them on when I come back. It's partly thrift and citizenly thoughts about energy, the sort of thing you do to get gold stars at grown-ups' Sunday school. But it's also a care not to leave an outward-glaring light to disturb some sleeper who perhaps must keep his window open and unshuttered for the sake of air and coolth; there's a ten-storey apartment building a quarter block away overlooking my east windows, and I've had my own sleep troubled by such unnecessary abominable beacons. On the other hand, I like to look out open windows myself; I hate to keep them wholly shaded, draped, or shuttered, but at the same time I don't want to become a target for a sniper—a simply realistic fear to many these days. As a result of all this I make it a rule never to turn on a light at night until I'm sure the windows of the room I'm in are fully obscured. I take a certain pride, I must admit, in being able to move around my place in the dark without bumping things—it's a test of courage too, going back to childhood, and also a proof that your sensory faculties haven't been dimmed by age. And I guess I just like the feeling of mysteriousness it gives me.

So when I stepped inside I did *not* turn on the 200-watt light above the lowered ceiling of the entry. My intention was to move directly forward into the bedroom, assure myself that the venetian blinds were tilted shut, and then switch on the bedside lamp. But as I started to do that, I heard the beginning of a noise to my right and I glanced toward the living room, where the street lights striking upward through the open venetian blinds made pale stripes on the ceiling and wall and slightly curving ones on the celestial globe atop a bookcase, and into the dinette beyond, and I saw a thin dark figure slip along the wall. But then, just as a feeling of surprise and fear began, almost at the same moment but actually a moment later, there came the realization that the figure was the black frame of my glasses, either moving as I turned my head or becoming more distinct as I switched my eyes that way, more likely a little of both. It was an odd mixture of sensation and thought, especially coming right on top of the star-birds (or bird-stars), as if I were getting almost simultaneously the messages *My God, it's an intruder, or ghost, or whatever* and *It isn't any of those, as you know very well from a lifetime's experience. You've just been had again by appearances.*

I'm pretty much a thoroughgoing skeptic, you see, when it comes to the paranormal, or the religious supernatural, or even such a today-commonplace as telepathy. My mental attitudes were formed in the period during and just after the first world war, when science was still a right thing, almost noble, and technology was forward-looking and labor-saving and progressive, and before folk wisdom became so big and was still pretty much equated with ignorance and superstition, no matter how picturesque. I've never seen or heard of a really convincing scrap of evidence for ancient or present-day astronauts from other worlds, for comets or moons that bumped the earth and changed history, or for the power of pyramids to prolong life or sharpen razor blades. As for immortality, it's my impression that most people do (or don't do) what's in them and then live out their lives in monotonous blind alleys, and what would be the point in cluttering up another world with all that worn-out junk? And as for God, it seems to me that the existence of one being who knew everything, future as well as past, would simply rob the universe of drama, excuse us all from doing anything. I'll admit that with telepathy the case is somewhat different, if only because so many sensible, well-educated, brilliant people seem to believe in some form of it. I only know I haven't experienced any as far as I can tell; it's almost made me jealous—I've sometimes thought I must be wrapped in some very special insulation against thought waves, if there be such. I *will* allow that the mind (and also mental suggestions from outside) can affect the body, even affect it greatly—the psychosomatic thing. But that's just about all I will allow.

So much for that first little experience—no, wait, what did I mean when I wrote, "I heard the beginning of a noise"? Well, there are sounds so short and broken-off that you can't tell what they were going to be, or even for sure just how loud they were, so that you ask yourself if you imagined them. It was like that—a tick without the tock, a ding without the dong, a creak that went only halfway, never reaching that final *kuh* sound. Or like a single footstep that started rather loud and ended muted down to nothing—very much like the whole little experience itself, beginning with a gust of shock and terror and almost instantly reducing to the commonplace. Well, so much for that.

The next few days were pleasant and exciting ones, as I got together materials for my new project, assembling the favorite books I knew I'd want to quote (Shakespeare and the King James Bible, *Moby Dick* and *Wuthering Heights*, Ibsen and Bertrand Russell, Stapledon and Heinlein), looking through the daybooks I've kept for the past five years for the entries in black ink, which I reserve for literary and what I like to call metaphysical matters, and telling my mind (programming it, really) to look for similar insights whenever they happened to turn up during the course of the day—my chores and reading, my meals and walks— and then happily noting down those new insights in turn. There was only one little fly in the ointment: I knew I'd embarked on projects somewhat like this before—autobiographical and critical things—and failed to bring them to conclusions. But then I've had the same thing happen to me on stories. With everything, one needs a bit of luck.

My next little experience began up on the roof. (They all did, for that matter.) It was a very clear evening without a moon, and I'd been memorizing the stars in Capricorn and faint Aquarius and the little constellations that lie between those and the Northern Cross: Sagitta, Delphinus, and dim Equuleus. You learn the stars rather like you learn countries and cities on a map, getting the big names first (the brightest stars and star groups) and then patiently filling in the areas between—and always on the watch for striking forms. At such times I almost forget the general dimming effect of San Francisco's lights since what I'm working on is so far above them.

And then, as I was resting my eyes from the binoculars, shut off by the roof's walls and the boxlike structure housing the elevator's motor from the city's most dazzling glares (the big, whitely fluorescent streetlights are the worst, the ones that are supposed to keep late walkers safe), I saw a beam of bright silver light strike straight upward for about a second from the roof of a small hotel three blocks away. And after about a dozen seconds more it came again, equally brief. It really looked like a sort of laser-thing: a beam of definite length (about two storeys) and solid-looking. It happened twice more, not at regular intervals, but always as far as I could judge in exactly the same place (and I'd had time to spin a fantasy about a secret enclave of extraterrestrials signaling to confederates poised just outside the stratosphere) when it occurred to me to use my binoculars on it. They solved the mystery almost at once: It wasn't a light beam at all, but a tall flagpole painted silver (no wonder it looked solid!) and at intervals washed by the roving beam of a big arc light shooting upward from the street beyond and swinging in slow circles—the sort of thing they use to signalize the opening of movie houses and new restaurants, even quite tiny ones.

What had made the incident out of the ordinary was that most flagpoles are painted dull white, not silver, and that the clearness of the night had made the arc light's wide beam almost invisible. If there'd been just a few wisps of cloud or fog in the air above, I'd have spotted it at once for what it was. It was rather strange to think of all that light streaming invisibly up from the depths of the city's reticulated canyons and gorges.

I wondered why I'd never noted that flagpole before. Probably they never flew a flag on it.

It all didn't happen to make me recall my three star-birds, and so when after working over once more this night's chosen heavenly territory, including a veering aside to scan the rich starfields of Aquila and the diamond of Altair, one of Earth's closest stellar neighbors, I was completely taken by surprise again when on entering my apartment, the half a noise was repeated and the same skinny dark shape glided along the wall across the narrow flaglike bands of light and dark. Only this time the skeptical, deflating reaction came a tiny bit sooner, followed at once by the almost peevish inner remark, *Oh, yes, that again!* And then as I turned on the bedside light, I wondered, as one will, how I would have reacted if the half step had been completed and if the footsteps had gone on, getting louder as they made their swift short trip and there peered around the side of the doorway at me . . . what? It occurred to me that the nastiest and most frightening thing in the world must differ widely from person to person, and I smiled. Surely in man's inward lexicon, the phobias outnumber the philias a thousand to one!

Oh, I'll admit that when I wandered into the living room and kitchen a bit later, shutting the blinds and turning on some lights, I did inspect things in a kind of perfunctory way, but noted nothing at all out of order. I told myself that all buildings make a variety of little noises at night, waterpipes especially can get downright loquacious, and then there are refrigerator motors sighing on and off and the faint little clicks and whines that come from electric clocks, all manner of babble—that half noise might be anything. At least I knew the identity of the black glider—the vaguely seen black frame always at the corner of my eye when I had on my glasses and most certainly there now.

I went on assembling the primary materials for my new project, and a week later I was able to set down, word by mulled-over word, the unembroidered, unexemplified, unproven gist of what I felt about life, or at least a first version of it. I still have it as I typed it from a penciled draft with many erasures, crossings out and interlineations:

There is this awareness that is I, this mind that's me, a little mortal world of space and time, which glows and aches, which purrs and darkens, haunted and quickened by the ghosts that are memory, imagination, and thought, forever changing under urgings from within and proddings from without, yet able to hold still by fits and starts (and now and then refreshed by sleep and dreams), forever seeking to extend its bounds, forever hunting for the mixture of reality and fantasy—the formula, the script, the scenario, the story to tell itself or others— which will enable it to do its work, savor its thrills, and keep on going.

A baby tells itself the simplest story: that it is all that matters, it is God, commanding and constraining all the rest, all otherness. But then the script becomes more complicated. Stories take many forms: a scientific theory or a fairy tale, a world history or an anecdote, a call to action or a cry for help—all, all are stories. Sometimes they tell of our love for another, or they embody our illusioned and illusioning vision of the one we love— they are courtship. But every story must be interesting or it will not work, will not be heard, even the stories that we tell ourselves. And so it must contain illusion, fantasy. No matter how grim its facts, it must contain that saving note, be it only a surpassingly interesting bitter, dry taste.

And then there are the other mortal minds I know are there, fellow awarenesses, companion consciousnesses, some close, a very few almost in touching space (but never quite), most farther off in almost unimaginable multitudes, each one like mine a little world of space and time moment by moment seeking its story, the combination of illusion and hard fact, of widest waking and of deepest dreaming, which will allow it to create, enjoy, survive. A company of loving, warring minds, a tender, rough companioning of tiny cosmoses forever telling stories to each other and themselves—that's what there is.

And I know that I must stay aware of all the others, listening to their stories, trying to understand them, their sufferings, their joys and their imaginings, respecting the thorny fact of both their inner and their outer lives, and nourishing the needful illusions at least of those who are closest to me, if I am to make progress in my quest.

Finally there is the world, stranger than any mind or any story, the unknown universe, the shadowy scaffolding holding these minds together, the grid on which they are mysteriously arrayed, their container and their field, perhaps (but is there any question of it?) all-powerful yet quite unseen, its form unsensed, known only to the companion minds by the sensations it showers upon them and pelts them with, by its cruel and delicious proddings and graspings, by its agonizing and ecstatic messages (but never a story), and by its curt summonses and sentences, including death. Yes, that is how it is, those are the fundamentals: There is the dark, eternally silent, unknown universe; there are the friend-enemy minds shouting and whispering their tales and always seeking the three miracles—that minds should really touch, or that the silent universe should speak, tell minds a story, or (perhaps the same thing) that there should be a story that works that is all hard facts, all reality, with no illusions and no fantasy; and lastly there is lonely, story-telling, wonder-questing, mortal me.

As I reread that short statement after typing it out clean, I found it a little more philosophical than I'd intended and also perhaps a little more overly glamorized with words like "ecstatic" and "agonizing," "mysteriously" and "stranger." But on the whole I was satisfied with it. Now to analyze it more deeply and flesh it out with insights and examples from my own life and from my own reflections on the work of others!

But as the working days went on and became weeks (remember, I'd pretty much given up all other work for the duration of this project) I found it increasingly difficult to make any real progress. For one thing, I gradually became aware that in order to analyze that little statement much more deeply and describe my findings, I'd need to use one or more of the vocabularies of professional philosophy and psychology—which would mean months at least of reading and reviewing and of assimilating new advances, and I certainly didn't have the time for that. (The vocabularies of philosophies can be *very* special—Whitehead's, for instance, makes much use of the archaic verb "prehend," which for him means something very different from "comprehend" or "perceive.") Moreover, the whole idea had been to skim accumulated insights and wisdom (if any!) off my mind, not become a student again and start from the beginning.

And I found it was pretty much the same when I tried to say something about other writers, past and contemporary, beyond a few obvious remarks and memorable quotations. I'd need to read their works again and study their lives in a lot more detail than I had ever done, before I'd be able to shape statements of any significance, things I really believed about them.

And when I tried to write about my own life, I kept discovering that for the most part it was much too much like anyone else's. I didn't want to set down a lot of dreary dates and places, only the interesting things, but how tell about those honestly without bringing in the rest? Moreover, it began to seem to me that all the really interesting subjects, like sex and money, feelings of guilt, worries about one's courage, and concern about one's selfishness were things one wasn't supposed to write about, either because they were too personal, involving others, or because they were common to all men and women and so quite unexceptional.

This state of frustration didn't grip me all the time, of course. It came in waves and gradually accumulated. I'd generally manage to start off each day feeling excited about the project (though it began to take more and more morning time to get my head into that place, I will admit), perhaps some part of my short statement would come alive for me again, like that bit about the universe being a grid on which minds are mysteriously arrayed, but by the end of the day I would have worried all the life out of it and my mind would be as blank as the face of my manikin in the fabric shop window downstairs. I remember once or twice in the course of one of our daily encounters shaking my head ruefully at her, almost as if seeking for sympathy. She seemed to have a lot more patience and poise than I had.

I was beginning to spend more time on the roof, too, not only for the sake of the stars and astronomy, but just to get away from my desk with all its problems. In fact, my next little experience leading up to the ghostly one began shortly before sunset one day when I'd been working long, though fruitlessly. The sky, which was cloudless from my east windows, began to glow with an unusual violet color and I hurried up to get a wider view.

All day long a steady west wind had been streaming out the flags on the hotels and driving away east what smog there was, so that the sky was unusually clear. But the sun had sunk behind the great fog bank that generally rests on the Pacific just outside the Golden Gate. However, he had not yet set, for to the south, where there were no tall buildings to obstruct my vision, his beams were turning a few scattered clouds over San Jose (some thirty miles away) a delicate shade of lemon yellow that seemed to be the exact complement of the violet in the sky (just as orange sunset clouds tend to go with a deep blue sky).

And then as I watched, there suddenly appeared in the

midst of that sunset, very close to the horizon in a cloud-less stretch, a single yellow cloud like a tiny dash. It seemed to appear from nowhere, just like that. And then as I continued to watch, another cloud appeared close beside the first at the same altitude, beginning as a bright yellow point and then swiftly growing until it was as long as the first, very much as if a giant invisible hand had drawn another short dash.

During the course of the next few minutes, as I watched with a growing sense of wonder and a feeling of giant release from the day's frustrations, eight more such mini-clouds (or whatever) appeared at fairly regular intervals, until there were ten of them glowing in line there, fluores-cent yellow stitches in the sky.

My mind raced, clutching at explanations. Kenneth Ar-nold's original flying saucers thirty years ago, which he'd glimpsed from his light plane over the American north-west, had been just such shining shapes in a row. True, his had been moving, while mine were hovering over a city, having appeared from nowhere. Could they conceivably have come from hyperspace? my fancy asked.

And then, just as the lemon sunset began to fade from the higher clouds, an explanation struck me irresistibly. What I was seeing was skywriting (which usually we see above our heads) from way off to one side, viewed edge-wise. My ten mystery clouds (or giant ships!) were the nine letters—and the hyphen—of Pepsi-Cola. (Next day I confirmed this by a telephone call to San Jose; there had been just such an advertising display.)

At the time, and as the giant yellow stitches faded to gray unsewn sky-cloth, I remember feeling very exhila-rated and also slightly hysterical at the comic aspect of the event. I paced about the roof chortling, telling myself that the vision I'd just witnessed outdid even that of the Good-year blimp acrawl with colored lights in abstract patterns that had welcomed me to this new roof the first night I'd climbed up here after moving in. I spent quite a while quieting myself, so that the streetlights had just come on when I went downstairs. But somehow I hadn't thought of it being very dark yet in my apartment, so that was perhaps why it wasn't until I was actually unlocking the door that, remembering the Star-birds and the Silver Laser (and now the Mystery of the Ten Yellow Stitches!), I also remembered the events that had followed them. I had only time to think *Here we go again* as I pushed inside.

Well, it *was* dark in there and the pale horizontal bands were on the wall and the skeleton black figure slipped along them and I felt almost instantly the choked-off gust of terror riding atop the remnants of my exhilaration, all of this instantly after hearing that indefinable sound which seemed to finish almost before it began. That was one thing characteristic of all these preliminary incidents—they ended so swiftly and so abruptly that it was hard to think about them afterwards, the mind had nothing to work with.

And I know that in trying to describe them I must make them sound patterned, almost prearranged, yet at the time they just happened and somehow there was always an element of surprise.

Unfortunately the exhilaration I'd feel on the roof never carried over to the next morning's work on my new project. This time, after sweating and straining for almost a week without any progress at all, I resolutely decided to shelve it, at least for a while, and get back to stories.

But I found I couldn't do that. I'd committed myself too deeply to the new thing. Oh, I didn't find that out right away, of course. No, I spent more than a week before I came to that hateful and panic-making conclusion. I tried every trick I knew of to get myself going: long walks, fasting, starting to write immediately after waking up when my mind was hypnogogic and blurred with dream, listening to music which I'd always found suggestive, such as Holst's *The Planets*, especially the "Saturn" section, which seems to capture the essence of time—you hear the giant footsteps of time itself crashing to a halt—or Williams's

Sinfonia antartica with its lonely wind-machine finish, which does the same for space, or Berlioz's *Funeral March for the Last Scene of Hamlet*, which reaches similarly toward chaos. Nothing helped. The more I'd try to work up the notes for some story I had already three quarters planned, the less interesting it would become to me, until it seemed (and probably was) all cliché. Some story ideas are as faint and unsubstantial as ghosts. Well, all of *those* I had just got fainter as I worked on them.

I hate to write about writer's block; it's such a terribly childish, yes, frivolous-seeming affliction. You'd think that anyone who was half a human being could shake it off or just slither away from it. But I couldn't. Morning after morning I'd wake with an instant pang of desperation at the thought of my predicament, so that I'd have to get up right away and pace, or rush out and walk the dawn-empty streets, or play through chess endings or count windows in big buildings to fill my mind with useless calculations— anything until I grew calm enough to read a newspaper or make a phone call and somehow get the day started. Sometimes my desk would get to jumping in the same way my mind did and I'd find myself compulsively straightening the objects on it over and over until I'd spring up from it in disgust. Now when the garbage trucks woke me at four (as they began to do again) I'd get up and follow their thunderous mechanical movements from one window or other vantage point to another, anxiously tracing the course of each can-lugging attendant—anything to occupy my mind.

Just to be doing something, I turned to my correspondence, which had begun to pile up again, but after answering three or four notes (somehow I'd pick the least important ones) I'd feel worn out. You see, I didn't want to write my friends about the block I was having. It was such a bore (whining always is) and, besides, I was *ashamed*. At the same time I couldn't seem to write honestly about anything without bringing my damn block in.

I felt the same thing about calling up or visiting my friends around me in the city. I'd have nothing to show them, nothing to talk about. I didn't want to see anyone. It was a very bad time for me.

Of course I kept on going up to the roof, more than ever now, though even my binoculars were a burden to me and I couldn't bear to lug up my telescope—the weary business of setting it up and all the fussy adjustments I'd have to make made that unthinkable. I even had to *make* myself study the patterns of the lesser stars when the clear nights came which had formerly been such a joy to me.

But then one evening just after dark I went topside and immediately noticed near Cygnus, the Northern Cross, a star that shouldn't have been there. It was a big one, third magnitude at least. It made a slightly crooked extension of the top of the cross as it points toward Cassiopeia. At first I was sure it had to be an earth satellite (I've spotted a few of those)—a big one, like the orbiting silvered balloon they called Echo. Or else it was a light on some weird sort of plane that was hovering high up. But when I held my binoculars on it, I couldn't see it move at all—as a satellite would have done, of course. Then I got really excited, enough to make me bring up my telescope (and *Norton's Star Atlas* too) and set it up.

In the much smaller and more magnified field of that instrument, it didn't move either, but glared there steadily among the lesser points of light, holding position as it inched with the other stars across the field. From the atlas I estimated and noted down its approximate coordinates (right ascension 21 hours and 10 minutes, north declination 48 degrees) and hurried downstairs to call up an astronomer friend of mine and tell him I'd spotted a nova.

Naturally I wasn't thinking at all about the previous ghostly (or whatever) incidents, so perhaps this time the strange thing was that, yes, it did happen again, just as before though with even more brevity, and I sort of went through all the motions of reacting to it, but very unconcernedly, as if it had become a habit, part of the routine of existence, like a step in a stairway that always creaks when your foot hits it but nothing more ever comes of it. I recall saying to myself with a sort of absentminded lightheartedness *Let's give the ghost E for effort; he keeps on trying*.

I got my astronomer friend and, yes, it was a real nova; it had been spotted in Asia and Europe hours earlier and all the astronomers were very busy, oh my, yes.

The nova was a four days' wonder, taking that long to fade down to naked-eye invisibility. Unfortunately my own excitement at it didn't last nearly that long. Next morning I was confronting my block again. Very much in the spirit of desperation, I decided to go back to my new project and make myself finish it off somehow, force myself to write no matter how bad the stuff seemed to be that I turned out, beginning with an expansion of my original short statement.

But the more I tried to do that, the more I reread those two pages, the thinner and more dubious all the ideas in it seemed to me, the junkier and more hypocritical it got. Instead of adding to it, I wanted to take stuff away, trim it down to a nice big nothing.

To begin with, it was so much a writer's view of things, reducing everything to stories. Of course! What could be more obvious?—or more banal? A military man would explain life in terms of battles, advances and retreats, defeats and victories, and all their metaphorical analogues, presumably with strong emphasis on courage and discipline. Just as a doctor might view history as the product of great men's ailments, whether they were constipated or indigestive, had syphilis or TB—or of subtle diseases that swept nations; the fall of Rome?—lead poisoning from the pipes they used to distribute their aqueducted water! Or a salesman see everything as buying and selling, literally or by analogy. I recalled a 1920s' book about Shakespeare by a salesman. The secret of the Bard's unequaled dramatic power? He was the world's greatest salesman! No, all that stuff about stories was just a figure of speech and not a very clever one.

And then that business about illusion coming in everywhere—what were illusions and illusioning but euphemisms for lies and lying? We had to nourish the illusions of others, didn't we? That meant, in plain language, that we had to flatter them, tell them white lies, go along with all their ignorances and prejudices—very convenient rationalizations for a person who was afraid to speak the truth! Or for someone who was eager to fantasize everything. And granting all that, how had I ever hoped to write about it honestly in any detail?—strip away from myself and others, those at all close to me at least, all our pretenses and boasts, the roles we played, the ways we romanticized ourselves, the lies we agreed to agree on, the little unspoken deals we made (''You build me up, I'll build up you''), yes, strip away all that and show exactly what lay underneath: the infantile conceits, the suffocating selfishness, the utter unwillingness to look squarely at the facts of death, torture, disease, jealousy, hatred, and pain—how had I ever hoped to speak out about all that, I, an illusioner?

Yes, how to speak out the truth of my real desires? that were so miserably small, so modest. No vast soul-shaking passions and heaven-daunting ambitions at all, only the little joy of watching a shadow's revealing creep along an old brick wall or the infinitely delicate diamond-prick of the first evening star in the deepening blue sky of evening, the excitement of little discoveries in big dictionaries, the small thrill of seeing and saying, ''That's not the dark underside of a distant low narrow cloudbank between those two buildings, it's a TV antenna,'' or ''That's not a nova, you wishful thinker, it's Procyon,'' the fondling and fondlings of slender, friendly, cool fingers, the hues and textures of an iris seen up close—how to admit to such minuscule longings and delights?

And getting still deeper into this stories business, what was it all but a justification for always *talking* about things and never *doing* anything? It's been said, "Those who can, do; those who can't, teach." Yes, and those who can't even teach, what do they do? Why, they tell stories! Yes, always talking, never acting, never being willing to dirty your fingers with the world. Why, at times you had to drive yourself to pursue even the little pleasures, were satisfied with fictional or with imagined proxies.

And while we were on that subject, what was all this business about minds never touching, never being quite able to? What was it but an indirect, mealy-mouthed way of confessing my own invariable impulse to flinch away from life, to avoid contact at any cost—the reason I lived alone with fantasies, never made a friend (though occasionally letting others, if they were forceful enough, make friends with me), preferred a typewriter to a wife, talked, talked, and never did? Yes, for minds, read bodies, and then the truth was out, the secret of the watcher from the sidelines.

I tell you, it got so I wanted to take those thumbed-over two grandiose pages of my "original short statement" and crumple them together in a ball and put that in a brown paper sack along with a lot of coffee grounds and grapefruit rinds and grease, and then repeat the process with larger and larger sacks until I had a Chinese-boxes set of them big around as a large garbage can and lug that downstairs at four o'clock in the morning and when the dark truck stopped in front personally hurl it into that truck's big ass-end mouth and *hear* it all being chewed up and ground to filthy scraps, the whole thing ten times louder than it ever sounded from the sixth floor, knowing that my "wisdom"-acorn of crumpled paper with all its idiot notions was in the very midst and getting more masticated and befouled, more thoroughly destroyed, than anything else (while my manikin watched from her window, inscrutable but, I felt sure, approving)—only in that way, I told myself, would I be able to tear myself loose from this whole damn minuscule, humiliating project, kill it inside my head.

I remember the day my mind generated that rather piti-
ful grotesque vision (which, incidentally, I half seriously
contemplated carrying into reality the next morning). The
garbage trucks had wakened me before dawn and I'd been
flitting in and out most of the day, unable to get down to
anything or even to sit still, and once I'd paused on the
sidewalk outside my apartment building, visualizing the
truck drawing up in the dark next morning and myself
hurling my great brown wad at it, and I'd shot to my
manikin in the window the thought *Well, what do you
think of it? Isn't it a good idea?* They had her seated
cross-legged in a sort of Lotus position on a great sweep of
violet sheeting that went up behind her to a high shelf
holding the bolt. She seemed to receive my suggestion and
brood upon it enigmatically.

Predictably, I gravitated to the roof soon after dark, but
without my binoculars and not to study the stars above
(although it was a clear evening) or peer with weary
curiosity at the window-worlds below that so rarely held
human figures, or even to hold still and let the lonely
roof-calm take hold of me. No, I moved about restlessly
from one of my observation stations to another, rather
mechanically scanning along the jagged and crenellated
skyline, between the upper skyey areas and the lower
building-bound ones, that passed for a horizon in the city
(though there actually were a couple of narrow gaps to the
east through which I could glimpse, from the right places
on my roof, very short stretches of the hills behind smoky
transbay Oakland). In fact, my mind was so little on what
I was doing and so much on my writing troubles that I
tripped over a TV-antenna cable I'd known was there and
should have avoided. I didn't fall, but it took me three
plunging steps to recover my balance, and I realized that if
I'd been going in the opposite direction I might well have
pitched over the edge, the wall being rather low at that
point.

The roof world can be quite treacherous at night, you

see. Older roofs especially are apt to be cluttered with little low standpipes and kitchen chimneys and ventilators, things very easy to miss and trip over. It's the worst on clear moonless nights, for then there are no clouds to reflect the city's lights back down, and as a result it's dark as pitch around your feet. (Paradoxically, it's better when it's raining or just been raining for then there's streetlight reflected by the rainclouds and the roof has a wet glisten so that obstructions stand out.) Of course, I generally carry a small flashlight and use it from time to time but, more important, I memorize down to the last detail the layout of any roof visit by night. Only this time that latter precaution had failed me.

It brought me up short to think of how my encounter with the TV cable could have had fatal consequences. It made me see just how very upset I was getting from my writer's block and wonder about unconscious suicidal impulses and accidentally-on-purpose things. Certainly my stalled project was getting to the point where I'd have to do something drastic about it, like seeing a psychiatrist or getting drunk . . . or something.

But the physical fear I felt didn't last long, and soon I was prowling about again, though a little less carelessly. I didn't feel comfortable except when I was moving. When I held still, I felt choked with failure (my writing project). And yet at the same time I felt I was on the verge of an important insight, one that would solve all my problems if I could get it to come clear. It seemed to begin with ''If you could sum up all you felt about life and crystallize it in one master insight . . .'' but where it went from there I didn't know. But I knew I wasn't going to get an answer sitting still.

Perhaps, I thought, this whole roof-thing with me expresses an unconscious atavistic faith in astrology, that I will somehow find the answer to any problem in the stars. How quaint of skeptical me!

On the roof at my old place, one of my favorite sights

had been the Sutro TV Tower with its score or so of winking red lights. Standing almost a thousand feet high on a hill that is a thousand already, that colorful tripod tower dominates San Francisco from its geographical center and is a measuring rod for the altitude of fogs and cloudbanks, their ceilings and floors. One of my small regrets about moving had been that it couldn't be seen from this new roof. But then only a couple of weeks ago I'd discovered that if you climb the short stairway to the locked door of the boxlike structure hiding the elevator's motor, you see the tops of the Tower's three radio masts poking up over and two miles beyond the top of the glassy Federal building. Binoculars show the myriad feathery white wires guying them that look like sails—they're nylon so as not to interfere with the TV signals.

This night when I got around to checking the three masts out by their red flashes, I lingered a bit at the top of the skeleton stairs watching them, and as I lingered I saw in the black sky near them a tremorous violet star wink on and then after a long second wink off. I wouldn't have thought of it twice except for the color. Violet is an uncommon color for a star. All star colors are very faint tinges, for that matter. I've looked at stars that were supposed to be green and never been able to see it.

But down near the horizon where the air is thicker, anything can happen, I reminded myself. Stars that are white near the zenith begin to flash red and blue, almost any color at all, when they're setting. And suddenly grow dim, even wink out unexpectedly. Still, violet, that was a new one.

And then as I was walking away from the stairs and away from Sutro Tower too, diagonally across the roof toward the other end of it, I looked toward the narrow, window-spangled slim triangle of the Trans-American Pyramid Building a half mile or so away and I saw for a moment, just grazing its pinnacle, what looked like the same mysteriously pulsing violet star. Then it went off or vanished—or went behind the pinnacle, but I couldn't walk it into view again, either way.

What got me the most, perhaps, about that violet dot was the way the light had seemed to *graze* the Pyramid, coming (it was my impression) from a great distance. It reminded me of the last time I'd looked at the planet Mercury through my telescope. I'd followed it for quite a while as it moved down the paling dawn sky, flaring and pulsing (it was getting near the horizon), and then it had reached the top of the Hilton Tower where they have a room whose walls are almost all window, and for almost half a minute I'd continued my observation of it through the glassy corner of the Hilton Hotel. Really, it had seemed most strange to me, that rare planetary light linking me to another building that way, and being tainted by that building's glass, and in a way confounding all my ideas as to what is close and what is far, what clean and what unclean . . .

While I was musing, my feet had carried me to another observation place, where in a narrow slot between two close-by buildings I can see the gray open belfry towers of Grace Cathedral on Nob Hill five blocks off. And there, through or *in* one of the belfry's arched openings, I saw the violet star again resting or floating.

A star leaping about the sky that way?—absurd! No, this was something in my eye or eyes. But even as I squeezed my eyes shut and fluttered the lids and shook my head in short tight arcs, my neck muscles taut, to drive the illusion away, that throbbing violet star peered hungrily at me from the embrasure wherein it rested in the gray church's tower.

I've stared at many a star but never before with the feeling that it was glaring back at me.

But then (something told me) you've never seen a star that came to earth, sliding down that unimaginable distance in a trice and finding itself a niche or hiding hole in the dark world of roofs. The star went out, drew back, was doused.

Do you know that right after that I was afraid to lift my head? or look up at anything? for fear of seeing that flashing violet diamond somewhere it shouldn't be? And that as I turned to move toward the door at the head of the stairs that led down from the roof, my gaze inadvertently encountered the Hilton Tower and I ducked my head so fast that I can't tell you now whether or not I saw a violet gleam in one of that building's windows?

In many ways the world of roofs is like a vast, not too irregular games board, each roof a square, and I thought of the violet light as a sort of super-chess piece making great leaps like a queen (after an initial vast one) and crookedly sidewise moves like a knight, advancing by rushings and edgings to checkmate me.

And I knew that I wanted to get off this roof before I saw a violet glow coming from behind the parapet of one of the airshafts or through the cracks around the locked door to the elevator's motor.

Yet as I moved toward the doorway of escape, the door down, I felt my face irresistibly lifted from between my hunched shoulders and against my neck's flinching opposition until I was peering through painfully winced eye-slits at the cornice of the next building east, the one that overlooked the windows of my apartment.

At first it seemed all dark, but then I caught the faintest violet glint or glimmer, as of something spying down most warily.

From that point until the moment I found myself facing the door to my apartment, I don't remember much at all except the tightness with which my hands gripped the stair-rails going down . . . and continued to grip railings tightly as I went along the sixth-storey hall, although of course there are no railings there.

I got the door unlocked, then hesitated.

But then my gaze wavered back the way I'd come,

toward the stair from the roof, and something in my head began to recite in a little shrill voice, *I met a star upon the stair, A violet star that wasn't there* . . .

I'd pressed on inside and had the door shut and double-locked and was in the bedroom and reaching for the bed-side light before I realized that this time it *hadn't* happened, that at least I'd been spared the half sound and the fugitive dark ghost on this last disastrous night.

But then as I pressed the switch and the light came on with a tiny fizzing crackle and a momentary greenish glint and then shone more brightly and whitely than it should (as old bulbs will when they're about to go—they arc) something else in my head said in a lower voice, *But of course when the right night came it wouldn't make its move until you were safely locked inside and unable to retreat* . . .

And then as I stared at the bright doorway and the double-locked door beyond, there came from the direction of the dinette-kitchen a great creaking sound like a giant footstep, no halfsound but something finished off completely, very controlled, very *deliberate*, neither a stamp nor a tramp, and then another and a third, coming at intervals of just about a second, each one a little closer and a little louder, inexorably advancing very much like the footsteps of time in the ''Saturn'' section of *The Planets*, with more instruments coming in—horns, drums, cymbals, huge gongs and bells—at each mounting repetition of the beat.

I went rigid. In fact, I'm sure my first thought was, *I must hold absolutely still and watch the doorway,* with perhaps the ghost comment riding on it, *Of course! the panic reaction of any animal trapped in its hole*.

And then a fourth footstep and a fifth and sixth, each one closer and louder, so that I'm sure my second real thought was, *The noise I'm hearing must be more than sound, else it would wake the city*. Could it be a physical vibration? Something was resounding deeply through my flesh, but the doorway wasn't shaking visibly as I watched it. Was it the reverberation of something mounting upward from the depths of the earth or my subconscious mind, taking giant strides, smashing upward through the multiple thick floors that protect surface life and daytime consciousness? Or could it be the crashing around me in ruins of my world of certainties, in particular the ideas of that miserable haunting project that had been tormenting me, all of them overset and trodden down together?

And then a seventh, eighth, ninth footstep, almost unbearably intense and daunting, followed by a great grinding pause, a monstrous hesitation. Surely something must appear now, I told myself. My every muscle was tight as terror could make it, especially those of my face and, toruslike, about my eyes (I was especially and rather fearfully conscious of their involuntary blinking). I must have been grimacing fearfully. I remember a fleeting fear of heart attack, every part of me was straining so, putting on effort.

And then there thrust silently, rather rapidly, yet gracefully into the doorway a slender, blunt-ended, sinuous leaden-gray, silver-glistening arm (or other member, I wondered briefly), followed immediately and similarly by the remainder of the figure.

I held still and observed, somehow overcoming the instant urge to flinch, to not-see. More than ever now, I told myself, my survival depended on that, my very life.

How describe the figure? If I say it looked like (and so perhaps was) the manikin in the fabrics shop, you will get completely the wrong impression; you will think of that stuffed and stitched form moving out of its window through the dark and empty store, climbing upstairs, etc., and I knew from the start that that was certainly not the case. In fact, my first thought was, *It is not the manikin, although it has its general form.*

Why? How did I know that? Because I was certain from the first glimpse that it was *alive*, though not in quite the way I was alive, or any other living creatures with which I am familiar. But just the same, that leaden-gray, silver-misted integument was skin, not sewn fabric—there *were* no sewn seams, and I knew where the seams were on the manikin.

How different *its* kind of life from mine? I can only say that heretofore such expressions as "dead-alive," "living dead," and "life in death" were horror-story clichés to me; but now no longer so. (Did the leaden hue of its skin suggest to me a drowned person? I don't think so— there was no suggestion of bloat and all its movements were very graceful.)

Or take its face. The manikin's face had been a blank, a single oval piece of cloth sewn to the sides and top of the head and to the neck. Here there was no edge-stitching and the face was not altogether blank but was crossed by two very faint, fine furrows, one vertical, the other horizontal, dividing the face into four approximately equal quarters, rather like a mandala or the symbol of planet Earth. And now, as I forced myself to scan the horizontal furrow, I saw that it in turn was not altogether featureless. There were two points of violet light three inches apart, very faint but growing brighter the longer I watched them and that moved from side to side a little without alteration in the distance between them, as though scanning me. *That* discovery cost me a pang not to flinch away from, let me tell you!

The vertical furrow in the face seemed otherwise featureless, as did the similar one between the legs with its mute suggestion of femininity. (I had to keep scanning the entire figure over and over, you see, because I felt that if I looked at the violet eye-points too long at any one time they would grow bright enough to blind me, as surely as if I were looking at the midday sun; and yet to look away entirely would be equally, though not necessarily similarly disastrous.)

Or take the matter of height. The window manikin was

slenderly short. Yet I was never conscious of looking down at this figure which I faced, but rather a little up.

What else did I glean as this long nightmarish moment prolonged itself almost unendurably, going on and on and on, as though I were trapped in eternity?

Any other distinguishing and different feature? Yes. The sides and the top of the head sprouted thick and glistening black "hair" that went down her back in one straight fall.

(There, I have used the feminine pronoun on the figure, and I will stick with that from now on, although it is a judgment entirely from remembered feeling, or instinct, or whatever, and I can no more point to objective evidence for it than I can in the case of the manikin's imagined gender. And it is a further point of similarity between the two figures although I've said I *knew* they were different.)

What else, then, did I feel about her? That she had come to destroy me in some way, to wipe me out, erase me—I felt a calmer and a colder thing than "kill," there was almost no heat to it at all. That she was weighing me in a very cool fashion, like that Egyptian god which weighs the soul, that she was, yes (and had her leaden-hued skin given me a clue here?), the Button Molder, come to reduce my individuality to its possibly useful raw materials, extinguish my personality and melt me down, recycle me cosmically, one might express it.

And with that thought there came (most incidentally, you might say—a trifling detail) the answer I'd been straining for all evening. It went this way: *If you could sum up all you felt about life and crystallize it in one master insight, you would have said it all and you'd be dead.*

As that truism (?) recited itself in my mind, she seemed to come to a decision and she lithely advanced toward me two silent steps so she was barely a foot away in the arcing light's unnatural white glare, and her slender mitten-hands reached wide to embrace me, while her long black "hair" rose rustlingly and arched forward over her head, in the manner of a scorpion's sting, as though to enshroud us both, and I remember thinking, *However fell or fatal, she has style.* (I also recall wondering why, if she were able to move silently, the nine footsteps had been so loud? Had those great crashes been entirely of mind-stuff, a subjective earthquake? Mind's walls and constructs falling?) In any case her figure had a look of finality about it, as though she were the final form, the ultimate model.

That was the time, if ever (when she came close, I mean), for me to have flinched away or to have shut tight my eyes, but I did not, although my eyes were blurred—they had spurted hot tears at her advance. I felt that if I touched her, or she me, it would be death, the extinguishment of memory and myself (if they be different), but I still clung to the faith (it had worked thus far) that if I didn't move away from and continued to observe her, I might survive. I tried, in fact, to tighten myself still further, to make myself into a man of brass with brazen head and eyes (the latter had cleared now) like Roger Bacon's robot. I was becoming, I thought, a frenzy of immobility and observation.

But even as I thought "immobility" and "touching is death" I found myself leaning a little closer to her (although it made her violet eye-points stingingly bright) the better to observe her lead-colored skin. I saw that it was poreless but also that it was covered by a network of very fine pale lines, like crazed or crackled pottery, as they call it, and that it was this network that gave her skin its silvery gloss . . .

As I leaned toward her, she moved back as much, her blunt arms paused in their encirclement, and her arching "hair" spread up and back from us.

At that moment the filament of the arcing bulb fizzled again and the light went out.

Now more than ever I must hold still, I told myself.

For a while I seemed to see her form outlined in faintest ghostly yellow (violet's complement) on the dark and hear the faint rustle of "hair," possibly falling into its original position down her back. There was a still fainter sound like teeth grating. Two ghost-yellow points twinkled a while at eye-height and then faded back through the doorway.

After a long while (the time it took my eyes to accommodate, I suppose) I realized that white fluorescent street light was flooding the ceiling through the upward-tilted slats of the blind and filling the whole room with a soft glow. And by that glow I saw I was alone. Slender evidence, perhaps, considering how treacherous my new apartment had proved itself. But during that time of waiting in the dark my feelings had worn out.

Well, I said I was going to tell you about those ten endless seconds and now I have. The whole experience had fewer consequences and less aftermath than you might expect. Most important for me, of course, my whole great nonfiction writing project was dead and buried, I had no inclination whatever to dig it up and inspect it (all my feelings about it were worn out too), and within a few days I was writing stories as if there were no such thing as writer's block. (But if, in future, I show little inclination to philosophize dogmatically, and if I busy myself with trivial and rather childish activities such as haunting games stores and amusement parks and other seedy and picturesque localities, if I write exceedingly fanciful, even frivolous fiction, if I pursue all sorts of quaint and curious people restlessly, if there is at times something frantic in my desire for human closeness, and if I seem occasionally to head out toward the universe, anywhere at all in it, and dive in—well, I imagine you'll understand.)

What do I think about the figure? How do I explain it (or her)? Well, at the time of her appearance I was absolutely sure that she was real, solid, material, and I think the intentness with which I observed her up to the end (the utterly unexpected silvery skin-crackle I saw at the last instant!) argues for that. In fact, the courage to hold still and fully observe was certainly the only sort of courage I displayed during the whole incident. Throughout, I don't believe I ever quite lost my desire to *know*, to look into mystery. (But why was I so absolutely certain that my life depended on *watching* her? I don't know.)

Was she perhaps an archetype of the unconscious mind somehow made real? the Anima or the Kore or the Hag who lays men out (if those be distinct archetypes)? Possibly, I guess.

And what about that science fiction suggestiveness about her? That she was some sort of extraterrestrial being? That would fit with her linkage with a very peculiar violet star, which (the star) I do *not* undertake to explain in any way! Your guess is as good as mine.

Was she, *vide* Lang, a waking dream?—nightmare, rather? Frankly, I find that hard to believe.

Or was she really the Button Molder? (who in Ibsen's play, incidentally, is an old man with pot, ladle, and mold for melting down and casting lead buttons). That seems just my fancy, though I take it rather seriously.

Any other explanations? Truthfully, I haven't looked very far. Perhaps I should put myself into the hands of the psychics or psychologists or even the occultists, but I don't want to. I'm inclined to be satisfied with what I got out of it. (One of my author friends says it's a small price to pay for overcoming writer's block.)

Oh, there was one little investigation that I did carry out, with a puzzling and totally unexpected result which may be suggestive to some, or merely baffling.

Well, when the light went out in my bedroom, as I've said, the figure seemed to fade back through the doorway into the small hallway with lowered ceiling I've told you about and there fade away completely. So I decided to have another look at the ceilinged-off space. I stood on a chair and pushed aside the rather large square of frosted glass and (somewhat hesitantly) thrust up through the opening my right arm and my head. The space wasn't altogether empty, as it had seemed when I changed the bulb originally. Now the 200-watt glare revealed a small figure lying close behind one of the two-by-four beams of the false ceiling. It was a dust-filmed doll made (I later discovered) of a material called Fabrikoid and stuffed with kapok—it was, in fact, one of the Oz dolls from the 1920s; no, not the Scarecrow, which would surely be the first Oz character you'd think of as a stuffed doll, but the Patchwork Girl.

What do you make of that? I remember saying to myself, as I gazed down at it in my hand, somewhat bemused, *Is this all fantasy ever amounts to? Scraps? Rag dolls?*

Oh, and what about the lay figure in the store window? Yes, she was still there the next morning same as ever. Only they'd changed her position again. She was standing between two straight falls of sheeting, one black, one white, with her mitten hands touching them lightly to either side. And she was bowing her head a trifle, as if she were taking a curtain call.

In the first Whispers *anthology William F. Nolan told a
contemporary horror story, "Dark Winner," entirely within
the form of transcripts. And here, in another demonstration of his talent and versatility, he gives us an Arthurian
fantasy in epic verse. "The Final Quest," he claims, was
inspired by research for an aborted TV series. It's a dark
and memorable tale whose inclusion in* Whispers III *marks
Nolan's 100th anthology appearance!*

THE FINAL QUEST

by William F. Nolan

Here now, stand close, and let me weave
   A tale so eldritch you'll believe
Me mad. For never has been told
   This death dark saga. Brave and bold
Was Arthur, bearing Britain's crown,
   A king of courage and renown.
Begat above a thundered sea,
   A just and stalwart lord was he.
In glittered armor, head to heel,
   He smote rogue knights with magic steel.

With Saxon blood upon his blade,
   He came from battle to a glade
Where demons did upon him cast
   A deep spell dark-designed to last
Ten thousand years or more they say.

Till Merlin came at break of day
And found his lord in sleeping death.
  Then blew upon his cheek a breath
Which waked him full. Cried out the king:
  "The Earth shall ever of thee sing!
I vow upon sweet Jesu's name
  That you shall never want for fame."
But Merlin sighed and bowed his head,
  His waxen face deep-marked with dread.
"This fame, my king, that you bestow
  Avails me naught where I must go.
For though I saved thee on this day
  From Old King Death there is no stay."
"Not so!" cried Arthur, fist raised high,
  "I say that Death Himself shall die!"
"But surely, Sire, you speak in jest,
  No chance have we in such a quest."
But Arthur gripped good Merlin's arm.
  "I shall not let thee come to harm.
Death shall not pluck thee from my side.
  To his dominion we shall ride,
And there, I vow, shall king meet king.
  An end to Death's long reign I'll bring!"

And so began, as legends tell,
  A quest for Death where he might dwell.
On horse, Excalibur in hand,
  With Merlin, searched they land to land
Across the world. And years did pass
  Until one morn, within a mass
Of stone from which no shadow's breath
  Was cast, at length they found Old Death.
Two kings, both bold, did thunderous reel
  Together, crashing, steel on steel.

And, sad by, watching Merlin wept,
  Aware that Arthur would be swept

From out this life. That even he
  Could not prevail now in the lee
Of Death's dark power. Yea, hour 'pon hour
  The marveled conflict hotly raged,
For never had the world seen staged
  Such awesome class of mighty wills.
And ringing from the sky-tall hills
  Was word of battle swiftly sown
From castle wall to hut of stone.
  From moor and meadow, mountain, plain,
Fast came they all to see Death slain
  By Arthur. Duke, serf-slave, and lord
Were dazzled by his blazing sword.

A day, a night, a week passed by
  Without surcease. O'er land and sky
These titans met in frighted clash
  Of arms, to hew and maim and slash
Each one in turn, while moons did wane
  And blooded sunsets redly stain
The earth. And even those long dead
  Themselves raised from their graves, 'tis said,
And stood, stark-boned in silent rows,
  To watch these fearsome, dreaded foes.

Until, at long last, it was done.
  Incredibly, their knight had won!
And Death Himself was laid full out.
  Then, heavenward, the strangled shout
From Arthur's throat: "We'll have no more
  Of Death upon fair Britain's shore!"
But Death knew well the knightly code,
  And to victorious Arthur showed
A face of guile. And, from the ground,
  His voice a low and piteous sound,
He asked for mercy, loud implored,
  Till Arthur put away his sword

To help him stand. Then Merlin rushed
   Straight on, ash-eyed, his tone close-hushed
In Arthur's ear. He harshly warned
   That here all mercy must be scorned.

''This thing I cannot do, good friend,''
   Said he to Merlin. ''For once bend
Our code, and it shall surely break
   And with it, knightly honor take.''
Thus, Arthur's fixed code could not yield.
   He laid aside his blade and shield,
While foul and fetid Death roared free.
   And not for all eternity
Would king meet king in such a fight
   As this. And Death, in turn, did blight
The world for his defeat. All died:
   E'en Arthur, Merlin at his side,
Sore-wounded now, his magic fled
   In this, their final leafy bed.

And later, all of Camelot,
   Knights of the Table Round could not
Evade that final darkling wood
   Where smiling, white-boned tall Death stood
Supreme. No further songs were sung
   Of chivalry. The knell had rung.